Shattered by Fate

SHATTERED BY FATE

PART TWO OF FATE'S PATH

JACELYN RYE

JACELYN RYE ROMANCE

Published by Jacelyn Rye
Cover Design by Najla Qamber Designs

ISBN:978-0615940090

Typesetting services by BOOKOW.COM

For Colorado,
the mountains of Steamboat Springs,
where I, and this story, all began.
There is a place in my heart that
will always belong to you.

ACKNOWLEDGEMENTS

Writing this story has become so much more to me than simply writing a book. There was no way of knowing, when this journey all began, where it would lead. I hoped it would lead me to the moment of holding my book in my hands, and feeling an accomplishment unlike anything I had ever known. And, yes, that has absolutely happened, and for that life experience, I will forever be grateful. But little did I know, that what I thought would be the end result, was only just the beginning.

What I couldn't have known is that a story that materialized from a dream, would become so real. My imagination wove a tale of young love, heartache, and hope. While all of that was happening on paper, something just as incredible was happening to me. Because of this story, I now have people in my life that, while we have never met, we are woven together with fate's thread of friendship, respect and appreciation.

For everyone who has read Surrender to Fate, I cannot begin to thank you enough. If you could only know how much your support has meant to me. Your reviews, your thoughts, your enthusiasm for the next book, all fuelled my passion to write beyond anything that I could've imagined. Julia and Allison, my beautiful and amazing Divas, your friendship will always be one of the greatest gifts I've received. Tabitha, it is rare and special to make a new friend so effortlessly. You are a true giver and a beautiful soul. Danielle Stewart, you have taken me under your wing, you have embodied the spirit of Pay It Forward, and I can only hope that someday, I can be what you have been to me. Najla, your talent in cover designing is inspiring, but the person you are is the real masterpiece. Thank you for indulging me on all of my "tweaks" for this beautiful cover. To the many others who have made this journey one of the most magnificent of my life, thank you.

I will forever be indebted to this story for bringing you all into my life.
Love to you all,
Jacelyn

CHAPTER 1

"You sorry sack of shit! How many times, Jake? How many times have you been told?"

Will let his head fall toward the thundering voice of Vernon. Squinting his eyes did nothing to alleviate his blurred vision. He could make out the shapes standing only a few feet away from him, and he knew what was going on. Vernon, no more than an inch away from Jake's face, screaming and spitting his words, and Jake staring stone cold back at him.

Will tried to speak, but found nothing more than a whisper escaping from his lips. Before he could give a second attempt, he felt a heavy hand land gently on his shoulder. He slowly turned toward the hand, realizing as he did that every movement brought a sensation of pain.

"Don't move, son. Just sit still." William knew his father's voice so well. The thickness and fear was palpable.

"I'm...okay." It didn't matter if he had the strength to talk, or if he should even be attempting to. He actually didn't know if he was okay or not. All he wanted to do was change the sound of his father's voice.

Henry moved to William's line of sight. If William thought the sound of his voice was bad, the look on his face was infinitely worse. "The doctor's on his way." Henry's brow was creased in worry and his words were thick, as if something were impeding his throat. His breaths were heavy and rapid, and William could see his chest rising and falling as if he had just run a race.

"Wha...what happened?" The clouds were slowly lifting, and William closed his eyes, wondering if the visions of logs and screaming could've been a dream. The bits and pieces that were flooding his mind didn't seem real.

If it weren't for the pain that was extremely real he would've bet everything, that this was all his imagination.

Henry swallowed hard and paused. "The logs. The logs rolled off the truck, and right on top of you. You've been knocked out cold for…for, I don't know how long. They told me you pushed Jake out of the way and…" He closed his eyes and looked to the sky. His chin began to tremble as he continued, "And I almost lost you, boy. I could've lost you, William." Henry dropped his chin to his chest, and his shoulders began jerking forward.

"But…you didn't, Dad."

Henry looked up with bloodshot eyes into William's face and whispered, "It's a miracle, son. A miracle."

William closed his eyes, letting the weight of his father's words sink in. The thought of his father having to cope with another loss brought stabbing pains to his chest. He didn't know exactly what had happened, or just how bad his injuries were, but he knew his father was right. He was damn lucky to be alive. His father believed it to be a miracle. But William knew it was so much more than that. The vision of his mother was the last thing he remembered. He felt it in the depths of his soul. His mother had saved him.

"I…I think I can get up, Dad," William stammered, as he attempted to lift his head from the ground.

"Oh, no you don't. We'll just wait for Dr. Paul."

Before William could protest, another face leaned over him. "You alright? Christ boy, you are some kind of lucky. I already fired that shit for brains, Wilson. A box of rocks has that kid beat."

"It was an accident," William said. "Besides, I'm okay." Before his father could stop him, William took a deep breath and hoisted his shoulders from the ground. He would've succeeded if it weren't for the piercing pain that radiated from his shoulder and arm and forced him to fall back to the gravel.

Grimacing and moving his other hand up to the source of the pain, he heaved, "Maybe not."

"William! I told you, don't move!" Henry scolded.

If for nothing else, William decided to appease his father and let out a deep sigh. "Okay, okay." He decided not to press his luck. He was lucky enough, that for right now, it seemed that his only major injury was that something was wrong with his shoulder. Even though it may not be life threatening, it was certainly enough to cause some serious concern over his ability to work, and therefore, take care of his family's farm.

Dr. Paul arrived to the lumberyard and assessed the damages. After making William bend all of his limbs, except for his right arm, he asked him a series of questions to ascertain any head trauma. Shining his light into William's pupils, he finally clicked the switch off and raised his eyebrows.

"Well, near as I can tell, you're going to make it. I'm not sure how you escaped more injuries than what you have, but I'd say you're damn lucky. Must've had a guardian angel, that's for sure."

With some help, William had been relocated to a stack of pallets for the examination, where he sat in some obvious discomfort. "What about my shoulder?"

"Yes, well, that is going to take some time to heal. Based on what I can tell, I think you've fractured your collarbone. Come see me tomorrow for a more thorough examination, and I'll be able to tell you more. For now, you're going to need to keep that arm immobile in this sling."

William looked down to the navy blue fabric that cradled his arm and the belt that held it next to his body. He sighed at the inconvenience this would most definitely cause, but quickly righted his mind, realizing he had nothing to complain about, considering what could've happened.

"For now, I want you to go home. You are not to do anything else, and I mean nothing. Try to eat something, go to bed, and rest. Here is some pain medication to get you through the night. I'll see you in the morning. Oh, and under no circumstances should you try to move your arm or shoulder. I don't want you doing any further damage."

William nodded and slowly stood. Henry helped brace him by holding him by the elbow of his other arm. "Yes, sir. Thank you, Doctor. I'll see you in the morning."

"C'mon, son. Let's get you home." The relief was starting to settle on Henry's face, and while the movement sent a shock of pain through William's arm, he fought off the grimace to spare his father any more worry.

The crowd of lumberyard employees had dispersed fairly quickly. Vernon wasn't about to be paying any gawkers and he made it clear that anyone not back to their duties immediately, could find themselves a new job as professional spectators. Just as they had rounded the corner of the building, William heard a shriek and instantly recognized Margaret's voice. It occurred to him, at that moment, that in all that had just taken place, and his near brush with death, that he never once thought of her. He hadn't worried what it would've done to her if he had been killed. He didn't open his eyes and feel the need to look into hers for comfort. It hadn't even crossed his mind to ask someone to let her know what had happened. He recognized this as a major issue, clearly. The woman he was to marry, to spend the rest of his life with, hadn't been a part of his concern. The reality was, that he wasn't sure she ever would be. But with all that had occurred, there was no way to process the magnitude of that realization.

"Oh, my God, William!" She ran to him and William braced himself in anticipation of her touch. "Oh, my God! Are you alright?"

The pain that shot through his arm and traveled through his core was unbearable, as Margaret threw herself against him and wrapped her arms around him. This time, there was no stopping the grimace, nor the audible moans, as he clenched his jaw and attempted to hide the jolt of pain flooding his body.

Unable to hide his annoyance, Henry pulled her arms loose from their vice-grip around William. "Easy, Margaret. Can't you see his arm is injured?"

Margaret looked at William's arm and sling, and the look on her face illustrated that she had not taken the time to notice. "Oh! Did I hurt you? I just couldn't help myself. I saw you, and all I could think about was how badly I wanted to feel your arms around me."

William reached up to his injured shoulder and gingerly held it. "It's...it's okay. It's just very painful, and can't be touched."

Margaret took a step back and looked at his arm, limp in the sling. "What's wrong with it?"

"Dr. Paul isn't sure. I'm going in tomorrow, so hopefully he'll figure it out."

"Well, how long are you going to be in this sling? This isn't exactly how I pictured us walking down the aisle. This," she said, touching the fabric of the sling with disgust, "this will never do."

William sighed and closed his eyes. He barely had the wherewithal to stand, let alone argue with Margaret about his wedding-day attire. He opened his eyes and took a deep breath, "Look, Margaret. Can we...?"

Henry cut him off before he could continue. "What he's trying to say, Margaret, is that he just barely survived trees rolling off a truck and landing on his body. I'm sure the last thing he is concerned with, is how this will affect the wedding."

Margaret was rarely speechless. She opened her mouth to say something, but clearly thought better of it and closed it.

William moved his free hand to his father's shoulder. "It's okay, Dad." Looking to Margaret, he sighed deeply and said, "Look, let's just take this one day at a time. We don't even know anything yet. Okay?" The conversation was exhausting, in more ways than one.

Margaret pursed her lips and gave him a short nod.

"Good." William was beginning to feel light-headed and just wished he could be home and in his bed. He leaned forward and kissed Margaret on the cheek. "I'll let you know what the doctor says tomorrow, alright?"

"Tomorrow?" Margaret protested. "Can't I come see you tonight?"

"Not tonight. I just need to get home and rest."

Margaret gave him her notorious pout, but seemed to know better than to argue any further. "Okay, tomorrow then." She moved up against his body and pressed her lips into his. When she finally broke their connection, she added, "Just so you know, I don't know what I would do without you."

William gave her a weak smile and turned to his father. "Let's go, I need to lie down."

Henry nodded and William put his free arm over his shoulder. Had he not stood for so long, he probably could've made it to the truck on his own. But now, he was thankful to have his father to lean on, and that his guardian angel had been with him today.

CHAPTER 2

The light was bright, so blinding that Sarah squeezed her eyes shut. Despite the momentary reprieve from the glare, she realized that she didn't want to keep her eyes closed anymore. The confusion that flooded her mind wouldn't let them stay closed and forced her to open them again. Her mind's persuasion was not convincing enough, as her eyes barely fluttered awake, and it took all the strength she had—mentally and physically—to stop them from falling closed again. They were so heavy that she wanted to lift her arms to her face and use her fingertips to assist in the endeavor, but her arms felt as though they were weighed down, even more than her eyelids.

Her mind darted in all directions of her sanity, searching for answers. But, everything seemed so foggy and thick in her mind that even if there were answers, they couldn't have been recognized as such. She could at least take stock in what she was sure of. She was lying down, but not in her bed. The way the light was artificial and intense, she knew she wasn't even in her house.

She felt her eyelids begrudgingly begin to flicker open, and like the curtain slowly rising on a stage, the blackness released its grip on her senses and she focused her eyes in front of her. The source of the glaring light was her first insight to her location: The buzz of the bright fluorescent lights accompanied the harsh illumination. Squinting, she tilted her chin to her chest to allow a broader scope of the room.

Despite wanting and needing to know what was happening, the sight that met her eyes filled her with so many more questions than answers, that she almost wished she could close them and start the process all over again, but this time to awake to her house, to the ranch, to something familiar and safe. White walls, a white, porcelain sink, a pinkish curtain on a round silver rod, pulled to one side of her bed. She sucked in one breath as she realized that this was not anything that she recognized as hers, and most certainly did not make her feel safe. She was in a hospital? The question pulsated in her mind over and over until she thought she would go mad.

But, once the realization had time to fully absorb, panic settled in, and she noticed her heart begin to beat faster. The questions came pounding so quickly, that this time, she did close her eyes, trying to make sense of the frightening unknowns that were now her reality.

She tried to lift her shoulders from the bed, but found that would to be an impossible request made of her body. Pain surged through her and she grimaced as she fell the couple of inches back to the pillow. A blinding pain was beginning to sting behind her eyes and she forced her hand, which must've weighed as much as an anvil, up to her forehead to rub away the pain. But touching her forehead only sent another bolt of pain through her. With ginger fingertips, she felt her forehead. Carefully rubbing along her brow, her fingers found a series of stiff threads protruding from her skin. Not wanting to exasperate the already piercing pain, she let her fingers drop down the side of her face to her cheek. There were no more threads to be felt, but every inch of her face hurt. She imagined her face in shades of blue and purple, as that would be the only color it could be from such painful injuries. She let her hand glide off her face and back to the bed.

She would have to call for help. But a terrifying thought intruded her mind before she could think further. Her voice. The thought of summoning the strength to talk, let alone yell for help, seemed as daunting as trying to move. She was afraid to even try. She couldn't ignore the fear that enveloped her now. Would she even be able to speak?

Taking a deep breath, as deep as her pained ribcage would allow, she knew she would need to try. Fearing what might, or what might not, come out of her mouth, she gradually let her jaw muscles loosen, and let her lips come apart slightly. She had no moisture to speak of in her mouth, but she licked her cracked lips anyway. Forcing her mouth to open a fraction more, she mustered everything she could.

"Hhhh...elp?" A cracked whisper filled the silence. The sound of her voice was unrecognizable to her. It was as if someone had opened an old steamer trunk that had been stored in an attic for decades, until someone finally opened the lid, only to release a puff of dust and dry air.

It wasn't much, but it was something. Sarah was filled such relief, that for a moment she had to close her eyes and savor the elation she felt in her small victory. She could talk, she had a voice, and she had the strength to use it. Fueled by the glimmer of hope, she swallowed hard, and tried again.

"HH...elp." Although in reality, it wasn't much louder than the first time, Sarah felt that it was, and continued with the momentum that she was feeling. "H...elp! Someone...help?"

It was exhausting, and Sarah paused to catch her breath. She turned her head toward the sound of soft, squishing shoes entering her room.

"Oh my heavens, you're awake."

Sarah watched as a tall, slender woman, with black-rimmed glasses resting on her nose, and dressed in an all-white nurse's uniform, pulled a clipboard from the side of the bed, and began scratching notes. When she was done, she slipped the clipboard into it slot by the bed, and smiled warmly.

"Hello, my dear. Nice to see those pretty eyes. Now, I know you're scared, but I am Nurse Tillie, and you are in the hospital." She smiled in such a way that it reminded Sarah of her grandmother and how she used to look at her. It was a look of comfort and compassion. Sarah was doing her best to keep the rising panic at bay, and the more she looked into Nurse Tillie's soothing eyes, the more she wondered if somehow she knew her.

Despite the comfort of Nurse Tillie, the alarm in Sarah couldn't be quieted. Knowing that she was in the hospital wasn't enough. What she needed was for the nurse to fill in the remaining blanks, and that is what scared her the most. Where were her parents?

"Wha...what happened? Why?" The dust from Sarah's voice was only slightly beginning to clear, and every word was taking more exertion than the last.

Nurse Tillie patted Sarah's arm reassuringly, "You were in a car accident. Most of your injuries were to your head. A good amount of bumps and bruises everywhere else, but nothing broken. You are very lucky, my dear, very lucky. You've been asleep for just about a week now." The nurse searched Sarah's eyes for understanding. "It's a very good sign that you're awake. I'll let the doctor know and he'll be in to see you shortly."

Sarah's mind raced. A car accident? How? Why? Nurse Tillie was just about to leave through the door when sound found her voice again. "Wai…wait."

With another kindhearted smile, she turned and peered at Sarah over the rim of her glasses, "Yes, dear?"

A huge knot was forming in Sarah's throat, making it even more difficult to speak. "My…my parents…call my parents? Please?"

Nurse Tillie opened her mouth, but then, quickly closed it before answering. She pressed her lips together and Sarah wondered why the nurse seemed to contemplate the request.

"Yes, dear. I'll make the call right now." She paused again as Sarah rested her head back to the pillow. "Try to rest now."

Sarah nodded her head and closed her eyes. She needed a drink of water. But mostly, she needed her mother. She needed her loving touch and help, to start putting the pieces together for her. As she felt herself drifting off, she imagined her mother's hands. Those magic hands. Sarah could almost feel them stroking through her hair. Everything would be all right once her parents were here.

CHAPTER 3

"That's what I thought." Dr. Paul announced, as he held the X-ray to the light. He turned to William and Henry as he flicked his finger against the thick charcoal plastic image. He sighed and raised his eyebrows, "Well, it could've been worse."

William raised his eyebrows, waiting for the doctor to continue. "And?"

"Your clavicle. See here?" Dr. Paul held the film up to the light for William and Henry to see as he guided his finger along a milky white image of bone. "You see that crack right here? Well, that's not supposed to be there."

"So…how bad is it, Doc?" Henry's voice was serious and quiet. William knew that prior to his mother's accident, his father would have been able to handle this situation better. But now, William understood how fragile Henry was, and how real the fear was of anything else happening to someone that he loved.

Dr. Paul cocked his head from side to side, weighing the prognosis in his mind. "Well, I'd say there's good news, and there's bad news."

Henry swallowed hard, "What's the bad news?"

Dr. Paul patted Henry's shoulder. "Relax, Henry. Your boy is fine, he's going to be fine. Let's look on the bright side. We all know how bad this could've been, considering. So let's remember that. He has some injuries, yes. But, he escaped with very minor injuries compared to what we could be dealing with. He could've been buried by the logs, but he wasn't. Okay?"

Henry nodded, and forced a slight smile. "Alright." He righted his posture and took in a deep breath. "So, what's the good news, then?"

Dr. Paul nodded his approval at Henry's new outlook and continued. "A fracture of the collarbone is a tricky break. The good news is, that it's not serious enough to need surgery to repair it and have it heal properly. The bad news, which isn't so bad, is that in order for this to heal properly, it's going to need to be completely immobile for several weeks, maybe even a couple of months. Since the bones are still aligned, it won't need plastered, and that's good news, too."

William looked at the doctor, eyes wide. "A...a couple of months?"

Dr. Paul nodded. "Well, that's the tricky part. Might be shorter, might be longer. We'll just have to see how quickly your body heals. You're a healthy young man, so if I had to bet, I'd say shorter. But, it will all depend on how easy you take it, and let your body do what it needs to do. If you try to rush it and start using your arm before it heals, it'll set the whole thing back. Understand?"

William nodded. He knew the doctor was right, but he also knew it would be nearly impossible to get anything done with only one arm. He hoped Vernon would let him stay on at the lumberyard and let him do what he could. Had this happened to any other employee, he was certain Vernon would've fired the guy as soon as he came to. But, he had something going for him that the others did not. He had Margaret, or rather, the obligation to make her happy. Vernon had the same obligation, and he knew he wouldn't dare risk upsetting his daughter by firing her future husband.

William slid of the examination table and held out his free hand to the doctor. "Thank you, Doctor."

"You're welcome," Dr. Paul smiled encouragingly. "You'll be alright, just remember what I told you. Keep this sling on. And, you're still going to need to take it real easy, at least for another week. This might be your only break, but you still took a pounding to your head and the rest of your body."

"Yes, sir. I will."

"I'm serious, William. I've known you your whole life, and you're not one to sit still. But, just this once, you need to sit still." Dr. Paul finished the lecture with a smile and a reassuring pat on William's back. He turned to Henry and shook his hand. "Take good care of him, Henry. I'll check in on you both in a week or so, alright?"

"Sounds good, Doc. Thanks again, for everything." Henry's anxiety had lessened somewhat, and William could see the lines of worry disappearing from his forehead.

Once seated in the truck, William looked over to his father. "Well, I suppose I better stop by the lumberyard, don't you think?"

Henry hesitated, "I don't know, son. You're supposed to be taking it easy, remember? I think I should get you home."

"I know that, but I better at least check in with Vernon and let him know what's going on. Besides, I know Margaret will be chomping at the bit to see me."

Henry sighed and looked out his window. "You're probably right. Let's go."

As Henry pulled into the parking lot of the lumberyard, William couldn't help but stare at the lot where this had all happened. The logs were stacked neatly, and to look at it, everything was as it should be. Despite making light of the tragedy that nearly unfolded, he knew how lucky he had been. It was just one more thing to convince William that you never can tell what fate has in store.

Henry held out his arm for William to brace himself as he slid out of truck. Dr. Paul was right. Nearly every part of his body hurt in one way or another. He hadn't appreciated how every action seemed to rely on his collarbone in some way. He also didn't realize how exhausting everything would be now. He had only been to the doctor's office, and he was already needing to lie down. But, it would be good to get this out of the way. The sooner he met with Vernon, the sooner he could put his mind at ease that he still had a job. At least, he hoped that's what he would find out, anyway.

Hiding his pain was also becoming an exhausting chore. He just couldn't stand to put his father through anything else. Henry had enough heartache to last him a lifetime, and then some. Gritting his teeth and catching his breath, he looked at his father. "I'll be just a minute. Don't leave me," he teased.

"You want me to come?"

"Nah. I'm alright. Besides, it'll be good for me to build up my strength and stamina a bit. I don't plan on sitting like a bump on a pickle for the next few months."

Henry reluctantly nodded and said, "Not too long, son. Ya hear?"

William ambled to the side door used as an employee entrance, to avoid the onslaught of customers and employees that would surely swarm around him by going through the main doors. He walked through the hallway, listening as the lumberyard buzzed with people. He had grown accustomed to running a well-oiled machine when he was there, and it was difficult for him to imagine the possibility of not working anymore. He only hoped Vernon would exercise a little patience with his recovery.

He turned the corner and stood at the base of the stairs that led to Vernon's office. He hadn't thought of this. Walking was one thing, climbing a flight of stairs, was another. The handrail was on his right-hand side, to boot. He wouldn't even be able to hold onto anything. Taking one last look at the very top of the stairs, he lifted his foot to begin the journey. Just as he planted his first step, he heard someone call to him in a forced whisper from down the hall.

Not recognizing the voice, he stopped and waited, hoping whoever it was would come to him.

With eyes darting nervously, Jake appeared from down the hallway. "William," he hoarsely whispered.

William took one step back, again hiding a grimace of pain as his body jarred to a stop. "Hey, Jake."

"Holy shit, are you okay?" Jake scanned William's body. Maybe he hadn't hidden that grimace after all.

"Yea, I'm going to be fine."

"I know I screwed up, I feel awful what happened to you. I'm so sorry, William. Really I am. I was pissed off at Thornton, and…and I wasn't thinking, or paying attention…and it all happened so fast that…"

"It's okay, Jake, really. The doctor says I'm going to be fine. We all make mistakes."

"But you saved me, William. I don't know why you did that, but I owe you."

"You would've done the same."

Jake shook his head and looked down. "I'm not so sure." He looked back at William. "I mean it, I owe you."

"Okay, Jake, okay. Listen, have you seen Vernon? I need to talk to him."

Jake looked around nervously again. "Hell no, I haven't seen him. I'm not even supposed to be here. I just came to get my stuff. I better get outta here before he sees me. I know I screwed up yesterday but I'm in no mood to deal with his bullshit; and now that I don't work here anymore, I plan on never dealing with that asshole ever again." The embers that had been lying just under the surface in Jake had become a full-fledged fire. William was sorry Jake was out of a job, but in all truth, he and Vernon had been on a collision course for some time, and now, maybe all of that could be avoided.

"I hear ya, Jake. I'm sure I'll be seeing you around."

Jake stepped forward and shook William's free hand. "Thank you again, William. And…I am really glad you're going to be okay. I won't be forgetting this."

William nodded his head and Jake turned back down the hallway to the storeroom. He knew his father probably had expected him back by now, and he hadn't even seen Vernon, let alone had a conversation with him. He looked back to the flight of stairs, which seemed to have gotten even steeper. The first step is always the hardest, just get going.

"Christ, boy! What in the hell are you doing?" Vernon barged toward the staircase.

William turned and sighed in obvious relief that he wouldn't have to make the daunting trek upstairs. "I was coming to see you."

"Here I am. What is it?" Vernon bellowed.

His tone caught William by surprise. He knew Vernon didn't have any sort of soft spot to speak of but he expected some sort of compassion from his future father-in-law. "It's about…work."

"What about it?"

"The doctor said I'll be in this sling for a while. But, I still plan on coming back to work to do what I can. If that's…alright with you?"

Vernon narrowed his eyes on William. "I should fire your ass for making such a stupid decision to push Wilson out of the way. What in the hell were thinking, by the way?"

"I…I…don't know. I just…"

"You just weren't thinking, is the answer. How could you put yourself in that situation? To save 'shit-for-brains Wilson'?" He shook his head in wonderment, but continued. "Yea, you still got your job. Just let me know when you're coming back. You can work the counter, or something."

"Yes, sir. Thank you."

"Don't thank me, thank Margaret. Speaking of, what's this going to do to the wedding plans?"

William paused, hoping for time to think up something to say other than what he wanted to say. He could not believe that through all of this, the wedding was the major concern. Considering Margaret was the reason he was still employed, he thought better of spouting his true feelings. "I hope this won't delay it too much, sir."

Vernon huffed. "Yea, you better hope. Margaret's not known for her patience."

"Yes, I know. My dad is waiting for me. Will you tell Margaret I'll come by and see her tomorrow?"

Vernon raised his eyebrows and smirked. "Tomorrow, huh? Right. I'll tell her but she'll decide. You might want to expect her today."

The conversation was exhausting and William was ready to be done talking and thinking. He nodded politely and stepped off the landing at the base of the stairs.

William pushed the door open and held his face to the sun. The rays warmed the chill that had been left by Vernon's absent compassion. William wasn't one to be expecting a pity party on his account, but it hadn't gone unnoticed that Vernon didn't express any sort of gratitude that William was okay, or any sort of well-wishes for him to feel better. It was only about Margaret. Making Margaret happy. William figured he just better get used to that from Vernon. Upon that realization, an ache began building in his chest. An ache so profound that he actually reached to his chest and pressed into it. It was an ache that he had felt before, and had learned to live with. He ached for Sarah. He could actually feel the pain emanating from the emptiness that she once filled. She would've been the one, the only one, who could make him forget the pain his body was enduring right now. Not willing to put himself through the agony that he had learned to squelch, he dropped his hand to his side. There was no sense even going there, in his mind, or in his heart. If there was anything he could be certain of, it was that Sarah was in the past, and there was no sense in dwelling in it. He had been given a second chance to keep living the life that had been dealt to him, and time was no longer a commodity that he was willing to waste.

CHAPTER 4

Sarah awoke to hushed whispers next to her. She realized that while her eyelids fought her a bit, it was easier to open them than she last remembered. It still took her time to get her bearings. The room was dimly lit, the only light coming in from the hallway. She welcomed the dark, as it was a nice change from the glare and the unbearable buzzing of the light fixtures above her. She slowly turned to the window to find that it too, was mercifully showing the darkness of night. Turning toward the voices, she squinted to make out the shapes of who was in her room. Her heart leapt when she realized that it must be her parents. They were finally here.

"Mom? Dad?" She interrupted the discussion next to her and the room fell silent.

An arm landed softly on Sarah's arm, and she smiled. The touch of her mother was all she needed now. Whatever had happened, whatever questions she had, they could all wait. There would be time for answers. She closed her eyes and felt a tear fall down the side of her temple and into her hair. She was overwhelmed by the sudden emotions of gratitude, which she felt, at last, from having her mother by her side.

A face leaned over to come into Sarah's view and she felt the hand that had been on her arm, slide down to her own hand. Sarah furrowed her brow; it wasn't the feeling she had come to know by heart. Someone else was holding her hand. She still had not gathered who it was, all she knew was, it wasn't her mother.

"Hello, Sarah, dear." A sweet whisper filled the room.

Sarah, dear? Sarah searched her memory. Somebody calls me that…who?

It sounded so familiar. Sarah felt as if she was in the dark reaching for a light, but only her fingertips could brush up against it, not quite fully grasping it. She squinted again, wishing that just this once, the lights were on to help her.

"Who's...who's here?" The panic was rising in her voice and it scared her.

"It's us, dear. Ellie and Oscar."

Nurse Tillie pulled the cord to the small light fixture over the sink, and in a few blinks of light, the room was illuminated in a yellow hue.

Sarah squinted at the sudden glow. Ellie cocked her head to side and smiled warmly.

"Oh, Sarah. It's so good to see your eyes open, dear."

Oscar stepped up to stand behind Ellie, wringing his hat in his hands and turning it over and over. "Hi there, Sarah."

Seeing the familiar faces brought a smile to Sarah's lips. Her mouth was dry, and she swallowed hard. "Hi. It's good to be awake." Her voice had regained some strength, but it still hadn't reached its normal tone. "Are my parents here, yet?"

Ellie squeezed her hand and turned toward Oscar. She turned back to Sarah with such pain in her expression that Sarah instantly felt nauseous.

Ellie pursed her lips as Sarah watched her eyes fill with tears.

Sarah couldn't stand this. "What? What!" She demanded.

Oscar placed his hand on Ellie's shoulder and looked down to the floor.

Ellie placed both of her hands over Sarah's and continued. "You and your parents were in a car accident."

Sarah nodded and slowly replied, "I know that."

Ellie glanced at Oscar again, and then back to Sarah. "Sarah, dear. I'm so, so very sorry to have to tell you this. Your parents...didn't survive the accident." Ellie closed her eyes and let the tears fall down her cheeks. "I'm so sorry," she whispered.

The lights were not on, but all Sarah could hear was a buzzing in her head. She looked from Ellie to Oscar and tried to speak, but no words would come out. Sarah's chest heaved and she covered her mouth with her hand just as

Ellie's words collided into each other in her mind. Parents. Didn't survive. The words thundered and echoed against her skull, and ripped through her heart. Nurse Tillie pushed passed Ellie and Oscar, grabbed a hospital pan from the bedside table, and reached Sarah just in time as she vomited. She heaved into the metal pan, tears streaming, as true pain set in. She wanted to ask Ellie if she heard her correctly. She wanted Ellie to have one more chance to tell her something else, anything else. She wanted to tell Ellie that she must be mistaken, but, she knew none of that would happen. She knew Ellie would not tell her anything that she wanted to hear. She knew that nothing would change the fact that she would never feel her mother's magic hands or her father's stubbly whiskers ever again. She squeezed her eyes shut knowing that she would never be the same without them. No touch, no soothing voice or sympathetic gaze, could ease the devastating pain that coursed through her. She felt hollow. Empty. Alone.

CHAPTER 5

Sarah stood in the middle of the small living room of the little house. Oscar and Ellie brought her home after she had been discharged from the hospital, but being here brought no relief. She had spent another four torturous days in that small, white room that closed in on her a little bit more each day. For four days, she felt more excruciating pain than a car accident could've ever caused. She struggled from one minute to the next: from disbelief, anger, to such extreme sorrow, that she thought she would wither away. There were many times she wished she could fade away. Fade away into oblivion. Surely that would hurt less than knowing what she knew. But that disbelief was only compounded infinitely by what she didn't know.

She felt she would surely go mad, as all she could focus on now, was replaying the same horrific conversation she had with Dr. Gregory the day after she learned about her parents. The conversation, the moment she realized, that as completely devastating as it was knowing that her parents were gone, things were about to get considerably worse.

Dr. Gregory had been so optimistic during his examination of her. It was a moment that Sarah had engrained into her memory as the last glimmer, the last semblance of hope she had, before it was yanked from her already precarious hold on her new reality. "Your injuries are healing nicely, Sarah. I'm not sure how you managed no broken bones, but you did."

Sarah stared down into her hands and could only nod.

Dr. Gregory continued on, "Have you ever had any broken bones?"

Not looking up, Sarah could only muster, "No."

"Really? Not even as a child? That is something. You must have very strong bones."

He clicked his pen light into her eyes, moving it quickly from side to side, watching her pupils react. Sarah looked away from light and to the doctor. "What did you say?"

Dr. Gregory moved the light from her face and tilted his head. "I said, you must have strong bones."

Sarah shook her head. "No. Before that."

The doctor furrowed his brow, not understanding what Sarah was asking. He started again slowly, "I…asked you if you broke any bones when you were a child."

Sarah's jaw dropped open, her eyes searching the doctor's face.

"What is it, Sarah? What's wrong?"

Tears flooded her eyes and blurred her vision. She blinked to clear them away and looked back to him. "I…I…" She was afraid to even say it out loud, but she was even more terrified to keep it to herself. "I don't remember…when I was a child."

Dr. Gregory dropped his hand that had the flashlight, down to his side. His lighthearted demeanor changed and seriousness blanketed the room. "What do you mean, Sarah?"

Sarah opened and closed her mouth, hoping some sort of sense could be made from the fear exploding in her mind. "I…don't remember," she yelled, as panic took hold. "I don't remember!" Those three words became her repeating nightmare, whether awake or asleep.

And now, she stood alone in the little house that not long ago, held all of them. Together and happy. But, that was something that she would never feel again. She closed her eyes as she realized, that leaving the hospital had not granted her a reprieve from the torment. Three little words. Alone, meaningless. But, when put together, they robbed everything. I don't remember. She looked around at her surroundings again. It wasn't enough for Matty and Adley to be taken from her. It wasn't enough that her parents were robbed from her. Fate completed the merciless and cruel trifecta when it stole her past from her, as well.

She stared blankly into the tidy kitchen. Her mother always kept it neat. As she closed her eyes, she could imagine hearing the sounds of her mother cooking. She turned to the small window that looked out to the garden, sunlight streaming in without a care. Hanging next to the window was a small metal hook that held her mother's green apron with miniature pink and white flowers. Sarah pulled it from the hook, and pressed it to her face. It smelled of biscuits, her mother's delicate soap; happiness. There would be no more biscuits, no more scent of her mother, and no more happiness as far as she was concerned.

Ellie stepped into the house and paused before she gently approached Sarah. She put her hand on Sarah's back and gave it a soothing rub. "Sarah, dear, are you sure you don't want to stay with us at our house?"

Sarah wrapped her hands in the apron and pulled it into her chest. She turned and attempted a half smile for Ellie's sake. "I'm sure, thank you, though. I think I just want to be here, if that's okay?"

Ellie hesitated, pursing her lips in disagreement. "Well, if that's what you want, dear. You really wouldn't be any trouble, though. Adley wouldn't want you to be alone…over here."

Adley. Even though the haze hadn't lifted completely, she remembered him. She could still feel him. She knew who he was. It still didn't help what she didn't know. "I'll be alright. Dr. Gregory told me my head was healing fine," she softly said to Ellie, looking back down at the apron.

Ellie nodded. "Yes, that's what he told me, too, dear. And," Ellie's voice lifted slightly in hopefulness, "he said that memory loss is very common in a head injury. He said that there was nothing saying your memory loss would be permanent. You know that, right?"

Sarah nodded. She wanted to cry, but in all truth, all the energy she could spare was spent in refraining from running down the road and never stopping, never looking back. She didn't have the energy to remind Ellie that the doctor also said that there was no guarantee that it wouldn't be permanent, either.

Sarah was appreciative that Ellie didn't push her too much more. In time, she hoped, she would be up for the company of Ellie and Oscar. And she was grateful to have them; she hoped they understood that she just needed time. Time wouldn't change anything, but maybe time would dull her pain. Ellie kissed her cheek and left her in the kitchen. After the door quietly closed, and the silence draped over her like a suffocating blanket, Sarah climbed the stairs and lay down in her parents' bed. She pulled the blue quilt over her and tucked the apron into her chest, and closed her eyes. As she drifted off to sleep, she hoped that when she awoke, her reality would be different from this current nightmare. She knew that wouldn't happen, but she at least hoped she would awake to find that she remembered something; anything about who she used to be.

CHAPTER 6

William had been learning a new way of getting things done in the two weeks since his accident. It was an enormous adjustment going from two arms, to one, and he realized how much he had taken for granted when his body was in complete working order. He had no idea how easy everything had been, in the stark comparison of how difficult everything had become. Even the simplest of tasks required planning and clever maneuvering. He would never again take for granted the simple tasks such as pulling on his trousers and buttoning them.

He was determined, though. He had never been one to sit around before his accident, and he certainly wasn't one now. Especially since he was unsure how long Vernon would let him be away from the lumberyard before he realized that the business ran just fine without him. He knew that he would need to get back and work in some capacity to ensure Vernon would still keep his offer on the table.

If there were any positives to the predicament of his injuries, it was that it brought his father out from the very dark and deep hole that had swallowed him ever since his mother's death. Henry could now focus on William and getting him well, instead of only having the gnawing pain every minute of every day that he had grown accustomed to. He was proud of Tommy, too. For being the baby of the family for so long, Tommy was growing up and taking responsibility where he could. William noticed that his ornery streak had been subdued, if only slightly. Tommy had taken on the task that neither he nor their father could manage: the arduous and harrowing process of cleaning up what remained of the barn. He worked a little bit more on it each day, and before long, he had the awful remnants of that night cleared away. At least the physical fragments.

William had just sat down at the table, pleased with his latest accomplishment of cooking eggs, when his father stepped from his bedroom wearing his trousers and shirt usually reserved for church on Sunday. William set his fork down and stopped chewing. It was Wednesday. He looked at his father from head to toe, wondering what his father could possibly be up to.

He swallowed his bite and looked at his father with an obvious concern coupled with curiosity. "Dad?"

Henry took his hat from the hooks by the door, and brushed at the lint and dust that was scattered on the brim. "Yes, son?"

"Dad, it's Wednesday. Why do you look like you are going to church?"

Henry flicked at the hat a few more times and walked to the kitchen table. He took notice of the breakfast William had made and smiled. "You're doing pretty good, aren't you?"

William looked down to his arm in the sling, "Yea, I guess so. Getting there, anyway."

Henry nodded and spun his hat over and over in his hands. "There's... something I need to do, son."

William nodded as he pushed his chair back from the table. "Alright, what is it? I'll help. I mean, if I—"

Henry stopped him and held up his hand. "No, no, no. Just stay put, William." He paused, "This is something I've got to do on my own."

William furrowed his brow. "Okay. Well, what is it?"

"Listen, son. I'm going to be going out of town for a few days, maybe even a week."

William's jaw dropped open and his head shot forward. "You're...what? You're leaving? For a week?"

Henry nodded slowly.

"What on earth for?" William's voice had gotten louder than he intended, but it couldn't be helped with the astonishment he felt from his father's announcement.

"There's just something that I need to take care of. I can't go into the details with you, but you don't need to worry. I've already asked Mrs. Wilkes to check in on you. Tommy knows I'm leaving, and I've put a lot on his shoulders to take care of while I'm gone. You need to make sure you don't do anything to that shoulder of yours. Can you do that?"

William closed his eyes and shook his head in disbelief. "Yes, I can do that. But, you are really leaving? And you can't even tell me where you're going? This sounds very strange, coming from you."

Henry got a distant look in his eye and answered quietly, "I know it does. But sometimes, a man's got to do what's right. I've got to do what's right, William. That's all I can tell you. For now."

William looked at his father and resigned that he had no control over what he had already made his mind up to do. "Okay. I'm still not sure what the hell is going on, but okay. A week? You'll be back in a week?"

Henry tilted his head back and forth, "More or less. About a week, and I'll be back. You think you and Tommy will okay?"

"Yea, we'll be fine."

"Trust me, Son. I wouldn't be leaving you two if this weren't important."

William watched his father as the distant look returned, and he sensed a pervading sadness in him. Before any more emotion could be revealed, Henry put his hat on and looked out the window to where the barn once stood. "You be careful," he turned back to William, "while I'm gone, ya hear? Keep an eye on your brother."

"I will, Dad."

Henry nodded and looked down. "Okay then. I best be gettin' on the road then. I'll see you in a few days." He walked over to William and squeezed his good shoulder.

William stood, "I'll walk you out."

"No, no need. Finish your eggs."

William watched his father climb into the farm truck and pull out of the driveway. He had no idea what was going on, but he had no reason not to trust his father's judgment.

Henry watched the reflection of his house in the rearview mirror as the dust from the farm truck swirled behind him. Reaching the end of the driveway, out of sight of William or Tommy, he stopped and gripped the steering wheel, bringing his forehead to rest on the back of his hands. He sighed and shook his head. He couldn't believe he was leaving his two boys. It felt unnatural, and after everything they had all been though, it felt frightening. Everything can change in a single breath. Reaching over to the glove box and unfastening the metal latch, he reached in and pulled out the folded envelope with his name on it. He knew what it said. He had already read it so many times that he was fairly sure he had it memorized. But leaving the boys was harder than he thought it would be. Reading it one more time would solidify his decision. He unfolded the paper and let his eyes scan its contents again. With each swipe of his eyes to the next line, the paper shook more and more from his trembling hands.

Dear Mr. Harston,

My name is Oscar Mills. I am writing to you with news regarding the Ellis family, who came to work for me on my ranch in California. Your name was listed as Next of Kin for Edward and Anne, and I'm sorry to have to deliver very sad and unfortunate news to you. Edward, Anne, and Sarah were in a very serious car accident, and Sarah was the only one to survive. Matthew was not with them as he reported for military service. Sarah's injuries were not life threatening, and she has been released by the hospital. However, due to head trauma, Sarah has lost a great deal of her memory. My wife, Ellie, and I are more than happy to care for Sarah, as the Ellis's all meant a great deal to us. Edward and Anne always spoke of your family with such love, that I knew it wouldn't be right not to let you know what happened.

Henry looked up and folded the letter. He replayed the phrase from the letter again and again, the very words that were behind his reasoning to leave his own children. It wouldn't be right. He knew that's why he had to go. It wouldn't be right. There was no way he could justify not going. He had supposed there would come a day when he would repay Edward for saving Catherine and Tommy during childbirth. It stung, knowing this was how he would square his debt. His best friend was gone, but nothing would ever erase a friendship that was as deep-seated as family, and there was no way he was not going to get Sarah and bring her home. It wouldn't be right not to.

He put the truck back in gear and headed west. He would have a thousand miles to figure out how he would convince Sarah to come back with him. He would have a thousand more miles on the way back to Colorado to worry about how William would react if he succeeded.

CHAPTER 7

Sarah could appreciate Ellie's intentions, she really could. But what she needed was time. Alone. She thought that if she could just sit, and be still, and allow her mind to rest, it would recover enough to bring her past back. She couldn't bring herself to tell Ellie that she really didn't need to be checked on so often. Or brought so much food. Other than the memory loss, Sarah was beginning to feel like herself. At least, physically. She would never again feel like herself, now that she would be living a life without her parents. Even worse, what about Matty? She needed her brother, they needed to grieve their loss together. They were together when they lost their baby sister, Samantha, to pneumonia. Being together was the only thing that made them feel like they could keep breathing. But, she wasn't even sure where he was, or how he could be informed of the terrible news. How was she going to keep breathing in and out, now that she didn't have any of them?

The garden was what it had originally started out being to her. A refuge: a place to be quiet, a place of her own. If she wasn't in the garden, she found herself staring at it through the window, remembering. Remembering what she could remember. And if the garden held any memories at all, they were memories of Adley. She knew if Adley were here, he wouldn't leave her side. She could curl into his embrace, and hope it could shelter her from some of this pain. She wondered if she would ever feel anything else but pain.

Her thoughts were interrupted by a knock at the door. Ellie must've thought it was time for another visit. Sarah reminded herself how lucky she was to have someone in her life that cared for her so deeply, especially after a relatively short time of knowing each other. And, Ellie was going to be her mother-in-law, after all, which gave her comfort knowing that she would still have people in her life to call family.

She looked away from the window and called out toward the door, "Come on in, Ellie."

The door cautiously opened. "No, it's me. Oscar."

Sarah stood from the wooden kitchen chair and walked to greet him. She knew she was lucky with Oscar, too. They were both so good to her, and she was suddenly overwhelmed with emotion and gratitude to have them.

"Hi, Oscar, I'm in the kitchen."

Oscar peered around the door and they shared a warm smile. He held up a small, brown paper bag. "I brought you something."

Sarah took a few steps to meet him. She noticed the limp from her right leg always took a little bit to loosen up if she had been sitting for a long period of time. She took the bag from Oscar's outstretched arms, and saw a slight hesitancy in him, as she pulled open the top to look inside.

"Ellie," he began, and Sarah detected the nervousness in his voice that she noticed in his demeanor, "Ellie made you something."

Sarah cocked her head slightly and smiled at him, hoping that whatever he was nervous about, could be put to rest. "She is so sweet. What is it?"

She looked to Oscar for a reply but he just nodded toward the bag. "Why don't you take a look?"

She reached into the bag slowly, not fully sure she wanted to know. Her fingertips wrapped around bunched fabric that had been tied with yarn. She pulled the bundle from the paper bag and looked at it curiously. Something was wrapped inside a navy blue fabric dotted with small white daisies. She set the bundle on the kitchen table and again looked to Oscar, who seemed to be holding his breath. Slowly, she pulled the end of the yarn, until she could slip her finger underneath to loosen its hold on the fabric. Once free of the yarn, the gathered fabric fell open. Sarah blinked, now certain that she wasn't breathing either.

Against the dark blue of the fabric, they shone like a full moon in the dark of night. Four perfectly round biscuits nestled against each other, slightly golden brown on their tops. Sarah finally inhaled and looked to Oscar.

As if he could read her mind, he answered, "Ellie, Ellie made them for you. It took her all morning, and all of the flour in the house, but she finally made a batch of biscuits from your mother's recipe that she thought would be worthy. She wanted to bring them over herself, but I told her I would." He paused and nodded slightly, "It's been a hard morning for Ellie. She wanted to make biscuits that Anne would be proud of, and…and, let's just say she really misses your mom."

Sarah nodded. She understood perfectly. She turned back to the biscuits, and smiled as fresh tears filled her eyes. They looked just like her mother's biscuits. She picked one up and held it to her nose. She breathed deeply and closed her eyes. She could see her mother now. Her apron covered in flour, rolling the dough out, pressing and spinning the biscuit cutter with quick flicks of her wrist. She opened her eyes and glanced to the empty kitchen and her mother's green apron. Slowly and gently, she bit into the biscuit, letting the flaky dough melt in her mouth. A tear dropped and rolled off her cheek.

She turned to Oscar, who still seemed quite anxious for her reaction. "Tell Ellie…they are perfect. Just like Mama's."

Oscar smiled in relief. "She'll be real happy to hear that."

Sarah nodded but seemed lost in her thoughts as she stared at the biscuit.

"I'm going to check the animals now. You let us know if you need anything, alright?"

Sarah smiled faintly at Oscar, "I will, thank you. And, please tell Ellie thank you for me, too."

As Oscar closed the door behind him, she whispered to the empty house. "You're sweet, Oscar. But what I need, is to remember. And I'm not sure anyone can help me with that."

CHAPTER 8

With Henry away, William found himself with so much idle time that he was beginning to worry that he might go crazy. He had never had so much time of rest in his life, and it wasn't suiting him to have it now. He thought about all of the days that he would come home from the lumberyard completely exhausted, only to have to get up the next day to do exactly the same. By the time he accounted for all of the work that needed to be done around the farm, he felt consumed by the magnitude of his responsibilities. What he wouldn't have given at the time to have a day off, and now, he had nothing but time. He knew now which extreme was worse, and he was ready to get back to work.

"Thanks for the ride, Mr. Wilkes. I appreciate it." William said, as he slid off the farm- truck seat.

"Anytime, William. I told your dad I would keep an eye out for you and Tommy while he was gone, so if there's anything you need, just holler."

"Will do, sir." He pushed the truck door closed and flinched slightly at the pain in his shoulder from the abrupt movement. He looked to his arm, still hanging limp in the sling. He still felt very fortunate to have only this injury to contend with, but he was certain that when this was all said and done, he'd be lucky to have muscle enough to lift a coffee cup with that arm.

He thought he'd come in through the front door of the store instead of the side entrance for employees. He'd be able to get a better feel for how the store was being run that way. It seemed like it had been a long time since he was last here, and the faint recollections he did have of that day were foggy at best. The emotions from the accident were still fresh and the pain in his arm so commanding, that he could hardly remember the details of stopping by after the appointment with Dr. Paul. He remembered his conversation with Jake, and he was sorry to not be working with him any longer. Hopefully, Jake had found another job, but he knew that would be unlikely. Not only were the jobs far and few between, he worried that Vernon's persuasive nature might've influenced the other businesses in town not to give him a chance. He wouldn't put it past Vernon. It was no secret what Vernon thought of Jake. It would be just like him to hold a grudge and make Jake's life hell if he could.

The store was busy, but not as bad as it usually was. At mid-morning, the customer traffic always lulled a bit. William was actually relieved not to have to brush past any of the customers. He was acutely aware of how the even the slightest nudge against his arm or shoulder could send him reeling in pain, or worse, slow the healing process that he hoped had begun.

As he walked down the main center aisle, he caught the glimpse of blazing red hair behind the counter. He hadn't seen much of Margaret lately, and a twinge of guilt hit him. She was a lot to contend with under normal circumstances, so William had thought it best to have a bit of time to focus on recovering, mentally and physically, from the accident, before he would have any spare attention for her. But as he watched her glide back and forth, he could feel that perhaps, he was ready. She was his future wife, after all. They had a lot of catching up to do, and catching up with Margaret had its benefits.

"How much for kiss?" William drawled in a thick, Southern accent.

Margaret spun around to face the counter, eyes blazing more so than her hair. She stopped herself from what was most likely going to be a very unladylike comment to whomever had the audacity to say that to her. But, the second she saw William, the bristles on her back smoothed.

She splayed her fingers over her hips bones and brought her shoulders back, begging for William's attention to be given to her low cut neckline and the rise of her breasts. "Well," she began slowly, "it'll cost you quite a bit, sir."

"Is that a fact? Don't I get some sort of discount?" William continued the tease.

"Ha." Margaret scoffed. "Do I look like someone who would give a discount?"

"No," William answered, "I suppose not."

Margaret walked to end of the counter to come out to meet William on the other side. She pressed her hips into him as she ran a finger down his chest. "There isn't a discount, but for my very favorite customers, I'm running a special."

William's eyebrows cocked as he reached around her waist with his arm and pulled her in to him. "I'd be interested in hearing about the special."

Margaret went up to her toes to whisper in his ear. "It's a…two-for-one special."

William looked into her glinting eyes. "Hmmm…sounds interesting. But, how do I know I'm getting a good deal?"

She moved back to his ear and breathed gently into it, accentuating her words. "Well, let's just say I can give you some of it to here, and the rest of it after we are closed."

"Okay, Miss. You've convinced me, how much do I owe you for this 'special'?"

"Oh, don't worry. I'm keeping track. I'll just charge it to your account."

Margaret tangled her fingers through his hair and pulled him down to her mouth. William had almost forgotten the feel of her soft, warm mouth against his. She pulled away from his kiss and looked up at him with a sultry gaze. "Well, sir? That's part one of the special. Is that something you might be interested in?"

"Oh yes, that is just what I need."

Margaret smiled victoriously, "Good, I thought so. But, you better hurry. I'm practically a married woman, you know."

He knew that by now, that fact shouldn't take him by such surprise, but it did. Hearing that brought on a wave of nerves that for the last few weeks had been held at bay. He had agreed to the whole marriage arrangement, but it still felt unreal to him. To Margaret, the notion had completely settled, and he knew it was all she thought about. It would all be happening sooner or later. William was fine with later, but just as Margaret didn't do discounts, he knew she didn't do waiting, either.

He took a deep breath to answer her but was interrupted by a heavy hand landing against his good shoulder. "It's about damn time."

William turned toward the abrasive voice that delivered the shove. Vernon walked past him and stood next to Margaret. "I was beginning to wonder about you. Thought maybe you were getting used to this little vacation you've been on."

William stared at Vernon, feeling his blood begin to pound in his face. What was it about Vernon that he felt so entitled to be an ass to everyone? "No, not at all. Just been trying to recover from a truckload of logs landing on me. Most people don't bounce back from that the next day, sir."

Vernon eyed William before his mouth began to curl slightly into a smirk. He glanced toward Margaret, and William was sure that if she hadn't been standing there, Vernon would've had something snide to add the conversation. "Well. Now that you are here, can I assume that you are here to work, or are you here just to distract Margaret from her work?"

"I'm here to work. I thought I could start behind the counter."

"Right. Behind the counter. At least it's something." Vernon narrowed his eyes again, clearly displeased with William's tone and attitude. William knew he had the slightest upper hand now when it came to Vernon. He and Vernon both knew that it would be more than unpleasant to deal with Margaret, if anything were to upset the engagement. William knew he wouldn't be the one to do so, and he knew Vernon was too smart to tangle with Margaret and the wrath that she could unleash.

"Now that you are here, I need to know if I can count on you to oversee everything for a couple of days. Mrs. Thornton and I have to make a trip to Denver to get some supplies. Can I count on you for that, at least?"

"Yes. I can do that. When are you leaving?"

"We weren't going to leave until tomorrow, but I'd rather get over there today. Since you're here, we'll leave this afternoon. I'm taking the lumberyard's truck. You can take my truck and make sure Margaret gets home alright."

Margaret's eyebrows arched with excitement at the new plan. "Oh yes, that'll work just fine. Don't you think, William?"

She looked at William so sweetly, but he could see the fire in her eyes lying just underneath her feigned innocence.

"Yes, that will no problem," William replied dryly to Vernon.

"Don't worry, Daddy. You know William will take good care of me. He's practically my husband, after all."

There it was again. William was certain that Margaret wouldn't let any opportunity go unused to mention that. These were going to a long few months listening to her ongoing announcements at every turn.

"Good, I expect he better do just that. Right, Harston?"

William nodded and placed his arm around Margaret. "Yes, sir. I'll see to it that she gets home safely."

Vernon gave one last look of warning, coupled with annoyance, before he turned and walked up the flight of stairs to his office. When the door slammed closed, Margaret spun to press into William's body and wrapped her arms around him. "Well, I guess that settles that."

"What do you mean?" William asked cautiously.

"Two-for-one special, is what I mean. You get to collect the rest of your goods, tonight."

"Ah," William bent down to brush her lips with his, "I'm sure your customer service is top-notch."

She moved her mouth right in front of his and whispered, "You have no idea." She parted her lips and William succumbed to the beguiling invitation by consuming her mouth and tongue with his. Margaret was mistaken; he had an idea of what was to come. After everything that had happened, he wasn't going to deny himself anything, anymore. Life was uncertain and fragile, and time was not to be taken for granted. Wasted opportunities were an insult to fate's design. He had already learned that fate dictated the rules, and he'd be damned to break them now.

CHAPTER 9

William dropped Margaret off at her house with her explicit instructions to return shortly ringing in his ears. She wouldn't have let him leave at all had he not insisted on getting home to check on Tommy and make sure he was all right to be home for a while by himself. William knew she would realize it to be in her favor if he didn't have to leave prematurely to get home to Tommy, so she reluctantly agreed. William found himself trying to piece together where his father could've gone, but also admitted that he was relieved to avoid explaining his plans for the evening. The mystery was unsettling, but since there was nothing to be done about it, he decided that it would be a waste of time and energy to speculate. Henry would be home in a few days, and he was sure that all of his questions would be answered then.

It was a challenge learning how to shift gears with his decent arm while he steadied the steering wheel with his knee, but once he finally arrived back home, he was relieved to find that Tommy had already made plans of his own. A note left on the kitchen table explained that the Wilkes's had invited Tommy to stay for dinner after he and their son, Luke, had worked in the hay fields all day. William was proud of Tommy for stepping up to more responsibility. Mr. Wilkes was now paying Tommy, and Tommy gladly handed over whatever he made to his father. The death of Catherine brought the three of them closer than ever before. It was a harrowing lesson to learn, but they had learned it. You realize the importance of what you have when you survive the realization of what you don't.

After changing into a fresh shirt and straightening up around the house,

William headed back over to Margaret's, or his future wife, as she would put it. Knowing Vernon and Esther weren't home was a relief, and it left him able to fully concentrate on what Margaret had planned.

It was dusk when he pulled into the driveway, with plenty of light left in the day, but Margaret seemed to have every light in the house blazing. He would have to change that once she was in his household. He despised waste. More specifically, wasting money. He worked too hard for it, and clearly Margaret had no qualms about squandering resources.

He waited at the door, hoping that Margaret had some sort of plan for dinner, and resolving that now would be as good of a time as any to enlighten her on conservation, but that all left him, the minute she opened the door.

She paused slightly and smiled at him. Leaning her head against the open door, she reached for his hand. He extended it automatically, no longer thinking about food or electricity. He had never seen an image like what was before him. Margaret's red hair cascaded over her creamy shoulders and down along the sides of her breasts. She wore a black silken nightgown, held by two thin straps that went over her shoulders. Down the center of her breasts and over her stomach, a black ribbon was laced in a loose crisscross fashion that reminded William of his first look at Margaret's body the day she found him fishing. But, what he couldn't take his eyes from was the black lace that covered her breasts. Pressing against the fabric, her round breasts could barely be contained. Through the design of the lace, her fair skin seemed to be illuminated.

Margaret's haughty smile couldn't be contained, and she led William through the threshold, quickly closing the door. Still holding his hand, she stepped closer to him and placed his hand on her chest, just above the rise of her breasts. William let his hand continue down to finally wrap his hand around her breast. He pressed into her, feeling her respond to his touch. She wrapped her hand over his, forcing him to press and squeeze even harder. With all of the limitations he had faced with only the use of one arm, this was proving to be the most frustrating.

Margaret took his hand from her chest and pulled him into the parlor where a large fire was crackling in the stone faced fireplace. The flames sent flickers of orange light from the hearth into the room, highlighting a blanket spread onto the floor, surrounded by several velvet pillows from the couch. She led him to the blanket and ran her hands up his chest. He bent down to kiss her, but she pulled her head back before he could.

She slowly shook her head and looked at him with a devilish grin. "No, William. I'll be in charge tonight."

William nodded his head, but he knew that no matter what he would've said or done, it wouldn't have changed Margaret's intentions.

"Good. All I want you to do tonight is let me take care of you. I've been waiting for weeks to finally get to take care of you."

Starting under his chin, she unbuttoned his shirt with slow, deliberate strokes of her fingertips. Releasing the final button, she pushed the shirt off his shoulder and free of his arm. She ran her hands over his bare chest and his skin recognized the touch as pure pleasure. The touch of her fingertips paled in comparison to her mouth peppering kisses along his chest and feeling her hips press into his body. She leaned back and wrapped her hand in his, pulling him down to the blanket with her. He knelt, but she pushed him to completely lie down. Pulling the long, black nightgown up slowly, it allowed her to straddle his waist. Leaning over him, she pulled his ear lobe into her mouth and moved with deliberation from his ear, down to his neck. He felt her warm tongue glide down his chest, her deliciously-scented hair following closely behind. She slid her knees further down and pulled his belt from the buckle and slowly unzipped his pants. As she clasped her hands around the waistband, he raised his hips slightly as she pulled them off him.

William couldn't worry about where this was undoubtedly heading. He knew with Margaret, now and in the future, everything would be on her schedule. At least in her mind, and at least for now, she could dictate the schedule. If he could just withstand the arrogance of her father, and a pre-cocious bride a little longer, his family could be taken care of. Perhaps with enough time, the marriage would become something more, something that a marriage was supposed to be. Something like what his parents had. Something, once upon a time, he had always hoped to have. Maybe he still could. But, that all remained to be seen.

Margaret's mission couldn't have been mistaken. She rid William of his pants, and he watched her eyes devour his body. His body had responded to her touch, and with each touch of Margaret's, it required more. He was beginning to wonder if he would be able to relinquish control to Margaret. Had it not been for his arm in the sling, he was sure he wouldn't have been able to control the momentum that was building. What the future held, was certainly a mystery. But for now, there would be no denying the pleasure that was at hand.

Margaret slightly hitched the length of her nightgown to once again straddle William's body. He could feel the smooth skin of her thighs glide over his. She hovered just above him, enough for him to be certain that there was very little separating them. She collapsed her body over his chest and ran her fingertip along his jawline.

"You know, I belong to you, William. It's not official yet, but I am yours, and you are mine. Tonight, you will know that."

Margaret lifted her chest from William's and sat straight up. William could feel the heat from her, and her moist nakedness against him. With one arm still secured in the sling, he would have to get creative. Not that Margaret wouldn't help him along the way. He'd never been one not to problem solve, and he'd be damned if this would be the first time.

He reached to the ribbon that was laced in a crisscross fashion and slowly pulled the loops loose. With the tension released, Margaret's breasts sprang from the black lace and beckoned for William's touch. He looked up to Margaret's face. She was pleased. He felt as if she was testing him, and he was passing her expectations. He reached to one of the thin, silky straps and slid it from her shoulder. Once she pulled her arm free, the side of the gown draped, fully revealing her breast to him.

Seeing that he would not be able to reach the other strap, Margaret slowly slid the other strap down. The front of the gown dropped to a rest at her waist. Against her narrow torso and waist, her breasts demanded awe at their perfection. Even with everything she and William had done to this point, he found himself staring in wonder. A woman's body was one of God's greatest masterpieces, and there was no way he would be able to let this moment pass without giving it its due appreciation.

Margaret leaned over him, and placed her hands on the blanket next to his head. Her hair fell to perfectly frame her face. Shifting her body forward, she allowed her breasts to skim over William's mouth. He tilted his head back, tracking their motion with his tongue, as she twisted slightly to bring one waiting nipple to his mouth. With his free hand on her back, he guided her to drop even more, letting more of her supple mound invade his mouth. His tongue moved slowly at first, feeling her respond to the warmth of his kiss. He pulled her in even deeper, stroking her with his lips and tongue. A soft moan escaped Margaret's lips and she leaned even harder into him. Slightly lifting her body, William relinquished the breast only to find she had turned her body to bring him the other. He pulled her into his mouth, this time with an urgency that wouldn't allow him to slowly caress her with his tongue. When he grazed his teeth against her nipple, Margaret whimpered in pleasure.

She moved her body back and descended onto his lips with hers. William probed vigorously with his tongue in her mouth. The warmth of her mouth was going to pale in comparison to being inside the heat that was emanating from between her legs. He reached his hand behind Margaret and clasped his rod in his hand. Lifting it slightly from his body, he positioned it to its target. Margaret lifted from the kiss and stared into his eyes.

Licking her swollen lips, she breathed heavily. "Are you ready for me, William?"

He nodded slowly.

Margaret smiled and moved her hips back until the tip of him pressed into her velvety opening. William's eyes burned with urgency. Margaret's eyes glinted with mischief. She rocked forward, forcing his tip to slide out of her. She leaned back, and in an instant, he was in her again.

"Remember this, William? The night on the desk?" She pressed herself back again, allowing him to enter her a fraction more.

The night he could've had her, but didn't. He remembered quite well, and now, it was her turn to dictate what would happen, and when. This is what Margaret wanted. Control. She was going to show William that she had the control, and he didn't. He knew there was more meaning to this than this exact moment. It was message that Margaret was sending. But right now, carnal desire had overtaken sensibility.

She rocked back and forth, only allowing him to barely penetrate her. He felt her body's tightness slowing giving way, allowing him to enter further. She closed her eyes and threw her head back. Her body now moved in rhythmic bursts over his tip. Despite not letting him fully indulge in her, the pleasure that was building in her was obvious. She dipped and plunged over his ridge until he thought he would explode. He flexed his jaw and watched her face. She had entered into a new realm, no longer concerned with a lesson to teach him. With each rock of her hips, she pushed him deeper inside of her. She fell to William's chest and began pulsing her hips so erratically that William moved his hand to cup around her butt cheek and press her even harder into him.

The mounting ecstasy that had been building in Margaret broke free, her quiet moaning growing into powerful cries into his neck. Just as William felt her body tightening around him, he pushed her body down onto him, fully impaling her with every inch. The feel of her swallowing him sent his head back. He held her tightly on him. She continued her gyrations against him, with each movement her body engulfing him even more. Lifting his hips from the blanket, he pressed himself into her, with each thrust forcing whimpers from Margaret.

Margaret lifted her body from his and propped herself to full upright position. Flexing and pressing into her made her body rise slightly. Margaret's hips slowly began to roll back and forth, and he could feel the sensation building. The vision alone of her riding him was enough to make him want to release the commanding pressure that was forming. That, coupled with her bouncing breasts, and her cavern that pulled and tugged at him with each movement of her hips, was more than he could contain. Margaret's voice began to rise again, and the constricting force that was wrapped around him, pulled the explosion out of him. Pressing her hips into him, he thrust himself up into her as his hot seed flowed out of him. Clenching his jaw, he let out a groan of release as Margaret dug her nails into his chest, letting out her own cry of exhilaration. Their hips rolled slowly to a stop, and Margaret slumped down to his chest. William draped his arm over her, and felt their breaths finally begin to slow and quiet. For the first time since arriving at Margaret's house, he realized the pain that was radiating from his shoulder had increased tenfold. Up until now, he had followed the doctor's order explicitly, taking every precaution with his shoulder and its recovery.

Margaret gently lifted herself from William and straddled him once again. She reached to her waist and finding the shoulder straps, slid them back to their original position. Once again, William admired the vision of black lace over her skin. He had to admit that a spending his life partaking in that, and many similar scenarios, would not be horrible.

Margaret smiled, exuding satisfaction. William knew they had just crossed the line in their relationship, and everything would be different now. As Margaret slid to lie beside him, a rush of finality washed over him. If there was anything left still tying him to Sarah, he was certain this night dissolved it. He had committed to marry Margaret, and he knew that this had connected him further to her while simultaneously closing the connection to Sarah. An unexpected wave of emotion came thundering in his head as he remembered the night at the soda fountain with Sarah. Sarah despised Margaret, she always had. If she knew what had just transpired between him and Margaret, it would literally break her heart. William closed his eyes, forcing his mind back to the reality that Sarah was gone, and Margaret was going to be his wife. He wondered what it would be like to spend his life walking the fine line of pleasure and pain because of that truth. Something told him that the pleasure that Margaret could temporarily produce would pale in comparison to the pain of Sarah being gone.

He didn't want to think anymore, it wouldn't change anything and it hurt too damn much, and he was grateful Margaret broke his train of thought. "Hey," she pulled his chin to meet her gaze, "you haven't told me if you enjoyed the special."

He smiled faintly and realized he certainly had enjoyed it, a little too much. How could he not? As a sated man, he now knew what his father had been talking about; he had just gotten himself into something too deep to get out of now.

CHAPTER 10

Henry pulled into the yard of the Somerton ranch and turned off the truck. He had thought of nothing but his old friends on the long, tiring drive. It was still hard for him to believe that they were gone, and how tragedy could've reared its ugly head so completely in his life. He had two choices: to wallow in defeat and sorrow, or stand tall and carry on. He knew what Catherine would tell him to do, and he knew that if the tables had been turned, Edward and Anne would've done this for him. Getting to Sarah and bringing her home was the right thing to do. It was his way of proving his fortitude, and honoring the people he'd loved most.

But after the letter from Oscar, he knew he had an additional challenge on his hands. With Sarah's memory loss, he wasn't confident that he would be able to convince her to come home to Colorado. To her, he was a stranger. She would have to choose him, and a place she no longer remembered calling home, over Oscar and Ellie who clearly cared for her. How he was going to persuade her remained to be seen. He could only hope that fate would be on his side, and see to it that Sarah's path led her back to Colorado. He couldn't help but think if he were successful, that Sarah's path would also lead her back to Will. And that would be another heartache waiting to unfold. But, he was getting ahead of himself. Step one would to be to get out of the truck, and acknowledge the reality that he would not have Edward and Anne come out to greet him. The magnitude of loss was agonizing. A feeling he knew all too well.

He reached over to the glove box and pulled out an old photograph. It was faded and the edges curled, but the images were still clear. This would have to be enough. It was all he had. He stepped from the truck and slammed the door. No sooner had he shut one door, another opened. Sarah stood holding the door open to the modest house, and shielded her eyes from the sun to see him.

He took a silent deep breath and walked toward her, exaggerating his slow steps up the three stairs to the porch where Sarah remained. He wanted to hug her. The girl he had watched grow since the day she was born, now stood in front of him as a beautiful woman. She had changed, no doubt, but her eyes had not. She still held the same mesmeric and entrancing depth in her eyes, which currently, revealed the broken soul that he prayed could be mended. She removed her hand from her forehead, and he hoped to detect a glimmer of recognition. He approached her slowly, almost as if one sudden movement might spook her like a deer bounding back into the brush.

"Hello, Sarah." He was overwhelmed by the emotion of seeing her, and knowing the angst she must be surviving since her parents' death.

Her face held very little emotion. If anything, caution. She held her hand out to him. "Hello, Mr. Harston. Oscar thought you'd be here today."

Henry reached for her hand and gingerly shook it, again acutely aware of his every movement and mannerism. He looked into her eyes, and saw the same sweet innocence as when she was a child, transformed only by maturity, but still, Sarah. "Hello, Sarah. I'm so happy to see you." He gently shook her hand and fought the urge to hug her.

She smiled guardedly, and shifted her weight to her other foot. Her nervousness around him punctuated the sadness of the situation even more profoundly.

"Would you like to come in?" He could tell that her courage was on unstable ground, as if she was searching for a handhold.

"Sure." Although he was preparing himself for what he knew would be a heart- wrenching experience at the absence of Edward and Anne, he took his hat off, and walked through the door, looking around. Edward's dark brown coat hung on the hooks, and Anne's apron, hung tragically alone in the kitchen. He could do this. He would do this, for them. The care of their daughter, and when Matthew came back, their son too—would be his responsibility.

"Can I get you something? Tea? Coffee?" Sarah motioned to the kitchen.

Henry smiled, "Sure, whatever you've got sounds good."

"I just put on a pot of coffee, is that okay?"

He nodded and she quickly turned into the kitchen, pulling two green jadeite coffee mugs from the cabinet. He noticed her hands trembling and wished there was something he could do to ease her nerves.

"Do you want sugar, or…?"

"Oh no. Black's fine."

She poured the two cups and brought them to the small table against the wall. Henry sat and watched as she gingerly placed two sugar cubes into her steaming cup and stirred gently. There would be no easy way to go about this. He would need to start talking if he were to convince her of anything.

"Sarah," he began, but immediately realized that it had been easier playing out the conversation in his head than the actual thing. "A part of me of me died, when I heard about the accident. I know you don't remember, but I'll tell you what, I loved your parents like they were my own blood. There will always be an empty spot in me, now."

Sarah nodded and looked into her cup as if reading a message that could be seen through the dark liquid. "I know what you mean, Mr. Harston. I feel empty, too. Sometimes I wonder why. Why did this happen? Why did I survive, and they didn't?"

Henry took a deep breath. The question that haunted him since Catherine's death, he had no answer for. "I wish I had the answer. Well," he paused and creased his brow, "maybe I don't, on second thought. You see, I don't think we're meant to know the answers like that. Why this, and not that? I don't think we could handle such information. It's meant for God, and God alone, to understand. Maybe it's His way of taking some burden from us." He shrugged slowly and bent his mouth downward. "I don't know."

Sarah paused and looked at him. After a deep sigh, she nodded. "I think you're right. It just feels like if I knew why this happened, it would somehow make it easier to go on. But, I've realized that no matter if I knew or not, it wouldn't change any of it. I'm going to have this empty spot for the rest of my life. I'm just trying to come to grips with that."

Henry nodded and regarded the grief splayed on her beautiful face. The questioning she was going through, he had been through it all himself a thousand times. He wished she didn't have to experience this lesson so young in life. But learning it late in life was no good, either. All that either of them could do now was breathe in and out, and do what they could to honor the people they loved, and hope to make them proud.

With that renewed mission fresh in his mind, he pulled the old photograph from the breast pocket of his coat, and slid it across the table next to Sarah's coffee mug. "That's the four of us." He raised his eyebrows and cocked his head to the side as his memory took him to that moment in time, "Seems like a hundred years ago, we were a lot younger, then."

Sarah lifted the photograph with reverence, as if any abrupt movement might shatter the image. Henry watched her eyes move across the photo to each face. She glanced up to Henry, and back to the picture. She focused on Catherine, and Henry could see her determination to place a name with the face. He peered over the top of the photo and pointed with his finger over the top. "Catherine. My wife, Catherine. She and your mom were— close. As close as sisters. Best friends, really."

Sarah stared at the two women, with their arms locked at the elbow, laughing and happy. She looked up to Henry, as if she were about to say something, but creased her brow and looked back to the photo. "It must've been very hard on the both of you to hear the news about the accident."

Henry ran his hand over his mouth. "Catherine passed away, several months ago."

Sarah looked at him, and Henry detected sympathy in her eyes. Even if Sarah couldn't remember him, it gave him hope that somehow deep down inside, she did. And, even if she didn't, neither time, injury, nor tragedy, could erase the compassion that had always been a part of her.

"There was a fire in the barn. She was inside, and didn't get out in time. I've spent every waking minute since then trying to figure out what happened, and why. That is, until I got the letter from Oscar. Then I started thinking about you, and how I would need to help you. That is what Catherine would want me to do."

Sarah nodded and put the picture back on the table. "There's a lot that I don't remember, Mr. Harston, and...."

Henry stopped her, "Please, Sarah. You've never called me 'Mr. Harston' a day in your life, and I've known you since you were knee-high to a pipsqueak. So please, call me, Henry."

She shifted in her chair uncomfortably, but replied, "Okay, Henry." She took a deep breath and started again. "There's a lot in my mind that is like a thick fog. Like, I can almost see what's beyond the fog, but no matter how I try, I can't. And some things are completely black in my memory." She shook her head, "Nothing, nothing is there where I know it should be. Like when I was a kid. I have no memories, other than what has happened most recently in my life. It's a very scary, and lonely feeling. And," she paused, "I'm hoping that's what you can help me with."

"I know, Sarah. Memories are all we have once something is over, or gone. They make us who we are, where we started. I'll do whatever I can to shine a light through the fog for you."

Sarah ran her fingertip lightly over the image of her mother's hands in the photograph, and closed her eyes, before looking at him with determination. "Will you come with me, Henry? I want to show you something."

"Of course."

They both pushed the chairs away from the table, the screech of wood scraping against wood breaking the silent and still house. Sarah motioned to the stairs, "It's up here."

Henry followed, clinging to the handrail with each slow step. He knew all along this was going to be a test. But, Sarah needed him. He had to put the uneasiness in himself to the side, and focus on Sarah, and, getting her home to Colorado.

At the top of the stairs, Henry took notice of the tidy room, not much bigger than the bed and side tables. Without Sarah saying, he knew this was her parents' room.

Beneath a window, Sarah stopped and stared at the steamer trunk on the floor. He instantly recognized it and thought back to the day he helped Edward load it into their farm truck. Sarah knelt down in front of it, and unlatched the metal clasps. The lid creaked up, and she looked up at Henry.

"There are things in here, that I feel like I should know, but I don't. Maybe you can help me?"

Henry knelt down beside her, and not taking his eyes from the contents answered, "I'll do my best."

He recognized several of the items immediately, but thought best for Sarah to take it at a pace that she was comfortable with. The last thing he wanted to do was overwhelm her. His eyes scanned the items quickly, and it took every bit of self-control to keep from reaching in and pulling one of the items out. Catherine's embroidered tea towel.

Sarah must've noticed his gaze, and followed it down to the crisp white towel with the blue mountains and pine trees artfully stitched. She retrieved the towels and handed them to Henry. "Do you recognize these?"

Henry took the towels, seeing now that his hands were trembling with the ache emanating from his heart. He nodded slowly, "I'd know these, anywhere."

A beacon of hope escaped Sarah's dark eyes for the first time since he had arrived. "You do? I know my mother kept special things in here, but I don't know why she chose these towels."

Henry ran his thumb over the wording, 'Always Together.' "Catherine made these for your mother, right before you all left to come out here. I'm sure Catherine meant for your mother to use them, but I can see that your mother kept them in here. I can remember Catherine making these." Henry closed his eyes as the memory washed over him. "She cried the entire time." He smiled and handed them back to Sarah. "Your mother kept them perfect, just like the two of them were."

Sarah folded them gingerly and placed them back into the trunk. Henry detected an eagerness in her to learn more. She lifted a picture from the trunk and smiled at Henry. "This looks familiar to me, at least."

She handed him the frame, housing the same photograph that he had brought with him. He took a deep breath, "You know, after all these years, this is the only photograph of all four of us together. We were all getting ready to go down to Cow Creek for the community picnic. This was taken when you were probably, oh, I don't know, maybe eight or nine years old."

Sarah looked at the photo thoughtfully. "I like this picture. It feels so, happy. And, carefree. Like there wasn't a worry in the world."

"Well, there were plenty of worries, unfortunately. But I guess you could say that when the four of us were together, they were easier to bear. When you all left, it nearly did us all in." Henry handed the frame back to her. So far, this was going all right. The memories of Catherine, Edward and Anne stung, but also gave him a rush from feeling their love again. He hadn't thought too much of the past recently. It was nice to remember the good times, and feel lucky to have had them in the first place. Some folks never even get to have that.

Sarah removed another item from the trunk and looked at it for several seconds. She ran her fingertip over the top of it before handing it to Henry. "Do you know anything about this?"

Henry opened his palm and looked at the pale yellow wooden box. An intricate carving of four circles decorated the top. He turned the box over several times, inspecting the craftsmanship. He looked at the top again, and ran his finger over the carving as well.

"Hmmm. Well, I can't be certain about this one, but I believe this is something William made." He looked to Sarah, and was dispirited to see no flash of recognition flash in her eyes.

"William? Who is William?" The encouragement that had been building in her expression had suddenly vanished.

Henry opened his mouth, but creased his brow as he looked back to the box in his hand. She didn't remember William. He wasn't sure why that shocked him so much. After all, he knew she had lost her memory. It just hadn't completely occurred to him that that would include even William's name.

"William," he began, "is my son."

Sarah contemplated the new information. "Oh. So, he and I knew each other well?"

That was understatement, but Henry nodded his head. "Yep, known each other your whole lives. You and Matthew, and William and Tommy, my other son, spent nearly every day together. You all were pretty much joined at the hip."

Now Sarah's expression was pure astonishment. "Every day? Every day? How can I not remember someone that I spent every day with?" Her eyes filled with tears, and searched Henry for answers.

"Don't cry, Sarah." Henry touched her shoulder and she looked back at him. "I don't know the answer to that. I know that I'll do whatever I can to help you, though. You know that, right? That I'm here to help you remember?"

Sarah sniffed and nodded her head. "I know," she whispered. "What about this carving? Do you know why he put this carving on the top?"

Henry studied the carving again, but nothing about it seemed familiar to him. "I don't know that part. I'm sorry. Can I open the box?"

Sarah nodded quickly, "Oh yes, of course."

Henry pried the lid open and pressed his finger to the contents inside. "Now this," he said, "is an actual piece of home. Your home, in Colorado." He held up his fingers, pinched around several rust colored pine needles. "These are from the pines, I'm sure."

"The pines?"

"The pines. All you kids loved the pines. Not far from your house, an outcropping of pine trees surrounded by the quakies."

"Quakies? What are quakies?" Sarah was intrigued, and Henry was happy that the frustration had stopped wrinkling her forehead.

He laughed, "They're aspens. Aspen trees. I've just always called them quakies, from how their leaves shake."

Sarah held open her hand and he dropped the pine needles into her palm. She brought her hand to her nose and breathed deeply. "They smell good. It sounds like a nice place."

"It's beautiful, actually. You kids explored every inch of the pines at one time or another. You built forts, climbed trees, you name it."

"I wish, I wish I could remember it. It makes me sad that I can't remember."

Henry saw his opening, and knew there wouldn't be a better time than now to make his offer. "Maybe you can remember, Sarah. I came here to tell you that I will take you back to Colorado with me, and help you get your memories back. If you want, I will take you home."

Sarah sat deep in thought, tracing the circles over and over with her fingertip. She looked up at Henry. "I want to remember."

"I know you do." Henry said softly.

"I want to go home."

CHAPTER 11

Sarah set her last few items inside the cab of the truck and gently shut the passenger door. It had taken her and Henry a few days to collect her belongings, and get packed up. Henry had loaded up the minimal possessions into the bed of the truck and was making sure the ropes were tightly holding them in place. He tied a double tether around the old trunk, knowing that was the most valuable. She turned to look at Ellie and Oscar, standing in front of the only house that she could remember that had been home to her. Ellie had at least attempted to keep her emotions from spilling out, but she was unable to do so as she sobbed into Oscar's handkerchief. While Oscar did not have the outpouring of tears as Ellie did, his face was lined with emotion. For someone always so talkative and lively, he was silent and stoic, simply rubbing Ellie's back in a back and forth motion.

Sarah approached them, begging herself to keep it together, for all of their sakes. This was a hard decision for her. She remembered a lot of the farm and Oscar and Ellie, and leaving the one thing she was certain of, was daunting. There was nothing about telling them goodbye that would be easy. She grappled with the guilt of choosing Colorado, over staying with them. She only hoped that in time, they would come to realize it as a necessity if she were to ever regain her memory. The doctors had told her that there were no guarantees either way. But, by surrounding herself with people and places that were once familiar, might be a way to chip away at the wall impeding her memory. She knew herself too well to know that she would never be satisfied with not knowing where she came from. Too much of her life had been spent in Colorado. It was a part of her, she just hoped that it still would be once she was there.

Sarah blinked against the tears and held her arms out for Ellie. The two clung to each other, allowing the tears to come. When they could feel the rush slowing, they pulled apart from each other, still grasping each other's forearms.

"Oh Sarah, dear, how I will miss you."

Sarah nodded, fighting the tears. "I will miss you, too. You have been so good to me, always have been. I don't know if I'll ever be able to thank you for everything that you've done for all of us."

"Oh, pish. There is no thanks needed. You are family, and, and, I hope you will come back to us, someday."

The thought caught in Sarah's throat. Ellie feared that she would never come back. Sarah hadn't even thought that far down the road. She hadn't assumed she would stay forever in Colorado, but she hadn't planned a time that she would return to California, either. She knew that Adley would be coming home to California, and Ellie surely assumed that they would live their lives there. Up until the accident, Sarah did too.

"Of course I will." Sarah hoped that her tone exuded some sort of re-assurance, as it was too heartbreaking to leave Ellie with the impression that they would never see each other again. "I just have to…I just have to know. I have to know my past. If it weren't for that, believe me, I would be completely happy to be here with you and Oscar, waiting for Adley and Matty."

Ellie blew her nose and nodded. "Okay, dear. I know you do, and I understand, it's just that, that you'll be so far away, and I worry. With Adley and Matty gone, your parents, and now you, it just worries me."

Sarah hugged her tightly and whispered, "I'll be okay, I promise you."

She turned to Oscar. The look on his face was so forlorn that Sarah could hardly bring herself to look into his eyes. He held his arms open and she collapsed against his sturdy frame, allowing her tears to come all over again. He patted her back and said, "You come back to us, ya hear?"

She lifted her head from his chest and nodded, wiping the tears from her cheek with the back of her hand.

"I can't be the only one here to enjoy Ellie's cooking, right?"

Sarah laughed quietly at the unexpected lightheartedness brought to the moment. "Hey, she's getting pretty good," she said, defending Ellie. "Especially her biscuits," she added softly, sending Ellie a loving smile.

Oscar squeezed her shoulder one last time. "Well then, I'll just have to wait until you come back so we can enjoy those together. Besides, Adley would have my hide if he knew I was letting you go. So, not too long, okay?"

She smiled and nodded, and this time looked into his eyes. "Okay."

Henry had come to her side and shook Oscar's hand. "I'll make sure she's okay. You have my word."

Oscar nodded, "Just by seeing you here, I know she's in good hands. Have a safe trip back."

Henry extended his hand to Ellie. She looked at his hand and scoffed, "Oh, no you don't. Come here." She wrapped her arms around Henry's shoulder, "Take good care of our girl."

Stepping back, Oscar put his arm around her, and she wrapped her arm around his waist. Sarah paused to forge the image of them in her mind. She loved them, and it was not going to be a small task in being able to actually drive away from them.

Henry looked to her and gently said, "Are you ready, Sarah?"

Pausing for one more moment, she looked from Ellie to Oscar, and back again. "I think so."

"Okay, I'll be in the truck. Oscar. Ellie. It was real nice to meet you folks, thank you again, for everything. And, I'll keep my word, it's the only thing I can control in this life, and I'll make sure Sarah is taken care of." With a final nod, he settled his hat in place on his head and walked to the farm truck.

Sarah rushed back to Oscar and Ellie, and they all three held onto each other for one last moment. Oscar sniffed and patted her back, "You better be going now. How can we miss you if you won't go away?"

Sarah smiled at him; she would miss Oscar. From the very first day that they had all arrived to the Somerton's Ranch, Oscar had made it a point to make them all feel comfortable. Today was no different. He clearly wasn't happy about her leaving, but she knew he wanted to make it as easy on her as he could. All she could do was to follow his lead, and not prolong the goodbye any longer. She pulled away from the embrace, all three of them lingering one minute longer holding hands.

"Then, I won't even tell you goodbye. This isn't goodbye." As she blew them a kiss and turned to the truck, an eerie feeling seeped into her mind. Had she already said that to them? It seemed like she had said something like that before. She dismissed the feeling, chalking it up to the emotional duress of leaving the safe and the known, for the unknown. It wasn't that she feared for her safety in Colorado, but she couldn't release the very real fear that she may never know who she was before California. It was a risk, but worth taking. As she and Henry rolled slowly out of the driveway and away from Oscar and Ellie, Sarah forced herself not to look back. There was no looking back, now. She had made her decision. Now, all that was left to be seen, was if she could somehow find a way to look back, once she got to Colorado.

CHAPTER 12

William awoke early the next morning, taking a moment to remember where he was. He and Margaret had moved from the parlor to her bedroom after falling asleep in front of the fire for a few hours, and she now lay in the crook of his left arm. His shoulder was stiff and radiating pain. It mostly hadn't been bothering him. But, then again, after not fully paying attention to his shoulder last night with Margaret, it was hard to know if he had done something to reinjure it. He gently began to slide his arm out from under Margaret, hoping not to wake her. He was still tired, and would've welcomed more sleep, but the ache in his arm was overriding any other need at this point.

Margaret moaned quietly as he squinted and clenched his teeth to completely slide out from the mass of red curls heaped onto his chest. Once free, he froze in place, letting sleep settle back in on Margaret. Quiet mornings were a gift—a rare gift—that he had learned to appreciate since most of his life he had been up working before the sun made its appearance. Since his injury had kept him from his normal work routine, mornings had become an indulgence he could get used to, but he knew that it would be short-lived once he got back to work. Despite how his arm felt at this moment, he knew it was making progress, and spurred his mission to enjoy the morning even more so. Watching the world wake with a hot cup of coffee was in order.

He stood from the bed and looked at Margaret. He hadn't woken her, and she lay on her side breathing quietly. The memory of the previous night's events obscured his thoughts of enjoying the morning. The events that led up to last night, and where he was in his life, never could've been predicted. If there was ever a lesson to be taught, it was that some things couldn't be taken back. He had learned that in spades. And this was one of them. Some things just couldn't be undone, beginning with his mother's accident, and ending with where he was standing now. It was all too late to change now.

CHAPTER 13

Sarah didn't remember it, but Colorado was undeniably beautiful. The mountains that seemed to scrape the sky, with huge sprawling patterns of dark green pine forests with intermingled slate blue of the blue spruce, and sweeping arrays of light green atop the pale white trunks of the aspen trees. She and Henry had traversed a mix of landscapes between California and here. The rose-colored desert and dunes of Utah were breathtaking at sunset, as if they had been a masterpiece on display. She had seen magnificent sunsets in California. But, against the canyons of stone for as far as the eye could see, where the sunset met the land and became a stunning compilation of the sun's fire and supremacy, she now had a vision by which all sunsets would forever pale in comparison.

As marvelous as the desert was, it was still left wanting when compared to the mountains she was now driving through. Everywhere she looked, she could see a place she would want to be. Underneath a canopy of trees, or walking freely through a meadow of wild flowers, it all called to her. She had to wonder if this was a new revelation, or had she felt this way before, when she was here. Had she always valued this beauty, or was it simply her mind appreciating a new splendor that it believed it hadn't experienced? Either way, her new home, her old home as it were, was a gateway to heaven from what she could tell.

Henry had attempted to fill in some of the holes of her memory on the long drive, but it was so overwhelming that Sarah had stopped asking questions, and he had recognized her need to take it slow. People's names, places, feelings, were all too much to organize in the chaos of her mind. She wasn't sure she was ready to jump into the past yet anyway; she just left the very place she thought would be her future. There was quite a gap between the two, and the challenge of bridging it was daunting, especially because she didn't know if it would even be possible to do so.

The debate in her mind was called to a halt with the slowing of the truck, and the left hand turn onto a driveway that quickly progressed into a steep hill. Henry looked over to her as the truck lurched into a lower gear for the climb. He looked as nervous as she felt. She hated to think what the look on her face must be, so she attempted a reassuring smile, not entirely sure if it was more for Henry's sake, or hers. She turned toward the window and noticed the serviceberry bushes were in full bloom. The thin limbs were bursting with the little white flowers, and she wondered about the berries.

"Will the berries be edible?" She asked quietly, pointing out her window.

"Oh, yes. Tasty, too. Little berries, dark purple, and sweet. Catherine and your mother would always make the most delicious jam from them." Sarah noticed the same half smile from him, before he too had to turn and look out of his window. They crested the top of the drive and Sarah scanned the large, open expanse for anything that might seem familiar. The house was small and simple, with the brown paint beginning to chip at the corners, but Sarah could sense a comfort about it. A small walkway of flat stones led to wide set of steps, and a large fenced porch. She smiled at the wooden swing that was swaying slightly in the breeze. Across from the house was a graveled parking area that met up with a series of corrals that held two horses, lazily swishing their tails back and forth. Beyond the horse pen, Sarah could see the telltale muddy ruts of a pigpen. Her gaze settled on the scorched black earth not far from the animals. A few blackened boards still lay cracked and crumbling against the new tufts of green grass emerging from the destruction. Sarah didn't have to ask. The barn was gone, but the harsh devastation remained evident. From the sudden sag in his eyes, and quick intake of breath, Henry's grief, and the pain it left in its wake, was still very discernible in his face.

He quickly turned his attention to the back of the truck and began to untie the ropes that held Sarah's belongings. "Well, we should get you settled in, I think."

Sarah walked to the back of the truck where Henry struggled to loosen the ropes. "Henry, I don't think I've told you," she hesitated slightly, "thank you. Thank you for coming to California, and thank you for bringing me to your home."

"No need to thank me, Sarah. I would do anything for your parents. Then, and now. And, that means I would do anything I could to take care of you and Matthew. My home is your home, for as long as you want it to be." His smile was genuine and warm, and Sarah could feel her apprehension begin to melt away. She nodded slowly, and walked to the side of truck to loosen one of the many knots.

Once the ties had been released, Sarah and Henry brought the small items into the house. Sarah put her small suitcase on the floor and scanned the room. The house was tidy and organized, nothing lavish, but felt as if nothing more was needed. The fireplace, surrounded by large, smooth river rock was the most impressive element in the room. For an inexplicable reason, she found herself drawn to it. She walked over and placed her hand on a stone to the side of the large wooden mantle, running her fingers over the cool surface, and around its edges. There was nothing like this in California. She dropped her hand to her side and took a step back to better admire the diversity among the stones. The fireplace was framed clear to the ceiling with the stones that varied in shades of gray to shades of brown, and some that boasted both. The large hearth provided room for a metal basket holding several split logs, and a couple of iron pokers. It wasn't difficult to imagine the beauty the fireplace would display with a roaring fire inside, flickering against the stones.

Henry interrupted her fantasy of feeling the warmth of the fire on her back. "Your dad and I built that. Boy, oh boy! Was that a project? Hauled every single stone in ourselves, too."

Sarah turned to him. "You hauled them? From where?"

"Not far from here, at King's Creek. We went for several miles up and down it to find these. Wasn't easy, I'll tell ya. But," he paused giving the fireplace a thoughtful nod, "I think it turned out pretty good."

"I'll say," Sarah agreed. "These rocks are beautiful. I bet the creek is, too?"

"Oh, yes. Good fishin', too. You remember how I told you that you kids spent a lot of your free time in the pines?"

Sarah nodded.

"You spent just about as much time at the creek, as you did the pines."

Sarah touched the stones again. "Really? I don't remember a creek." Her voice trailed off with the realization that another substantial part of her past was gone.

"Well, maybe you will once you see it again." The hope in Henry's voice mirrored the hope she was afraid to admit.

She looked at Henry and smiled, "Maybe, Henry. Just maybe."

CHAPTER 14

William jumped from the bed of the truck and walked to the driver-side window. "Thanks for the ride, Mr. Wilkes. It would've been a long walk home from town."

"You betcha, William, any time. Say, when do you think your dad will be back from wherever he went? I wanted to ask him how much hay he was interested in buying this year."

William shrugged his shoulders and raised his eyebrows, breathing out heavily. "I wish I knew. It's been about a week, so I can't imagine it'll be too much longer. But, then again, what do I know? I don't even know where he went in the first place. I'll be sure to have him get a hold of you, though. I know we need some hay." He paused, but mustered enough to continue. He would have to get used to talking about it, but he didn't know if that would ever be possible. "All that we had, was in the barn."

Perry Wilkes cringed slightly and looked at William, "Dagdabbit, I didn't mean to bring that up, William. I'm sorry."

William knew he didn't. What Mr. Wilkes didn't realize was that at any given moment, there was something that reminded him of his mother, or the fire, and it didn't much matter how much time had gone by. He shook his head, and looked to the ground, kicking at the gravel. "Nothin' to be sorry about, Mr. Wilkes. I'll let you know about the hay."

Mr. Wilkes nodded and put the truck in gear. William waited until the truck had disappeared over the hill, allowing the sadness to linger in the air. He turned to walk up his driveway, trying to focus on hay, instead of the fire. It would help if knew where his father was. He hadn't let on to

Tommy how uncomfortable it had made him not knowing the whereabouts of their father. Henry hadn't been himself since the accident. But, leaving for days with no indication which direction he was going, was a new cause for concern. He tried to tell himself that it wasn't time to panic. Yet.

He crested the last steep part of the driveway and looked around. Everything seemed quiet with no signs of Tommy. He would have to keep better track of him. Tommy was getting more independent, but he didn't want him to think he could start having the run of the countryside without letting someone know where he was and whom he was with. But, with his father setting the example, it would be difficult to enforce.

There was still a good bit of daylight left. His day at the lumberyard wasn't difficult, but everything with his arm in the sling was more exhausting than it should have been. He would be more than happy to call it a day and kick his boots off for the rest of it, but he knew the horses would need some water and attention. Margaret would be by early in the morning to give him a ride to the lumberyard, and it would be best to get the chores done tonight. Maybe Tommy was inside, and he would get him to help out. As he walked down the narrow path that led to the front porch of the house, he remembered that his mother always had the walk decorated with yellow and orange marigolds on both sides. She said they were the flower that just kept giving since their seeds were plentiful and so easy to harvest. Throughout the winter, she kept the black and white seeds inside of a jar that sat on a shelf on the front porch. He decided it might be time to plant some again. His mother would like that, and with the snow gone and spring starting to wake up the earth, it's what she would've done. He walked up the steps and over to white paint-chipped shelf that held her gardening tools. Kneeling down, he moved the small spade and hand rake to the side, revealing the small jelly jar filled with the little splinters that would bloom into colors of the sun. Pulling the jar out and turning it over in his hands, he watched the seeds fall against the side like beads in a kaleidoscope. Perhaps it was time for the seeds, and for him, to emerge from the dark corner, and live again. His mother never intended for the seeds to stay seeds, and he knew she would never want him to not fully live and enjoy life.

A pot crashing into the sink jerked his attention toward the house. Tommy was home, after all. He was glad that for now, he wouldn't need to track him down and he could help him with the chores. Standing with the jar in his hand, he let the seeds settle at the bottom of the jar; he would plant them, soon. It was time, for all of them.

He shifted the paper sack of nails that he brought home from the lumberyard to start mending the corrals to the same hand holding the jar of seeds to fling open the screen door. Using his knee to hold it open, he leaned down to turn the doorknob to the house. Pushing the door open, he walked inside before turning to close the door behind him. He turned toward the kitchen just beyond the living room to holler at Tommy. But, before he could utter a word, the bag of nails and the jar of seeds dropped from his hand and came crashing to the floor. The sound of breaking glass, and the rolling nails on the floor went unnoticed, as well as the seeds scattering across the floor and over his boots. He could only stand in place, believing his mind was playing tricks on him, and stare.

He blinked and shook his head slightly, as if to clear the apparition before him. There she was. A sight he had convinced himself many times over he would never behold, except in the daydreams that he allowed himself occasionally. Her beauty was utterly striking. He had never seen anything so breathtaking, yet instantly recognized it at the same moment. Holding a large cast iron skillet in her hands, looking at him with her almond-shaped brown eyes, was the girl he promised to love for the rest of his life. The girl was gone, but only because of the woman that was now standing before him. The girl. The woman. They were one in the same. As if a bolt of lightning streaked across the sky and through his heart, he knew that the love he promised her was anything but gone. In that instant, he realized that he would be a fool to continue to deny the feelings he had for her or pretend that they had somehow vanished over time.

He wanted to say something to her. Hell, he wanted to run to her. But the magnitude of shock coursing through him let him do neither. He could only stare, with his mouth gaping and his eyes locked on hers. He somehow managed to lift his feet and took two steps toward her, and all of a sudden, all he could think of, was how amazing it would feel to hold her in his arms. A smile of disbelief mingled with joy crossed his lips as his steps quickened to close the gap between them. Raising his left arm to embrace her, he was suddenly filled with confusion as her eyes filled with terror and she raised the skillet into a position worthy of a major league slugger. Before he could stop, or talk, or think, Sarah's arm cocked back and swung the skillet with full force toward his head. Ducking his head to the side, the skillet barely grazed passed him, missing his temple by a fraction of an inch. As her arm was on the downswing, he quickly clasped his hand around her wrist and squeezed tightly.

"What in God's name are you doing?" He belted out, eyes bulging with a newfound disbelief.

"Let go of me," Sarah screamed, trying to wriggle her tiny wrist loose from his grip.

"Drop the pan, then," William screamed, equally as convincing. The way Sarah was looking at him could only register as complete perplexity. He hoped he wasn't hurting her, but he couldn't believe the position he was forced to be in to defend himself from an attack that in no way he could've anticipated.

Sarah struggled again try free her wrist, "I said, let me go!"

William couldn't stand it any longer to be squeezing her arm so tightly. He thought about taking a hit to the head with a skillet just to avoid hurting her. He looked at her as calmly as his blood pressure would allow, and lowered his voice. "Sarah? I'm not going to hurt you. I'm going to let you go, so if you're going to wallop me, I guess you can. But, I'd really rather you not, if it's all the same to you. Okay?"

He kept eye contact with her blazing eyes, and slightly loosened his fingertips from her dainty arm. "See? I'm letting go. It's okay, it's okay." His voice was quiet and calm, although he had no idea how it possibly could be. His mind was reeling from the fact that not only was he staring into the eyes of the person that he loved and thought he would never see again, but he found that he was defending himself from certain bodily harm while staring into those same eyes. If ever he thought that he and Sarah would be reunited, he never could've imagined it would've played out like this.

He freed her wrist from his clasp, and slowly moved his hand up to her line of sight. She stood staring at him, breathing heavily with the look of fear still etched in her face. "See? I'm not going to hurt you, Sarah. Can you put the pan down, now? Please?" He was still accentuating his cautious tone as he took a few steps back, since she still clung to the pan with white knuckles.

"Wha—what do you want?" Sarah demanded.

Will's head cocked back in complete confusion. "What do I want? Is that what you said? What do I want?" He wanted to laugh out loud at the situation, and he almost did. Surely Sarah was trying to play a trick on him. But his amusement soon faded, as he couldn't recognize one glint of humor in her eyes. Her eyes were still nervous, scared, different.

Will was beginning to understand that there was more going on here than he possibly could've realized. Sarah was serious; there was no resemblance of how they were the last time they were together. There was no connection, no bond, of years spent together or the promise they made to each other. There was nothing but a frightened woman, a confused man, and a skillet still at the ready.

CHAPTER 15

The squeal of brakes outside broke their stare as they turned toward the front window. William was relieved to see that his father was finally home. He had a lot of blanks to fill in, where he'd been and more importantly, how it came to be that Sarah was standing in their kitchen. Will turned his attention back to Sarah, who momentarily relaxed her weapon, but brought it back up as he started to talk to her.

"Sarah, please, put the pan down. That's my dad; he's not going to hurt you, either."

She lowered the pan, and pleated her brow in confusion. "Your…dad? Henry, is your dad?"

William wanted to understand what was happening. This all felt like a strange dream that you wake up from feeling relieved that is all just a dream. But, he was wide awake, and Sarah was as scared as he had ever seen. Scared of him.

"Yes, my dad," he answered slowly.

She lowered the pan to hang in her hand at her side. "Then, you are William, or Tommy?"

Will's heart started to pound. If this was some idea of a trick being played, it wasn't funny. He saw no amusement in any of it. Based on the look on her face, she wasn't about to crack a smile and end this bad dream for him.

Slowly, he walked toward her, as gently, and as carefully as he could. He had to be next to her. All he wanted, was to understand why she was acting like this toward him. He was finally within arm's reach of her, and with every fiber of his being he wanted to touch her. She looked up at him, her eyes searching his for answers that he didn't have.

"Sarah," his voice cracked, "it's me. Will."

At the announcement of his name, her eyes welled with tears. Blinking up at him and forcing the tears to spill onto her cheeks she whispered, "Will? You're Will?"

"Holy hell, William, you're home." Henry's eyes widened as soon as he walked through the door and saw the two face to face.

William spun around. "Dad." He was grateful his father was home and safe, but he had no time for a reunion with him. He lifted his hand gesturing to Sarah and stuttered, "Sarah, Sarah's here? What's going on?" The urgency in his voice was disconcerting, and he realized that shock must be settling in. His mind was whirling and he couldn't get his mouth to work properly.

Henry closed the door and walked to the kitchen. "Son, just calm down. I tried to get to you before you left the lumberyard, but they said that you had already caught a ride home. I was going to explain it all to you before you got here. But, obviously, you beat me to it."

William's eyes bulged. "Okay, so explain."

Henry looked at William and back to Sarah and took in a deep breath. "This is going to be hard to tell you, son. I've been in California."

William nodded slowly, understanding that for Sarah to be here, California had obviously been a part of the equation.

Henry looked down and continued quietly, "I went because, because there was an accident."

William furrowed his brow, waiting expectantly, but afraid to hear what was obviously difficult for Henry to formulate into words.

Henry ran his hands through his hair and looked at William. "This isn't easy to say."

William eased his expression and lowered his voice. "What is it, Dad?"

"Edward and Anne, and Sarah," he looked to her and back to William, "they were in a car accident."

William spun around and looked at Sarah up and down, wanting to hold her, everywhere. The thought of her being hurt suddenly filled him with alarm. She looked beautiful, perfect. But after a closer inspection, he could see a pink scar where a laceration was beginning to heal on her forehead. She had been hurt. The same feeling that surged through him the day he saw her at the cove facing the bear arose. He felt nauseous. The thought of her ever being hurt was at the core of his every fear. Knowing she had been hurt sent a pain through his chest, and he was certain that if he had anything to do with it from here on out, he would do whatever it took for her to never feel pain again.

He turned back to his father to continue, although he was beginning to have the sinking feeling that everything is father was telling him was only going to get worse. He only let his father carry on in the hopes that he was wrong. "What happened, Dad?" he asked.

Henry eyes looked tired and sadness overtook them in that moment. "They didn't, they didn't survive the accident." Henry sighed heavily. William knew that saying those words were difficult, the pain streaking across his father's face couldn't be ignored. Henry cleared his throat, "Sarah was hurt badly, but she was lucky."

William looked at her again. Her face was twisted in sadness, and the confusion in her eyes as she looked at him, destroyed him. He dearly wanted to be able to wrap his arms around her.

"But," Henry continued, "Sarah's injuries were serious." William noticed his father's tone was laden with dread. What was he talking about? She looked fine, other than the scar on her forehead, but even that looked to be healing. Will's expression dropped as the realization of the situation was becoming clear. His earlier confusion, Sarah's strange behavior, all of it was becoming clear. He was filled with even more anxiety to hear what his father was about to reveal. Henry walked closer to William, "You see, she had major head trauma that caused her to be knocked out for several days."

William nodded slowly, and Henry reluctantly went on. "When she woke up, the doctors were very encouraged by her progress and thought that her bruises and cuts would heal just fine. But, it wasn't too long before they realized that..."

William raised his eyebrows and held his breath, waiting for the continuation, "Realized what?"

Henry's chest filled with his deep breath that he held for a moment. "William, they realized that she had lost her memory. Her head injury caused her to lose a great deal of her memories."

A swift kick to his gut would've been more welcomed than what his father just said. The wind had been completely knocked out of him, and he felt his head start to spin. "What, exactly, are you saying?" He turned to Sarah again; she had been quiet through all of this. He wasn't sure she would've been able to speak even if she wanted to. Her lips were so tightly pressed together, he was sure to keep from bursting into tears. His father's words slowly sunk into him and he tried to remain calm.

"Her memories, of here, are gone. Her memories of Colorado are gone." Henry confirmed.

Will looked at Sarah, searching for what to say, what to even tell himself. In a flash, he remembered the day he and Sarah had said goodbye at the cove. He begged her to remember their promise. He told her to never forget what they had. She had promised him, and now through no fault of her own, that promise was broken. A promise broken, and, irretrievable.

He knew when he did it, that he shouldn't have. Knowing what he knew now, it was probably not the right time, or the right reaction. But something so deep inside of him would not listen to reason. Wrapping his arm around Sarah, he brought her gently against his chest. His arms were once again around Sarah. His Sarah. All he wanted to do was to hold her and let the sadness flow out of her and into him over losing her parents. That kind of pain was debilitating and relentless, and he knew it all too well. He would gladly bear it for her if he could. With every bit of his strength, he held her knowing the fear she must be feeling, knowing that the memories of her life were now doused in cloud of black ink. He wanted to hold her because he had dreamt of the moment that he might be lucky enough to do so just one more time. Closing his eyes, he breathed in the scent of her hair. None of this seemed real, but as he bent his head down to press his lips against her forehead, he realized that nothing had ever felt so true. But just as the actuality of Sarah being in his arms melted over him, it was over the moment his lips pressed against her warm skin. She pushed out of his embrace and stepped back, looking at him with anguish splayed all over her face. In that instant, he knew he had gone too far. He cursed at himself for choosing his needs over hers. She wasn't ready to have him hold her, and he did it anyway. The way she looked at him was devastating, and he wasn't sure he could forgive himself for doing that to her. Never again, he swore. He would never again be the one to cause that look to mar that breathtakingly beautiful face of hers.

He thought, as far as cruel tricks were concerned, that he had well and truly punched his card by now. He could see that he was just a pawn in fate's twisted book. If there was some other explanation, he didn't know it. If it weren't that, then how could Sarah have been brought back to him, with no memory of what they promised each other? As if that weren't punishing enough, even if she had her memory, there was the minor detail that he was engaged to be married to the one person that Sarah absolutely detested. He thought back to walking up the driveway, and the only thing on his mind was to plant his mother's marigold seeds. That all seemed so trivial to him, now. The only connection between then and now was that his life now mirrored the seeds that were scattered all over the floor. Picking up the pieces would be a task he wasn't sure he would successfully achieve. The chance of picking them all up were slim, and hoping that the end result would be as simple as a flower, or hope, blooming, was next to zero.

CHAPTER 16

Something inside of her wanted to stay in his arms. Her mind was screaming that it was alright, too. Henry had told her so many stories of her and
Will, stories that would have made it perfectly normal for him to hold her,
and for her to seek comfort in his arms. If there was anything that she craved
now, it was feeling safe. She wanted to feel safe in his arms, but she didn't.
She didn't know him, and it wasn't in her to force herself to feel what wasn't
there. Her mind and logic couldn't override the emotion surging through
her now. The last man that held her was Adley, and she found herself suddenly doubting if coming to Colorado was the right decision. Perhaps she
should've stayed with Ellie and Oscar, and waited for Matty and Adley to
come home.

But, there was something about this man that just had just wrapped her
in his embrace. She felt herself reaching for some memory to cling to of him.
She trusted what Henry had told her about her childhood, and therefore
what he shared about her and Will's closeness. She studied Will's face, willing it to come back to her. Surely she would remember those eyes. Piercing
and blue, calm and intense; all at the same time. The way he watched her
was powerful, but she wasn't uncomfortable. He looked at her protectively,
and she had to remind herself that to him, she wasn't a stranger. He could
remember their past, and this must be as difficult for him to comprehend
as it was for her. Almost.

She wanted to say something to him to ease the hurt in those passionate
eyes after she pulled away so abruptly from him. She didn't mean to make
a scene, but at the time, the emotions erupted and it couldn't have been

helped. There must've been something in her subconscious of him. Otherwise, why would she care so much that she hurt him by her actions? She couldn't find the words, and almost wished she could feel his momentary embrace and start over again.

He still stood, patiently looking at her, as if deep in thought. She studied his face, his jaw clenched tightly, as if trying to hide the emotion that was pouring from his eyes. His broad shoulders gave way to strong arms, his torso narrowing at the hips. Leaning against him, she could feel the tightness of his body and the strength it must contain. She studied the sling that held his arm immobile and a sudden pang of worry rose within her. The sight of the sling made her feel something, of that, she couldn't deny.

She took a sudden step toward Will, but stopped herself from going right to him. She raised her arm, and brushed her fingertips lightly against the navy blue fabric of the sling. "Your arm...I hope I didn't hurt you."

His eyes instantly softened, as he shook his head and looked down to the sling. "You didn't," he quietly answered.

She hesitated, not wanting to cross any boundaries, "Are you, is your arm, okay?"

He smiled again at her and she had to admit that the way he was looking at her made her feel at ease. "Well, it's going to be, I guess. At least that's what the doctors say, as long as I take it easy while it heals. It's actually my collarbone that's broken. I'll be like this for a while longer, I suspect."

She nodded and smiled slightly at him. He seemed relieved to have the awkward moment over, and she was as well. Maybe it was just what Henry had told her about him that was starting to settle in, or maybe it was just him. She didn't know what it was about him that made her feel at ease, and yet, anxious all at the same time. But, that's why she was here. She was here to remember, or at least try to remember, her life before California. Once she knew where she came from, she could feel ready to live her life and move on with her future. For as much as Henry had told her, and the thousand miles she had to contemplate what she might remember, none of told her as much as being in the presence of Will. The answers she needed, the memories she craved, were wound around this man standing in front of her. And, if the first few minutes with him told her anything, it was that there was more, so much more to know. It was something deep down inside of her that told her that her past was intricately woven with his.

CHAPTER 17

William and Henry spent the rest of the afternoon clearing out the small room just off the kitchen. Catherine had used it as a sewing room, and since her accident, Henry hadn't been able to change anything about it. He would go in there occasionally, thinking he was ready to box up her notions, but every time, he thought of some reason to put it off a little longer. Now, with Sarah needing a room, it was finally time. The room was just big enough for a small bed in the back corner, and a small round table next to it as a bedside table. Opposite the bed, Henry kept the small chest of drawers that Catherine would use to store her fabrics. It made a perfect dresser to hold the few items of clothing that Sarah brought with her. William brought the small round mirror that hung in the living room, and placed it above the dresser.

Just as he finished hanging it, he caught Sarah's reflection from behind. She was leaning over her bed, placing the pillow against the wall after she had spread the quilt neatly on top of it. Her silky brown hair fell to the front of her shoulders and swayed gently with her movements. He knew he was staring, but there was not one part of him that could turn his attention from her. She was absolutely breathtaking. Her skin had a warm golden glow, and looked perfectly smooth and soft. Her face had the same features he had always found undeniably beautiful, but her high cheekbones and full pink lips seemed to be accentuated with her maturity. But her body, her body had become something else. Her body was hard to ignore as it had changed, too. Everything about her was exquisite. The way her shirt clung to her breasts left little for Will to have to imagine. The round fullness was so alluring that he couldn't help but let his eyes sweep over them. Her narrow waist and hips would feel so good to wrap his arms around and hold on to.

He jerked his attention back to the mirror, instead of the beauty showing in its reflection. What are you thinking, William? You're engaged. To Margaret. Remember? He had to admit that everything with Sarah would be different now. It had to be, he had made his choice. All he could hope for now was to somehow be in her life again as her friend. And, even that wasn't a guarantee. It stung remembering that he was a stranger to her now. She might not know him, but he sure as hell knew her, and truth be told, still loved her, if even as his best friend. That was a love he allowed himself to hold on to and keep in his heart, and there was no reason to let that go. As he had done for as long as he could remember, he knew he would do everything he could to help her. To protect her. He couldn't stand to even imagine the kind of fear Sarah must be feeling, and his protective instinct was working in overdrive because of it. She had taken a huge leap of faith by agreeing to come back to Colorado with his father, and he was going to show her that it was the right choice. There was no doubt that he could help her, he felt it in the furthest reaches of his soul. The fact remained that he knew her better than anyone, even better than she knew herself at this point.

Not able to stop himself, he looked back to the reflection in the mirror and noticed Sarah had finished making the bed and was standing, looking at him. She was clearly deep in thought, her angelic face showing little emotion. Her reflection alone could've kept him content forever, but he had her, in the flesh, behind him to behold. Keeping his eyes off her was an impossible request. Not denying the gift any longer, he turned to her, and smiled. "Are you okay?"

Sarah blinked and slowly nodded her head. "Yes. It's just that I keep waiting. Waiting for something to come into my mind that I remember. But, nothing does." She shook her head and looked down at her hands. "I feel like I'm waiting, at each passing moment, for something to happen.

But with each minute that passes and I don't remember my past, I have to wonder if I ever will." She looked back up, trying to stop the tears from coming. "The doctors said that my memory may never come back," she whispered.

Will took a few short steps toward her and her spine straightened. Having already scared her, when he went too far by holding her, he stopped. Now, he knew the look of fear in her eyes, and he never wanted to see it again. She wasn't ready for everything that seemed to come so naturally to him, and he would have to remember that. Especially if he were to gain her trust.

"But, the doctors also said that it might come back just fine. That's what you have to hold onto, okay? We have to be thinking that it will come back. But, it's not going to do you any good to be worrying every single second that passes by where a memory doesn't come to you. You just need to get settled here, let your mind and your body heal, and not put so much pressure on yourself. A very wise person once told me, 'All due things in all due time.' We just need to trust in that, all right? And, you're not in this alone."

She smiled again, and he was relieved to see her posture relax. She closed her eyes and took a deep breath. "Okay, you're right." She looked up at him, "Thank you, Will."

On the inside, he leapt. She called him Will. Not William, Will. Something deep inside of her made her call him Will. In that moment, he believed his words to her even more. His Sarah was still in there, but he would need to be patient, too. Rushing her, or pushing her could only backfire. Trusting in his own advice, he hoped that in all due time, Sarah's memories would return. He wanted to reveal to her that she called him by the name that only she used. He wanted to wrap his arms around her in the excitement of that revelation. But, he knew better than to do that. Step by step he would help her, and the first step, was to let things happen on her timetable.

"You're welcome." He paused and looked around the room. "Well, I know it's not much, but I hope you'll be comfortable here. Is there anything else you need?"

Sarah looked around the room and then back to William. "No, it's cozy, just the way I like it. But, I am tired. Maybe I'll lie down and rest for a little while if that's okay?"

"Of course it is. You just let me know if there's anything you need, all right?"

She nodded and he turned toward the door to step out. He gave her one last lingering look, still in disbelief that Sarah was here. He grasped the doorknob and slowly pulled it shut behind him.

"Will?" she called, just before the door latched.

He pushed the door open, his heart pounding at the sound of his name once more coming from her lips. "Yes?"

"I'm...I'm happy to be here."

If she was happy, he didn't know what to call how he was feeling. Happiness didn't even begin to graze the surface of it. He paused and looked deeply at her, "I am too, Sarah." He gently closed the door and put his face in his hands. He took a deep breath, ran his hands up over his face, and through his hair. It would take some time for this all to sink in.

His happiness, his elation, his utter euphoria that he couldn't help but feel, was compromised. All of the amazing sensations that he was feeling from once again being with her were entangled with restraints. Every feeling he wanted to express, he had to stifle. The reality was, that he had made a decision to move on with his life. And now, there was much more at stake than just his future. He had never been one to settle, but he would have to settle for being a friend to Sarah, and nothing more. Too much had changed, too much had already happened, and too much had already been promised. That very well may be. But, what he still couldn't quite grasp was, that what had been taken from him, was now given back. He learned the hard way that life doesn't play out that way. His mother had been taken from them, forever. And, up until a couple of hours ago, he thought Sarah had been, too. His mind replayed the promise he made her. The fateful promise that someday, he would take care of her and make her happy. That is what he still intended to do. It would just have to be completely different than how he had imagined it would be.

He sighed and walked away from Sarah's door and through the kitchen to find his father sitting on the couch, looking expectantly at him. "Are you okay, son?"

William sighed and shook his head, "Okay? Well, 'okay' isn't exactly how I would put it, but I guess I'm trying to be." He walked over to his father, who stood and hugged him tightly.

"It's good to be home, William," he said, patting his back. "I'm sorry I couldn't tell you about the trip. I didn't want you to worry too much, and I didn't want to tell you about Sarah. Honestly, I wasn't sure she would agree to come back with me, and I didn't want to give you any false hopes in case she didn't."

William nodded. He understood now why the secrecy was so important. His dad was right. He would've been going out of his mind wondering if Sarah were coming back to Colorado. Instead of worrying about that, he had spent the week with Margaret and everything that they did, he felt, had changed everything. Permanently. He sighed again, wondering if all of that would've happened had he known there was a possibility of seeing Sarah again. It was all a waste of energy now to think about the "what ifs." What was done, was done. Besides, the situation with Margaret was far too complicated. Whether they had been together like that or not, his deal with Vernon hinged on marrying Margaret. His family's very survival hinged on marrying Margaret. And Sarah, or no Sarah, wouldn't change that. That didn't mean that his heart didn't ache with the familiar depth of regret that he was certain would never leave him.

It suddenly occurred to him that he had not been told anything about Matthew. He shot his head up and opened his eyes. "What about Matthew? Why didn't he come, too?"

"Matthew is enlisted. He's been gone for a few months and no one is really sure where he is. He might already be overseas, I don't know. The worst part is that he doesn't know about the accident, or about his parents."

William looked down to his arm, hanging limp in the sling. Had it not been for the logging-truck accident, he would have most likely been summoned to fight in the war, too. The guilt of that had already played out for him as many of his friends had already gone. It struck him as ironic that for as many cruel tricks that fate had played, had the logging accident not happened, he wouldn't be here now, with Sarah.

He sunk into the couch, suddenly exhausted, and let out a soft laugh. He closed his eyes and leaned back. A few hours ago, he thought he was tired. Now, his mind and body were numb from the shocking turn of events, and he truly felt drained. After a few minutes, he opened his eyes and stared at the ceiling. The thought occurred to him that how would he possibly be able to sleep having Sarah under the same roof. He had so many questions for her. He wanted to know about California, and her life over the past couple of years, but he wanted the answer to the biggest question of all. The question that nagged at the back of his mind nearly every minute, and that was why she had never written to him. He didn't harbor any ill feelings toward her because of it, but it would be nice to at least hear the explanation for it. But, perhaps now, she actually wouldn't know the answer anyway. After he had waited for months and months for some sort of contact, he had learned to accept that it wasn't coming. Admittedly, he was hurt because of it. But, he had learned to let go, and ultimately, to forgive her. He had truly wished her well in her new life that didn't include him. Not that it would change anything, but he thought he at least deserved to know why she couldn't have used the stamp to tell him that she was moving on with her life as well. He had thought that stamp would be their only hope to stay connected. The stamp may not have been used, but he couldn't help the awe that surrounded his thoughts; Sarah had been delivered to him, instead of a letter.

That, and so many other questions, would all have to wait. He realized that. It would be a delicate dance uncovering the happenings over the last several months, and the last thing he wanted Sarah to feel was pressure to explain herself, or that he was upset with her. His mission now was simple. He was going to help her, and not for his own selfish reasons of wanting her to remember what they had shared. His love for her was pure, and therefore he wanted only what was best for her. His wants and needs would not overshadow that. But, it would still be an interesting night knowing that she was there, and he couldn't deny the craving he had to be near her.

He hoisted himself from the couch, remembering the chores that needed to be done so that he wouldn't have to worry about them tomorrow morning, before Margaret arrived to take him to the lumberyard. His eyes widened as a harsh realization entered his mind. Margaret. He would need to tell Margaret that Sarah was here, living with him, and that he would most likely be spending a fair amount of time with her to help her regain her memory. He didn't have to contemplate the scenario long to know that none of those announcements would go over well with her. In all fairness, he couldn't blame her. Margaret had gotten quite used to having him when and where she wanted, and the competition for his time and attention would most certainly be a burr in her blanket. He rubbed his brow, as if preparing for the headache that would surely be brought on the moment Margaret realized that she would not have a say in this. Not only would Margaret be livid about sharing William, it didn't take a genius to know that it was who she would be sharing him with, that would really embitter her. If he were to keep the peace at all, with Margaret and Vernon, he would need to convince her that Sarah was not a threat to their engagement. The first one who would need convinced of that, though, was himself.

CHAPTER 18

Sleepless nights were not new to William, but this one was different. This one was worse. Now, he would've gladly taken on the one or two things on his mind like in the past. But now, they all converged as one stifling grip on his mind, and sleep was going to be an impossible request. It wasn't enough to sort through the emotions from learning of Edward and Anne's accident—and Sarah narrowly escaping death herself—but he was having a heck of a time keeping his mind on anything but the fact that Sarah was sleeping in his mother's sewing room; a mere few feet away. His stomach would swirl with anxiousness when he thought how every single day and night, she would be in his home. He had never even dared to imagine what that would be like until the day that he would be able to marry her and have her all to himself. But, here she was. Only, not for the taking.

The next obvious dilemma was Margaret. She would be there in a few short hours to take him to the lumberyard. She would see that his father had returned home, and undoubtedly want to know where he had been. William knew that as soon as she heard the word California, there would be an uprising to manage. There would be no hiding the fact that Sarah was now a part of the Harston household, and William was dreading the moment when the two would be meeting face to face. Sarah had been through enough, and his instinct was to protect her from what was most certainly going to be another unpleasant experience. He hated to make such assumptions about Margaret. After all, a lot of time had passed and a lot had happened between them that would surely put to rest any doubt in her mind. But, if William knew anything about Margaret, it was that she wasn't naïve, and he would have to be very convincing in order to hide his exhilaration that Sarah was so near.

Whether he was ready or not, morning came with the promise of a beautiful day, as far as the weather was concerned. He had gone over and over the various scenarios of explaining to Margaret the new situation with Sarah. But each time, he would also contemplate the various scenarios of explaining to Sarah that despite their history and promises made, he was now engaged to another woman. Considering Sarah was ready to deliver bodily harm to him since she had no recollection of who he was, it gave him some sort of solace knowing she didn't remember their history, or their promises. But, with that caveat, it also meant that she had no memory of the intense feelings that, for him, were quickly resurfacing.

He emerged from his room just before the first rays of sunshine doused the land, careful to not wake Tommy, who had eventually made his way home to discover their father's return. It was a happy reunion for all of them and William was glad that Tommy wasn't upset that his days of so much freedom might be reined in, now that his father was home. He carefully maneuvered across the living room floor making his way to the kitchen to start a pot of coffee. He would need the time this morning to collect the mash of thoughts that plagued him throughout the night. He wondered how Sarah's night went, and if she had as much difficulty falling asleep as he did.

He glanced into the living room, noticing the glow of embers flickering against the darkness. Mornings were cold, especially early mornings, despite the season. He would need to stoke it and get fresh logs so the house could be warm for everyone when they woke up. With his mind on coffee, he turned the small corner into the kitchen, and ran directly into a petite, warm body coming from the opposite direction. The two collided, and William quickly wrapped his arm around the body to prevent knocking her over completely. He didn't need daylight to know whom his arms were around; her softness and sweet scent quickly arresting his senses.

Sarah immediately gasped in complete surprise, but didn't fight against him. "Oh, my goodness," she whispered.

William regained his composure from the initial shock that he wasn't alone as he thought he was. He released his clasp around her waist only slightly as he whispered, "Sarah, it's just me, Will. Are you okay?"

The soft giggle that escaped from the shadows was as sweet as it was mind-blowing. He swore he had not heard such a beautiful sound in his entire life, and only wished he could've seen her, too. To see her face, her eyes, and her smile would've been a sight worth waking for, much more than that of a sunrise.

She wrapped her hand around his forearm to steady herself. "Will," she whispered back, "you scared me half to death."

He asked again, trying to control his anxiousness of being so near her, "Are you okay?"

"Yes, yes, I'm fine. I didn't know anyone was up."

Perhaps it was because he couldn't see her that he was so in tune to the sound of her voice. It sounded like Sarah, his Sarah; the Sarah that had never left. His heart began to pound; maybe it wouldn't be as hard to bring her from the shadows of her mind as he thought it would. Remembering not to press her too far, he reluctantly released his hand from her waist, but couldn't help to still hold onto her arm.

"Of course no one is up. It's practically the middle of the night." He noticed the giddiness in his voice, but it truly couldn't have been stopped.

"Well, you're up," she whispered back.

He recognized a new feeling surging through him. A feeling that had been missing from his life for so long. He felt happiness. Still reeling from the feeling of her soft skin beneath his hand, he answered, "Yea, I guess you're right on that one." He paused, but could sense that their eyes were locked on each other's faces. "Is everything…otherwise…okay?"

She pulled her hand from his forearm and he followed suit. "Yes, I'm fine. Just got a little cold, that's all. I guess I'm too used to California weather, or something. I came out to stand by the fire. Why are you up?"

The real reason of course, was because of her. But, he couldn't tell her that he hadn't slept at all because she was all he could think of. "Oh, uh, I was going to make some coffee. I always get up early, I like the quiet mornings."

"Oh, I didn't mean to bother you," she said slowly. "I'm fine, I'll go back to bed so you can enjoy the morning." She slowly and carefully turned back toward her room, but William was able to catch her elbow before she could go.

"No, don't go." She stopped and turned toward him. "I mean, please, don't go. Come out and I'll build the fire so you can warm up."

"Are you sure?"

Was he sure? He almost laughed out loud. He would rather be with her and miss a lifetime of sunrises in exchange. "Of course I'm sure. Here." He pulled her hand into the crook of his elbow to lead her to the living room and toward the fireplace hearth. The dawn was breaking, and sky was beginning to show the slightest hint of bluish gray emerging from the darkness. He probably didn't need to guide her, but he was more than happy to.

"Okay, Will." Her whisper was so delicate, and once again, his name was on her lips.

He led her through the small room and slid his mother's rocking chair close to the hearth. Pulling the crocheted blanket from the back of the chair, he motioned for Sarah to sit down. Her face and therefore her expressions too, were now clear. They were tentative, but relaxed. A far cry from the look of terror she had for him yesterday. Things were definitely improving.

She sat gingerly in the chair, with her shoulders raised and hands huddled in her lap; he could see that she was cold. Gently laying the blanket over her lap, she quickly wiggled underneath, bringing it up under her chin. He pulled the iron stoker from the metal stand and jabbed it into the crumbling logs, waking a spray of sparks that zigzagged up the chimney like drunken fireflies. Never had he been so thankful that there were still a few logs in the bucket, and he wouldn't need to get more from the shed. Retrieving a few broken pieces from the bottom for kindling, he threw them in. Within a few seconds, the sleepy fire had awakened from the fresh fuel, and small flames quickly licked at the blond wood. Gently, he placed a larger log onto the pile, letting the flames wrap and pop around it. He glanced over to Sarah, but the intended glance became much more than that. Her beauty was undeniable. The gentle orange glow illuminated the soft smile on her lips and flickered in her eyes. Her hair was draped over her shoulder, wavy and loose. Breathtaking. She had just emerged from bed, and was more beautiful than if she had spent hours in front of a mirror. Her eyes moved to his, and for that moment, everything stopped. The past didn't exist, tragedies had never struck, and she had never left. Just as the fire popped its interruption, the moment was gone and they both snapped their eyes from each other, back to the fire. For, as quickly as it passed, the moment was still monumental to William. In that moment alone, he was given a hope that he hadn't dared to imagine. But, to imagine what could've been, would prove far too painful, and all he could hope for now was for Sarah to feel at home. Because, in his heart he believed, and somewhere deep down he hoped in hers she did too, that she was finally, truly home.

He turned his attention back to the fire that had gladly accepted the fresh wood as its own to devour. Pressing the stoker back in to adjust the log further back, and added another log to the growing blaze.

Sarah closed her eyes and sighed, "Mmm...that feels nice."

William looked at her, happy to provide her more comfort. "Warming up?"

"Yes." She breathed deeply. "Much better. Thank you."

Sarah stared into the crackling flames and then up to the stones surrounding the fireplace. "This fireplace is so beautiful."

William replaced the iron poker and sat down on the hearth that was made to provide the perfect bench for warming next to the fire. He loved that he was so close to her, and now on eye level. He turned slightly to look up at the wall of stones. "Yea," he agreed, "it's one of my favorite things here. My mom's, too. She would always sit in that chair and read, or sew in front of it."

"Your dad said that he and my dad built it themselves."

William raised his eyebrows and nodded, "Yes, it took them a long time, but it was worth it. It took them forever to find stones that were just right."

Sarah eyes scanned over the stones again. "Tell me about King's Creek."

William sucked in half of a breath. He would be more than happy to tell her about King's Creek. Everything, about King's Creek. He could tell her about the time she pulled a spiny sucker fish out of Coon's Cove when she was only six years old, and made him get it off her hook. He could tell her about the days they spent on the banks basking in the crisp air, wishing the daylight would never end. He could tell her about the last time she was there. He could tell her about their promise, and help her across the fallen log to their stump, and put her hand on their carving once again. He knew he could tell her everything that was bursting inside of him to be set free. But telling was different than remembering. Remembering would mean feeling.

In a sudden rush he realized, that by Sarah remembering details of their past, she would be forced to grapple with the fact that the man who promised to love her forever, would soon be married to another woman. But, he quickly shook the thoughts away as if shaking a spider from her intricate web of trappings, knowing that he hadn't broken a promise. He would love her forever, even if he couldn't be with her. He loved her enough to give her back her past. She deserved to know who she was.

He looked up at her expectant face, still illuminated in shadows and orange flickers. Her brow had creased, waiting for the answer of a seemingly uncomplicated question. "King's Creek is..." he paused searching for the words that could even remotely give the creek its due justice. "King's Creek was your favorite place to be. You would choose to be at King's Creek above all else." He hesitated again, thinking surely there must be some better way to convey how she felt about the creek. "For you, King's Creek was proof that heaven existed, because part of it was here on Earth."

Sarah stared thoughtfully at him, then back to the stones where the shadows danced. "How can I not remember a place like that?" She asked the question out loud, but William wasn't sure it was meant for him to answer.

He wanted to give her the keys to her past that she was so desperate to have. She looked back to him and he slowly shrugged his shoulders. "I don't know, Sarah. Maybe your memory is like a photograph developing. At first, the paper is blank. With little time, faint lines appear that the look familiar. The more time it is submerged, the clearer the image becomes until you can completely recognize it and even perceive the smallest of details. You have the picture in your mind; you just need to let it develop."

She blinked and a single teardrop dropped down her cheek, glistening in the light of the fire that had relaxed into long, slow laps at the fragrant pine logs. "How?" Her voice had become small and scared.

William looked at her intently, "You immerse yourself in your past, and let the photo appear bit by bit. The pictures that your mind has taken haven't disappeared; they just can't be seen yet. They just need to be developed again."

Now, the look Sarah gave him created a warmth so deep inside of him, rivaling that of the fire at his back. "I want you to show me, Will. I want you to show me everything I need to remember. I'm ready for the pictures to come back. Will you help me?" She paused again, deep in contemplation. "I don't know why, but I feel like you are the only one who can."

"I will do anything you want me to." He knew how forward that sounded, but he didn't care. He had spent enough time without her—and thinking that he would never again lay eyes on her—to deny any request that she had of him, was impossible. Nothing had changed, he realized. He would've done anything for her before, and he'd do even more for her now. Losing someone, only to have them return to you, was not something he was prepared to treat lightly.

She smiled and seemed relieved. Whatever it was that would make her look at him like that, he would do it over and over again. He could sense her wall, maybe not brick by brick, but crumb by crumb, starting to fracture. That was all he could ask for at this point.

"Will you take me there? To King's Creek?"

"Of course I will. When would you like to go?" He remembered that he would need to work on her comfort level and not rush her.

Sarah's eyes scanned the room and then landed at her hands in her lap. "I want to go soon. Can we go today?"

In his mind, he flashed forward through his day. So much had already happened in these early morning hours, all of which he hadn't even prepared himself for the possibility of. He had thought that it would take a lot longer for he and Sarah to be able to be comfortable around each other, considering their reunion was less than ideal. It only reiterated to him that their bond, whether she knew it or not, could withstand just about anything.

Margaret would be here soon, and he had planned on working a full day at the lumberyard. Not only was he extending his hours day by day as a way of conditioning his body for work, he needed the money. He also didn't want to give Vernon any excuse for cutting him loose completely, although he doubted that would happen. Vernon wasn't an idiot.

William knew that displeasing Margaret was going to be his doing now and be unavoidable once she heard the news about Sarah. And, that would just be the start of it. Once she caught on to the fact that he was going to do whatever he could to help Sarah, there was going to more than just hell to pay. This was not something William was willing to negotiate on. He had already learned which battles to fight, and which to ignore, with the latter being the majority when it came to Margaret. Here's where he would have to show her that this was non-negotiable.

"If you want to go today, then of course I'll take you."

"I do. I'm ready, Will. I'm ready to see what the photographs will show."

"Then we'll go. When I get home from the lumberyard."

"The lumberyard?"

William flinched on the inside, realizing again the connection of the lumberyard to himself. "Yes, I work there." His explanation was true, just not complete.

"Oh," Sarah nodded.

William stood to press the poker back into the fire. He needed a distraction from the conversation continuing on to anything else about the lumberyard. As he jabbed at the ashy log, he began to formulate the words for his discussion with Margaret. He was about to find out how the stoker felt, as it would soon be time to face the fire.

CHAPTER 19

William heard the truck lurching up his driveway and rushed out the door and down the path to meet it. After spending the early hours of dawn with Sarah in front of the fire, he was hardly able to get himself ready for his day at work. He somehow got dressed, and packed a small lunch, amazed that he was able to put on matching socks, let alone put one foot in front of the other. Once daylight broke, Henry and Tommy had joined them and William was dreading the moment when he would have to leave.

But, Margaret was here. There would be no more time to debate exactly how this moment would go. He knew he had to intercept Margaret in the driveway, instead of her coming to the house. The last thing he wanted was for Sarah and Margaret to meet prior to him explaining the situation. It was going to be bad enough without adding the element of surprise.

He quickly strode down the walk just as Margaret turned off the ignition and got out to meet him. He crossed the graveled parking area and met her at the front of the truck.

He was out of breath from practically running to meet her, but he knew that wasn't the only reason his heart was pounding. "Hey, good morning, Margaret."

Margaret eyed him, "'Good morning, Margaret?' That's all I get?" She smiled coyly and walked up to him, so close that she pressed against his chest. She wrapped her arms around his shoulders and waited.

William had never been so anxious. All he wanted to do was leave. He had no idea if Sarah was watching him. He quickly bent down to meet Margaret and kissed her lips. He wanted to pull her arms off from around him but he knew better than to do that. His best bet would be to get her in the truck and get the hell to town.

"Sorry. I guess I'm just ready to get to work. Let's get going, okay?"

Margaret slowly brought her arms from his shoulders. "Oh, okay." She turned back to the driver's side and William swiftly got in on the other side and slammed the door closed. He was more than ready to be able to drive himself. Having his arm in the sling made it damn near impossible to drive since he couldn't use his right arm to shift. He had to remind himself to be calm and patient with his healing process, remembering how lucky he was that the extent of inconveniences caused by his injuries were minor. But right now, there was nothing to be calm or patient about.

As soon as the truck was headed back down the driveway, William couldn't help but turn and glance back toward his house. He couldn't see her, but knowing she was there was enough. She would be there when he got home, and they could go to King's Creek. It was almost too much for him to grasp. He took a deep breath. It would take a while for his new reality to settle in on him.

He turned back, noticing that Margaret was staring at him. She clearly noticed his strange behavior, and he would need to stop the questions that were blazing in her eyes.

"Margaret, I have some news to tell you." He swallowed but noticed his mouth was completely dry.

She looked back to him and raised her eyebrows. "Oh?"

Now, where to start? He wanted to keep it simple, and not raise any more suspicion than what would already come naturally as soon as she knew what was going on. He needed to remember that if he had any chance of keeping Margaret pacified, she would need to be confident in his devotion to her. He was about to be walking a very fine line. "Did you see that my dad is home?"

"Well, barely. But yes, I saw his truck. When did he get home?"

"Yesterday. He got home sometime before Mr. Wilkes dropped me off from giving me a ride." He knew his explanations were sounding unnecessarily long.

"Hmm." Her lack of enthusiasm was so blatant. That was all about to change. "Where was he?"

Here it was. Once he said it, there would be no taking it back. He looked at her and said as calmly as he could muster, "California."

Margaret continued to stare straight ahead through the windshield. She blinked a few times and pursed her lips. She finally turned to him, her green eyes flashing in an instant. "California?"

He nodded. She turned back to the road, nodding slowly. "California. Why was he there, William?"

He hadn't even mentioned Sarah and her voice was already slicing through the air. "There was a car accident." He hated talking about this. He knew there would be no sympathy for the loss of Edward and Anne, and it sickened him to have to say it out loud. "Edward and Anne Ellis were in a car accident, and they didn't...they didn't survive." He swallowed again, the reality of that fact still hard for him to believe.

She turned again and looked at him. "I'm sorry to hear that." Her words said it, but her eyes were still shooting accusations. He knew her well enough to know that she was waiting for the real news that was yet to come. The news of his parents' best friends passing wasn't enough for her. "So?"

"They weren't the only ones in the truck. Sarah was with them."

Margaret turned to him again, searching his face for more than what he was slowly revealing. "Sarah was in the accident?"

He nodded. "Yes, she was." He looked out the window to the road. "Listen, maybe we should pull over so we can talk without you trying to drive."

Margaret said nothing but pulled over at the next widening of the road, and parked the truck by the bar ditch. She turned off the ignition and turned to him. "What else, William? What are you not telling me?"

"Sarah was hurt badly, but she survived the accident. She was in the hospital for several days, and the people that Edward worked for were taking care of her. They sent my dad a letter about the accident, and about Sarah.

He knew that he had to go there."

She sat silently, saying nothing, showing no emotion. He couldn't read what she was thinking. All he could do was get it over with. Stalling would only make her more suspicious.

He took another deep breath and continued, "Anyway, when he got there, Sarah didn't know who he was."

Now Margaret's eyes narrowed, "What do you mean she didn't know him?"

"She suffered a severe head injury, and...because of that, she has memory loss."

"Memory loss?" she asked incredulously.

"Her memories of when she was younger are gone. Basically, her childhood memories, her memories of Colorado, are gone." He took in one more deep breath, "And my dad brought her home with him. To live here. With us."

Margaret turned her attention back to the windshield. William could only wait for what would most likely be a barrage of questions and complaints. He had tried to prepare for them, but he knew he couldn't. He could only sit, and wait.

After several beats of excruciating silence, he thought he detected the faintest of smiles curl onto Margaret's lips. She looked down to her hands and back to William. She pressed her lips out, and nodded slowly. "So, Sarah is at your house? Right now, she's at your house. Is that right?"

William nodded, still confused with her subdued reaction. "Yes, she is."

Margaret's head was in a constant nod as the information slowly seeped in. "And she doesn't remember you?"

"No, she doesn't remember anything about here, or the people she knew here."

"I see." Margaret's voice was controlled and cold. "Where's Matthew?"

"We don't know. He was drafted several months ago and no one is even sure if he's still in the country. My dad is going to try to find a way to contact him. But, that's going to be very difficult."

"So, it's just Sarah, living with you, in your house?"

"Yes," William confirmed.

"I see. Well, how do you feel about all of this?"

A dangerous question that he knew he couldn't think about for too long. He would need be convincing as hell to hide the real answer. "Me? Oh well, I guess I'm just surprised. Shocked, really. I had no idea where my dad went, and I sure as heck didn't expect Sarah to be coming back with him."

Margaret stared, clearly waiting for him to go on. "And, now that she's lost her parents, and who knows when she'll see Matthew again, we're kind of her only family now."

"Family, huh?"

"Yes, Margaret. Look, I know what you're thinking. But, things have changed. It feels like forever ago that I knew her. Too much time has gone by for things to be the same between her and me. I care about her like family. I just want to help her, now."

"Help her with what?"

If he thought he had been convincing so far, he could see now that he was wrong. "Just help her remember some things, that's all. I feel bad for her, losing her parents and her memory isn't fair. I can't do anything about her parents, but maybe I can help her remember a few things here and there."

"She doesn't remember anything? No memories whatsoever?" Margaret stressed again.

"No. In fact, I really don't think she'll get them back, either. I think she'll just have to make new memories of Colorado."

Margaret nodded and slid across the seat, positioning herself against his body. "Well, then by all means, let's help her make new memories. Does she know about us?" Her smile was wily, and made William nervous.

"Well, not yet. She's just barely gotten here, and is trying to get settled. I didn't want to overwhelm her with too much."

"I see," she whispered, as she leaned in to kiss his neck. "Sarah might not be ready, but I am ready. More than ready for you." She pushed her lips to his mouth. "Overwhelm me, William. Now." He knew this was a test. His words wouldn't be nearly as convincing as his kiss, and if he were going to keep Margaret calmed about Sarah's return, he would need to placate her skepticism. He wrapped his arm around her and pulled her in even deeper to his kiss. As he closed his eyes, all he could see was Sarah's face, in the flickering orange glow of the fire, and the way she looked at him. He quickly pulled away from Margaret's lips, trying to recover from the awkward moment.

Margaret smiled, and he felt relief rush over him that she believed him. For now, she believed him. Keeping the ruse would be challenging, he knew. But what really did he expect to happen with Sarah? As much as he was feeling again, he knew that it could go nowhere. Too much, and too many people were depending on him. It was true, after all. His life really had moved on from Sarah. Surely this was a normal and natural feeling to seeing her again. Once the shock began to fade, he was sure that the feeling felt years ago would be put into perspective. That was then, this was now.

Margaret leaned in and breathed into his ear. "Well, what are you doing later? I'm sure we can sneak away from the lumberyard a little early today."

Here's where William would be walking that fine line. He was going to need to be able to successfully balance spending the time necessary for Sarah to hopefully recover her memory, all the while keeping Margaret satisfied, in more ways than one. If she even remotely felt threatened by Sarah, he would be forced to choose. That choice had already been made. It was a choice that he had made somewhat willingly, although in reality, what choice did he have when it came to saving his family's farm? Going back was not an option. The first test was already upon him.

"Oh, well, I told my dad that I'd be home to help him with some things that got put off since he was gone."

"Oh?"

"Yea, something about the repairs on the corral or something. We have a couple of steers coming in, and the corral's not ready for them."

Margaret pulled away and sat up straight, clearly not pleased with his response. "I see." She smoothed her hair and looked out of the window. "Well, then I'll be sure to get you home in time for fixing the corral."

The stress and intonation of her voice at the words, "fixing the corral" was enough for William to know that it was already time for damage control. "Well, it might be a good time for Sarah to meet you." He hated the lie as soon as it left his lips. But, the sooner he could put Margaret's insecurities to rest, the easier it would be to spend time away from her. Time away from Margaret would mean time that he could devote to Sarah.

Margaret perked at the suggestion. "Oh, well, yes, of course. I think it would be, too."

There was no apprehension on Margaret's part, which worried William even more. Sarah would be completely unaware of the unscrupulous ways of Margaret, or their history prior to moving to California. He would have to do what he could to keep the introductions short. He would have all day to worry about how he would be able to that.

"We better get going, don't you think? Your dad is going to wonder what's going on and fire us both."

Margaret laughed. "Really, William? Haven't you figured this all out by now? My daddy would never do anything to upset me. He makes sure that his little girl is happy. So, I really don't think you have anything to worry about. If we're late, blame it on me. But then again, it will be my fault."

William turned his head slightly, "What is your fault?"

"Us being late, of course." She tucked her chin and looked up at him with eyes glinting. She raised her hand to the collar of her shirt and one by one, began to unbutton her shirt, revealing more of her porcelain skin with each movement of her hands.

William looked at her, genuinely shocked. "What...are you doing?"

"What does it look like I'm doing?"

William turned and gestured to the open road and the surrounding area. "Here? It's broad daylight, and we're on the county road!"

"No, we're in a truck, and I don't care what time of the day it is." She slid herself next to him and began kissing his neck while her hands went to work on his belt. She had it unfastened and his pants unbuttoned before he even knew what to say.

"Margaret—wait, we can't..."

"Yes, we can," she whispered. "Tell me you want me. Tell me you want me as much as I want you."

William closed his eyes, still in disbelief that this was all happening.

Margaret hoisted herself to a straddling position over him. She entwined her fingers through his hair and guided his face into her breasts that were barely covered by a white eyelet lace bra. She pulled the fabric down, exposing her breast completely to him and pressed it into his face. His mind was contesting everything that was happening. This was the last thing he thought he would be doing on his way to work today. But, here he found himself in the surprising position of Margaret straddling over him, with his face buried between her breasts.

If anyone had driven by, he hadn't noticed, and he could only hope that no one had. He knew Margaret didn't care, she would've been just as happy for this to have all occurred in his driveway, especially knowing who might be inside to witness the whole thing.

She pulled away from him and looked dreamingly into his eyes. She sighed deeply, contently. "Mmm...now, that's what you need to be thinking about. You just needed a little reminding."

William choked down his shock and asked, "You sure are full of surprises this morning, aren't you?"

Margaret raised her eyebrows and smirked, "Well, now you know how it feels, don't you?"

He cocked his head, wondering what she could be referring to. "Oh, come on now, William. I think you know what I'm talking about. Sarah? Living with you? Don't you think that was a considerable surprise?"

William paused for a moment. Sarah. He had thought of nothing but her since the moment he'd laid eyes on her standing in his kitchen. In fact, he felt his stomach turn as he realized that his only desire was to be with her now, and yet, Margaret's arms were still wrapped tightly around him.

This was going to be far more complicated that he originally thought. The sooner he got Sarah, and all of the "what-could've-beens" out of his mind, the better.

"Yea, I'm sure that was a surprise. It was to me, too, believe me."

Margaret ran her finger down his cheek and across his lips. "I don't think I want to be surprised anymore, alright William?" Her attempt at playfulness failed and William could decipher her exact meaning behind the coldness in her eyes.

"Don't worry, the surprises are over." William tried to reassure her.

"I hope so. In fact, getting everything out in the open today is how it should be." Margaret smirked as she raised herself from her straddling position over him. She pushed herself back and swung her knee over to a sitting position on the bench seat, all while maintaining her eye contact with him.

William looked at her, and knew what she was talking about it, but hoped by some chance she had been appeased enough to delay the meeting with Sarah.

"I'm talking about Sarah, Will," she blurted. "Sarah should know about us. You said yourself that the surprises are over, so let's just make sure of that. The sooner she knows, the better. Don't you think?"

William shifted uncomfortably and stole a few minutes of avoidance by running his fingers through his hair. "Well, yea, of course. I just thought..."

But whatever his thoughts were, they were interrupted. "Good, then we agree. Tonight, after work, would be just fine."

Margaret had already slid back over to the driver's side and was smoothing her dress and hair back into place. She looked over to William and smiled as if they had just made a plan as innocent as going for an evening stroll. But, he knew better. He knew Margaret couldn't wait for the moment that she would get to introduce herself to Sarah as his future wife. The only saving grace in the whole scenario was that Sarah had no memory of Margaret, either. For as much pleasure as he knew Margaret would have, he was thankful that Sarah would simply have to tolerate the introduction, instead of experiencing the heartache, and worse, the certain revulsion that would normally surge through her at the sight of Margaret. He hated to think what Sarah would think of him. As much as he wanted her regain her memory, there were certain memories that would most definitely impact his relationship, or what he hoped could be a relationship of some sort, with Sarah. But that was all way down the road, and he didn't have to worry about that right now. He would have enough to contend with this evening's reunion of the woman who would be his wife, and the woman who, from what he could tell, still had his heart.

CHAPTER 20

There hadn't been a workday at the lumberyard that William dreaded ending, until today. Margaret had been in an unusually good mood throughout the day, and it was no surprise as to why. He wondered, if with time, Margaret would ever change. He still found it hard to believe that she was the one he would be spending his life with. She and Sarah were complete opposites, and he could only hope that the more he got to know Margaret, the more he would find to admire in her. Today, that was not going to happen. In fact, the last thing he wanted to do was be around her at all. It took a mere few seconds to be around Sarah again to illuminate the depth of their relationship, and he knew deep down, that would never exist between him and Margaret. Sarah was all he could think about. He couldn't wait to be home to see her, but that would be the time Margaret would be seeing her, too. He finally understood completely, the definition of bittersweet.

Shortly before closing time, Vernon sent both of them home. He felt like just walking the thirteen miles to his house; it would've been far easier than the ride with Margaret. She laced her arm through his as they walked to the back lot and to the truck.

"Ready to go?" she chirped.

William sighed and nodded, "Yes, this has been a long day."

"Well, let's get you home, then."

He could only nod again, as they parted to get into the truck. They pulled out of the parking lot and William noticed the sun starting to set, leaving the sky doused in the colors of pink lemonade. It would've been a perfect sunset to watch with Sarah. Instead, the sunset would come and go, and he was fairly certain that there wouldn't be anything enjoyable about this evening.

About half way to his house, he finally broke the silence. "Look, when we get to my house, let's not mention too much to Sarah about the past."

Margaret nodded, but kept her eyes straight. "I agree, William. Whether she can remember it or not, the past is over and done with. The only thing that matters is what is happening now. A lot has changed; she'll just have to realize that. That is, if she ever remembers anything, anyway."

William cringed inwardly. Margaret had put into words what he had been afraid to admit. She might not remember anything. It was very much a possibility that Sarah would never remember everything they had felt for each other. He wasn't ready to concede that, yet. But to Margaret, he completely agreed. "You're right. The past is in the past. It's time to move forward." He reached over and held her hand, hoping to keep up the ruse.

Margaret smiled, "Be careful, we might just have to stop on the way home from work, too."

William shook his head at her, hoping she wouldn't dare. Although, he knew she wouldn't hesitate to do so if she thought it would serve her purposes. Fortunately, he knew she wanted to get to his house almost as much as he did.

They pulled up the long driveway and parked the truck. William had gotten used to coming home to a dark and still house, and it was nice to see the windows framing the warm glow of the lanterns from inside. He had to force himself to slow his breathing and regulate his rapidly climbing pulse. This was bound to happen sooner or later, it was just working out to be sooner. He would've done just about anything to change it from sooner or later, to never. With each step up the walkway, with Margaret's hand in his, the reality and dread he had been feeling all day, was upon him. Just as he climbed the steps and reached for the door handle, he wondered how in the hell he had gotten himself into this mess. Even more importantly, how would he get Sarah out of this mess?

He pushed the door open, and quickly scanned the kitchen and living room. For a second, he felt relieved that no one was there. For as much as he couldn't wait to see her again, he half hoped that she wasn't there, although he had no idea where else she would possibly be.

"Hello?" he called, still hopeful. "Anyone home?"

He and Margaret both turned their attention to the back of the kitchen as a door creaked.

"Hello?" came the sweet voice of Sarah. "Is that you, Will?"

It killed him not to be able to rush to her, and show her how happy he was to be home. "Yes, we're out here." He turned to look at Margaret who looked anxious, but not one bit nervous.

She turned the corner and looked absolutely ravishing, but not for any reason as simple as fancy clothes or something formal. Her hair draped over one shoulder in soft waves, exposing the side of her neck. A white T-shirt hovered dangerously, almost exposing a peek of her skin at the top of the waistline of her jeans. But, the most exquisite sight was her smile that she was bringing to him. Instead of delivering the smile, her eyes went straight to Margaret, and the smile disintegrated. A look of confusion filled her eyes, as her eyes darted back to Will for an explanation.

"Sarah," he quickly began, hoping to say anything that would change her expression. "I have someone for you to meet."

"Oh, okay," Sarah said, hesitantly. She hadn't been expecting this, and he felt horrible that their plans for King's Creek would have to wait.

She took a couple of slow steps into the living room, her eyes going between him and Margaret. "Sarah, I know you have a lot on your mind right now, and I don't want to overwhelm you. But I thought that you should... that I should..." he stuttered like a fool. How exactly would he be able to word this, and cause the least amount of turmoil for her?

Margaret shot him a look of annoyance, and took a step, placing herself between him and Sarah. "What he's trying to say Sarah, is that he thought you and I should meet."

Sarah nodded her head, "All right. Are you someone I should know?"

Margaret smiled widely, "Yes, that's right. You should know me, but it's okay that you don't. You can know me, now. I'm Margaret." She jutted out her hand for Sarah to shake. Just as Sarah reached for it, she added, "I'm engaged to William." The forced smile earlier had given way to one of genuine glee, especially as the look of sheer surprise cloaked Sarah's face, and she looked to William.

"En...gaged?" Sarah repeated.

"Oh yes," Margaret continued. "We are to be married, soon, I hope." She shot her sarcastic glance back to William. "If it weren't for William's accident, we probably would've been married by now."

"Oh," Sarah finally whispered. "I had no idea."

William wanted to start explaining. He wanted to tell her how he had waited for her, waited to hear something, anything from her. An urgency to tell her that he had held onto their promise, until it became clear that their paths were no longer entwined, twisted through him. She needed to know it wasn't by choice, and he wanted to explain the deal he had made with Vernon. The harsh reality was that he was now bound by the responsibility of taking care of his family's farm. He wanted her to know that even though everything had changed, some things had not. But, unfortunately what had changed, was that Margaret was right. He was an engaged man, and now that Sarah knew that, he felt an entirely new pain scrape against the wound in his heart, that had begun to heal after she had left for California. But even if he could explain all of that, she would have no idea what he was talking about. According to her memory, none of those promises or feelings had ever existed.

"No, I'm sure you didn't have any idea. But at least you know now, and isn't it wonderful that you'll be here now to join the celebration!" Margaret's jubilant demeanor was increasing by the minute.

Now Sarah had something to say. Her expression changed from surprise to an obvious irritation. "Well, actually, I'm here because my parents were killed in a car accident, I would hardly call that 'wonderful.'"

Margaret quieted immediately. William could only look at Sarah through the same lens as he did when they were younger. She still had her resolve to stand up to Margaret. He couldn't believe that within the first few minutes of reuniting with her adversary from the past, Sarah reacted with the same degree of distaste and intolerance toward Margaret. This was not about feelings, either. This was about the core of Sarah, her ability to read people, and not be fooled by any false pretense. He wondered if some of her old feelings toward Margaret were so close to the surface that they were easily summoned, or if making Margaret's acquaintance really was as displeasing as she made it seem to be. He ventured to think that it was probably a little bit of both.

"Oh, well, yes." Margaret's prior confidence shattered. "I was sorry to hear about that."

"I think I'll go for a walk." Sarah shot one last look at Margaret and walked past them, out the door, not even attempting to slow the screen door to avoid the slam that followed her out.

"Well, she's quite irritable, isn't she?" Margaret huffed.

William turned and stared at her, watching her smooth her hair and push it behind her shoulders. "You can't possibly begin understand what she is going through. But I can tell you that the last thing Sarah is, is irritable."

"Hmm." Margaret huffed. "Yes, well, I really don't care to talk about Sarah anymore. But, now that we're alone, I can think of a few other things I'd like to do," she said slyly, as she ran her hands along his chest.

"I don't think so, Margaret," he objected. "I have no idea where my dad and Tommy are, and truthfully, this has been a long day, and I still have chores to get to."

Margaret looked at him, giving him her best pout. "Are you sure?"

He pulled her hands from his chest and held them in his. "I think we'd better just say goodnight."

She pulled away slightly to look up at him. "Well, you're not much fun. But, it's just as well. Mother and I have some things to discuss and plan for the wedding."

"Oh, really? I thought we were going to wait a bit on that?"

"Well, I was only willing to wait a while on the actual wedding because your arm is in that God-awful sling. I'm not willing to wait on planning it."

William nodded, knowing he better not argue any further, or risk alerting Margaret to his new focus, that most certainly wasn't the wedding. "Okay, have fun then."

"Will I see you tomorrow?" she said, falling back against his chest.

"Tomorrow? Well, since it's Saturday, I think I'll be here fixing the corral, so probably not. We've got a lot to do."

Margaret pulled away and looked at him, "Will you miss me?"

He could detect the slightest hint of skepticism in her voice. "Of course I will."

"Then kiss me like you'll miss me. Convince me."

He quickly leaned down and pressed against her lips. He was worried about where Sarah might've gone and he didn't want to leave her alone for too long.

He pulled away from her kiss, slowly, hoping he had successfully convinced her. "Okay, I'll miss you, too," she confirmed.

"I'll walk you out."

His kiss must've not have satisfied her completely, though, as Margaret wrapped her arms around him again once they reached the truck. She pushed against him, allowing him to fully access her mouth and to feel her breasts press against him. This time he had to pull away from the kiss swiftly as he feared where Sarah might be, and did not want her to witness the whole thing.

"You better get home before it gets any darker. Watch for deer."

Margaret's stare seemed to bore a hole into him, but he wondered if it was his conscious getting the better of him. "Okay, William. Get your work done; I'll have to see you Sunday, though."

"I'll do my best," he assured her, as he helped her into the truck and shut the door.

"Goodnight, William. Dream about me," Margaret instructed.

He gave her a curt nod as she put the truck in gear and turned down the driveway. When he could see that she had turned onto the county road, he intently scanned the yard for Sarah. He hoped she hadn't decided to wander too far.

He tried to slow his pace, but to no avail. He couldn't hide how anxious he was to find her. The sun would be setting soon and he shuddered to think of Sarah being far from home in the dark. Even worse, he knew that she would have a hard time finding her way around. There was a time that she knew the countryside as well as anyone, but not anymore. Turning at the corner of the pigpen, still frantically scanning the scrub oak that bordered the corrals and the tack shed, he finally spotted her. He let out an audible sigh, and walked to the far edge of the corral where she had climbed over and sat on a large boulder. Her back was to him, and he admired her curves. He recognized the changes in her, not necessarily disregarding the beauty that she had always possessed. Now, her beauty and her body called to every ounce of what a man desires. His mind easily processed what was hidden beneath her clothing, and his body pulsed in response. Quickly shutting down that particular thought process wasn't easy, as he began to imagine what it would feel like to touch her just once more. That thought was just too dangerous to entertain, and just as painful, knowing it couldn't happen.

As much as he could've stayed and watched her, he slowed his pace and walked to her side. As soon as he did, he saw that she wasn't alone. Sprawled out across her lap lay Lulu, purring and pressing her yellow eyes closed with every stroke of Sarah's finger down her nose.

Sarah jumped slightly, obviously jerked out of a deep contemplation, once she caught sight of Will from the corner of her eye. She looked to him and gave a forced smile.

The look on her face forced a pain deep inside of him that he wasn't sure he'd ever get used to. Not that he planned on getting used to it; in fact the opposite was true. He was rapidly coming to the realization that it wasn't going to take long for him to fall back under the spell that Sarah had cast so long ago. The look, the pain, was all something he was determined to change.

"Mind if I join you?" Will motioned to the rock.

Sarah nodded and moved over to provide more room. "Do you know this cat?" she asked quietly. "She's awfully friendly."

William smiled and reached over to pet the cat's head. "Yes, I know this cat. And she's only friendly like this to people she knows."

Sarah stopped in the middle of rubbing Lulu's nose and looked at Will. "What? You mean...she knows me?"

Will was pleased that her earlier look was now replaced by one of cautious optimism. "She knows you very well. This is your cat, Lulu. We took her in when you moved to California."

Sarah looked down to the gray tabby in her lap with a new softness, and William realized that tears were forming in her eyes. She stroked the content cat's nose again, sending Lulu back into a deep, relaxing trance. "Do you remember her?" he asked, hoping that Sarah's first beam of light into her memory was beginning to break through darkness.

But Sarah slowly shook her head. "No, I don't remember her, Will. I'm trying, I'm really trying." She looked to him with eyes pleading for the memory to return. "I wish I could remember."

William placed his hand tentatively on hers. Her skin was warm and soft, and he was again, acutely aware of the tingle evoked by even the slightest touch of her skin. "I'm not so sure that you don't."

Sarah looked back at him, and he was pleased she hadn't tried to remove her hand from under his. "I...don't...."

He stopped her from continuing any further. "Sarah, when Lulu was a kitty, you discovered that if you rubbed her nose, she would fall asleep. Do you know what you were just doing?"

Sarah hesitantly let a smile cross her lips and answered, "Rubbing her nose."

"Yes, you were." He smiled back. "And I don't know anyone else that has ever pet a cat that way. You may not think that you remember, but you do. Your mind remembers, even if it's not ready for you to realize it."

"I hope you're right," she said, as she looked into the distance still petting

Lulu's nose.

"Well, I'm always right. You might as well just get used to that."

"Always?" Sarah asked. Will couldn't help but stare at her lips as she let her smile creep across them.

"At least, half of usually."

Their eyes locked momentarily, and they both fell silent. William didn't mind the silence. They had always been comfortable just being with each other. He was happy that from what he could tell so far, that hadn't changed.

Sarah finally took a deep breath and ended the silence. "So, you're engaged?"

William wasn't sure if it was more of a question, or a statement, but either way, it came to his ears sounding like nails across a chalkboard. It was a fact that he never expected to have to explain to Sarah, let alone hear those words come from her, directed to him.

He swallowed the lump that instantly formed in his throat and nodded. He felt that she deserved much more, but he could only muster a slow nod. He couldn't even bring himself to look at her; he could only look down to his hands, and then off into the distance. It didn't matter that he could try to defend his choice, assuming that as she hadn't written to him, she had moved on. He couldn't justify that no matter how he rationalized his decision, he still felt that he had betrayed her.

She seemed to accept his answer, as she didn't press for any further detail or explanation. He couldn't deny the relief he felt, but he somehow knew it was temporary. Sooner or later, the subject of Margaret would be back, and he couldn't avoid that. The subject of his engagement to Margaret was bad enough, but nothing compared to the sheer discomfort that would come once she and Sarah were in the same room again. It was no coincidence that their first encounter was as uncomfortable as it was. Just like petting Lulu's nose, Sarah's mind most certainly remembered Margaret. If he thought he was uncomfortable now, he could only imagine how he would feel if Sarah remembered everything about Margaret, and then realized that he had not only betrayed her, but he had done so with her worst enemy; her only enemy. If only it were possible to keep some memories permanently hidden, he would be able to breathe easier. But waiting for her memories to return seemed like a ticking time bomb that would most certainly end in casualties of both of their hearts.

CHAPTER 21

Sarah shivered and goose bumps crawled up her arms. She was still wearing just a T-shirt, and now that the sun had dipped behind the hills, the cool mountain air was hard to ignore. She would've been content to stay longer, talking with Will and rubbing Lulu's nose, but Will noticed her shivering and suggested they go back to the house. She wanted to know more, though. Hearing that Lulu used to be her cat gave her a rush of feelings that she was where she needed to be in order to remember her past. That was the good part of the conversation with Will. She couldn't quite figure out why the new knowledge of Will's engagement bothered her so much. It most certainly could've been the woman he had decided to marry. She didn't know him well, but she had a good sense about him, and that redhead seemed to be opposite of what he would be interested in spending the rest of his life with. But then again, she had nothing to base that on other than a few conversations, and her intuition. Her intuition told her plenty about Margaret, too. She was still searing from Margaret's obvious lack of compassion that she had just lost both of her parents, and was still reeling physically and emotionally from the accident herself. The only thing she cared about was pointing out that Sarah would now be here to witness their wedding. Everything about that short encounter filled her disgust. She was glad that Will hadn't told her more about his engagement. It seemed like everything about it caused her feelings of repulsion. She knew that she would have to get over it, since she would undoubtedly be around her again, but for now, she wanted to think of anything as long as it wasn't Margaret.

"I'm sorry we didn't make it to King's Creek tonight."

She looked over to him as he thankfully interrupted the brewing in her head over Margaret. His face was so sincere, and compassionate, and there was just something about the way he would look at her that made her feel safe. There was no way to explain it, but she couldn't deny that she felt she could trust him. Was it a hidden part of her mind that remembered him and the friendship that they once had, or, was it how he made her feel since she had been here? But, after waiting for him all day, she realized how anxious she had been to see him again.

"It's alright. It was still a nice evening, mostly." The spite in her voice came quite unexpectedly. She looked back to him quickly, not wanting him to mistake her true enjoyment for the inner disgust she was trying to squelch over meeting Margaret. "I really enjoyed sitting with you tonight." When he looked at her with genuine surprise at her admission, she quickly added, "And Lulu."

"Oh, so if it hadn't been for Lulu?"

The way his blue eyes flashed playfully made her heart instantly speed up. She tried to hide her smile, but couldn't help it as she giggled. "Yes, had it not been for Lulu, I'm pretty sure it wouldn't have been any fun at all."

"Really? Well, then next time we're on the rock, you can rub my nose. How about that?"

This time she couldn't help but to laugh out loud. "Only if it'll make you fall asleep."

He turned and smiled, and she felt a new sensation surge through her. Her stomach actually flopped, and she felt a rush go through her at the way he looked at her. "There's only one way to find out, Sarah." She was certain her face turned a bright crimson, and the way he said her name caused jitters in her stomach. How could she be so carefree with a man she hardly knew? She was taken aback at how rapidly their conversation about sitting on a rock and a cat had so quickly changed into something else.

She could've sworn that he noticed the change just as much as she did. His smile faded, and the way he was looking at her was filled with intensity.

He had tenderness in his eyes, but a look of desire that was unmistakable. She wasn't sure if it was desire to say something, or do something, but the immediate electricity that was between them was undeniable. She felt it without question. It was a feeling laced with excitement and her heart pounded. She could only look up at him, with too many emotions to form any of them into words.

The way her heart was hammering brought back a very familiar feeling. She was remembering. But this wasn't a memory about Colorado or her childhood, or even about Will. This was a feeling she had in California, when she was with Adley. Something about how Will was looking at her made her mind and body react in a way that had only been conjured by Adley. Now her stomach turned again, but this time, it brought on a wave of nausea. Adley. She too was promised to someone. But right now, someone else was making her feel light-headed.

She quickly put her hands up to her face and ran her fingers down her temples and to her cheeks. She could only look at Will with sudden confusion. Whatever it was that she just felt scared her. None of it made sense, but at the same time, she knew she hadn't imagined it. Whatever had just happened ignited something in her, and if she read his expression correctly, incited something in Will, too.

His heated expression transformed into one of concern as she still could only look at him with her face in her hands. "Sarah, are you okay?"

She closed her eyes and nodded. Despite searching for the words, for some sort of explanation, all she could feel was that extreme rush of emotion that had just exploded between them. She wasn't supposed to feel that, not with him. "I...I guess I'm just tired. I'm sorry, can we go in?"

Will's brow furrowed in worry. "Of course. You're cold, too. Let's go in so you can warm up."

He gently placed his arm around her shoulder as they walked up the path to the house. Feeling his arm around her felt comforting, but being so close to him was not helping her sort out her feelings. Part of her wanted to fold her body into his, and just let him hold her. But, that didn't make sense either. She didn't know him, and she shouldn't be so comfortable with a stranger. Why didn't he feel like a stranger? It was all so overwhelming that she felt the tears threatening, and all she wanted to do was escape to her room to figure all of this out.

Will held the door open for her and followed closely behind. "Come sit, I'll get the fire going."

When she looked to the rocking chair, memory of their morning together talking in front of fire, hit her. But now, she couldn't focus. She certainly knew she couldn't sit in front of the fire again with him. Not right now. "Actually, Will, I really think I need to go lie down."

Unsure of what she would see, or what she might feel if he looked at her the way he just did, she couldn't look at him at that moment. She turned toward the kitchen, knowing that if she didn't hurry, he would see the flood of tears that she wouldn't be able to explain.

"Sarah? Are you okay?" The concern in his voice was apparent and she hated to leave him without an explanation.

"I'm fine," she said, holding up her hand. "Really, I'm fine, thank you. I'm just going to go." Her voice trailed off, revealing the fact that the tears hadn't made it to the safety of her room. Closing her door gently, she lay down on her bed and buried her face in her pillow. She couldn't help the sobs that were escaping, or the tears that were soaking the pillowcase. Everything had just become so much more overwhelming: the accident, losing her parents, leaving California, coming back to Colorado where she should feel the most at home, and now a completely unexpected element of how she felt around Will. It was all too much to contain. She didn't know if she could go through with this. Finding her memories would be one thing, but finding more than she ever bargained for, was another. Right now, both options seemed just as frightening, and yet she had an inexplicable need to uncover the truth about her past, and that included her past with Will. What she had just experienced was too powerful to ignore as simply a co-incidence, or her imagination. What was more, she felt he had experienced the exact same thing.

For now, she would stay in the safety of her room, and let the turbulence in her mind calm down to the point where she could be around him, and not feel the chaos in her mind paralyzing her every thought and action. Part of her wanted to go to him now, and feel the safety of being around him. But, she knew deep down that she wasn't ready. Whatever it was, she couldn't rush, or force herself to be something that she wasn't. Right now, she had to get some sort of hold of herself if she were to maintain her sanity.

After enough tears exhausted her, she finally fell asleep. But, after a fitful dream, she awoke, lying on the covers of her bed, cold. Eventually, she would remember that she was no longer in California and start dressing more appropriately for the mountain weather. She sat up and reached for the sweater that was at the end of her bed, and listened for signs of anyone else who might be awake, or for some indication of what time it might be. After several beats of silence, she assumed it must be the middle of the night based on the stillness and the black of the moonless sky outside of her window.

Plunging her arms into the sweater, she wrapped her arms around herself. Despite the gentle pull, as she tried to open her door quietly, the door announced her movements with a high-pitched creak. She stepped out to the kitchen and noticed the flickering shadows dancing across the floor. Anxious for the comforting fire, that was popping and snapping at the wood, she rubbed her arms and tiptoed across the floor. She turned the corner and instantly looked to the fireplace. But, she came to an abrupt halt once she saw that she wasn't the only one to have this idea. Will sat on the hearth, with his elbow resting on his knee, staring at the floor. She continued quietly across the floor, not knowing what she would say to him once she reached him.

A creak of the wooden floorboard gave her away, and Will's head snapped up in surprise. Once he saw her, he immediately straightened his posture, but said nothing. She didn't exactly feel courageous, but she wasn't scared either. She knew she needed to say something to him, and thought she'd have to wait until morning, but this was just as good. She stood directly in front of him, forcing him to look up at her from his seated position. The warmth of the fire felt overwhelming against the chill on her skin, and she realized that it may not just be the fire that was warming her. Being next to him brought with it a flux of emotions, of that she was becoming more and more aware.

She locked eyes with his, and as he stood, his focus never broke from her eyes. She now, however, had to look up into his face. It seemed like so much was being said, just with their eyes. She could almost feel what would seem a natural next move. She imagined him putting his arms around her and holding her. She could almost guess how amazing that would feel. But despite her immediate daydream, Will did not pull her into his embrace. He only stood, looking at her, as if he could see straight to her soul.

Maybe he could see into her soul, and read her innermost thoughts, at one time. All she knew now, was that she needed him to know what she was thinking and feeling, and give him some sort of explanation for her unexpected behavior earlier in the evening.

"Will, I'm glad you're up," she said, slightly louder than a whisper.

"Oh? Why's that?" His voice was calm and controlled, not a trace of tension in his words.

"I wanted to tell you that I'm sorry. I'm sorry for rushing away from you like I did."

He cocked his head and slowly shook it back and forth, all while keeping his eyes on her. "You don't have anything to apologize for, Sarah. Not to me, ever."

"No," she disagreed. "I do. I just didn't know how to understand everything that was washing over me since...everything happened, and I came here. There's just been so much, and I guess that tonight it all came crashing down on me. All I could think to do, was to run from it."

Will slightly lifted his arm, and for a second, she thought that he was actually going to touch her. Her heart immediately responded by pounding against her chest, but he slowly lowered his hand back to his side. "I understand, Sarah, really I do. Please don't feel like you need to explain anything to me. That's not how we were, that's not how I want us to be now."

She stared at him, wondering how he could say exactly what she was hoping he would. She had no idea how he would react to her after her strange behavior, but she couldn't have hoped for anything better than what he was saying. "I just wanted you to know that," she paused, allowing herself time to really think about what she wanted him to know. She took in a deep breath, "I just want you to know that it's not you that's overwhelming me. It's everything that is piling up inside of me. Everything that I'm hopeful for, and everything that I'm afraid of. But, it's not you. You've been so good to me already, your whole family taking me in like this. I know that I don't remember everything, well, anything, really, but it almost seems like that doesn't matter when I'm with you. I don't know, I can't explain it." She looked down to the floor but couldn't stay away from his eyes for too long. "I guess I just wanted you to know that I'm sorry, if it seemed like I was running away from you."

"First off, you can't run away from me, I know where you live." He gave a devastatingly handsome smile and Sarah let out the breath she had unknowingly been holding. She smiled at him, and was once again in awe at how he could make her feel so at ease. And...so off balance.

She felt like she must be blushing, but she wasn't sure why. How was he able to so easily melt any tension with his words? "Yes," she nodded. "I suppose you do."

"And, the other thing is that I am willing to do anything it takes, for however long it takes, for you to remember. There is no time limit; there is no set expectation for your recovery. There is no pressure. I want you to let whatever is meant to happen, happen. Maybe you'll remember everything tomorrow, maybe you won't. But, either way, I know you're not running away from me, because I'll be at your side every step of the way. For as long as you want me to be."

This time, there was no stopping what was inside of her. It came without thought of consequence, and she could only allow herself to do what came as naturally as anything she had ever done. Closing the gap between them with one small step, she wrapped her arms around his waist. She turned her head so her cheek fell against his broad chest. She closed her eyes and breathed in his warm scent. It was an inexplicable response, but it felt good, and it felt right. She felt his arm gently and firmly circle around her back, and hold her. He wasn't forceful, just sure of what he was doing.

She could've stayed there longer, except for the nagging reminder that she really didn't know him, which crept into her mind and forced her to release her grasp and retreat slowly. He looked at her for only a second with slight confusion creasing his brow, but it was quickly softened into a curious smile.

"What was that for?"

Sarah wondered if she had let herself cross into territory that wasn't allowed. "I'm, I'm sorry."

Will's eyes widened, "No, no, no. Not that I mind, just wondering where that came from."

She sighed and smiled, "I just wanted to thank you. Thank you for being so nice, and thank you for helping me."

Will stepped to her, so close, he could've easily put his arm around her again. She looked up into his face, and noticed again his ice-blue eyes were serious.

"Sarah, now is as good of a time as any to tell you something. Whether you hear it now, or later, it doesn't matter because nothing could change what I have to say."

Sarah swallowed the lump that formed in her throat. The way he was looking at her, and his words, made her heart race. Her skin tingled from his close proximity. What was it about this man?

When she didn't respond, he continued, "There isn't anything I wouldn't do for you. Not then, not now. Sarah, I..." He stopped himself just short of finishing his thought.

"You...what?"

Taking a slow breath and shaking his head, he continued. "Just know that I will do anything."

"We must've been very good friends."

He nodded and raised his eyebrows, "Yes, we were."

Whether it was his words, or how he was looking at her she didn't know, but she could feel her head start to spin and felt her heartbeat pounding in her chest. There was no other explanation other than, in the crevices of her mind, she still knew him. The more she was with him, the more she was certain that she had to know the secrets her mind was keeping from her.

CHAPTER 22

Sarah propped her elbows up against the pine posts and gazed through the gap. Henry and Will had been up before the sun, and at first light, started repairing the corral. The two worked harmoniously together gathering materials, and stacking posts. She watched admiringly as Will took on the heavy lifting instead of Henry. For having only the use of one arm, she was amazed at the ease he seemed to be able to lift and move the various tools and materials. He was strong, and energetic, and by looking at him, it would seem that he was well rested. But, she knew that wasn't the case at all.

She and Will's middle of the night encounter lasted a while longer until they both decided they should try to get some sleep. Their conversation flowed effortlessly in front of the fire. She had no way of knowing about Will, but for herself, sleep didn't come for a long time once she was in bed. Instead, she could only replay the events of the day over and over in her mind. Unfortunately, not all of the events left her feeling contented. Had it not been for making the unfortunate acquaintance of Margaret, it couldn't have been more pleasant, or perfect. She had been reunited with her cat, and she remembered petting her nose. Well, perhaps she didn't remember, but she knew what to do and that was the seedling of hope that was showing signs of growth. But, her time with Will was what left a lasting impression. She still couldn't believe that she had wrapped her arms around him, as if it were instinctively what she felt to do. When he wrapped around her too, with a gentle protectiveness, it was such an unforeseen rush through her body that she could still feel it lingering in her mind, and even more so, on her body, this morning.

Now, she leaned against the posts and breathed in the air that still held a slight bite of the morning's coolness. She closed her eyes and positioned her face to the sun. In the nearby trees, the birds were welcoming the morning, and she took note of the different songs, wishing she could also see what little bird was each making its own presence known to the world. It was moments like this that she craved. Appreciating what seemed like minute details, but in reality, were glimpses of peace, and gratitude for being able to be in this exact moment. She breathed in deeply, and for the first time since the accident, thanked God for this moment, and for allowing her to experience it.

She slowly opened her eyes, and squinted at the brightness after her eyes had become accustomed to the darkness. Shielding her eyes from the sun, she gazed across the pen and noticed Will had stopped working, and instead was staring at her. Once their eyes met, he smiled and gave a short nod of his head. "You doin' okay over there?"

She smiled back. "Yes," she replied, feeling her pulse quicken, knowing he had been watching her.

He set down the bucket of nails and walked toward her. She noticed that she could pick up the blue of his eyes even from a distance.

"Enjoying the beauty that is around me, soaking it all in," she continued, once he was directly across from her.

His smiled faded with seriousness as he gazed directly into her eyes. "I know exactly what you mean."

The tumultuous feelings his comment created, blazed right through her and landed in her stomach. Was he talking about her, or the weather, as she had been innocently referring to? She only had to wonder for a moment. That was long enough to watch his face fill with a crimson hue, as he quickly turned his head toward the trees. Her expression must not have been able to hide the question that was spiraling through her mind. He leaned his elbow against the post next to hers and looked back at her, his bashful smile playing across his lips. He dropped his head and shook it slowly, breathing out loudly, "I'm sorry, Sarah. I didn't mean to...I mean, I hope I didn't make you uncomfortable."

She shook her head, still not believing that he was referring to her. "No, you didn't," she reassured him.

"I guess it's just that, even after all this time, I still think you are so very beautiful."

Now, it was Sarah's turn to feel the blush scamper across her cheeks. She couldn't help but smile, but the rising fluttering in her stomach was beginning to make her dizzy. She quickly searched her mind for something to say, but Henry interrupted her thoughts.

"This corral isn't going to fix itself, son. And, this sun is only getting hotter," Henry yelled from across the pen, yet Sarah could detect a light-hearted tone despite his clear message to Will to get back to work.

Will turned toward his father, "Yes, sir. I'm coming."

He looked once again at Sarah before he stepped back from the fence. "I better get going."

She nodded, "Okay, be careful."

He laughed, "I will. I'd be completely worthless with two of these things." He tugged at the sling, shaking his head at the extreme inconvenience it provided. He took a few steps before turning back around to her. "Hey, I almost forgot to tell you. I have a surprise for you."

"A surprise? What kind of a surprise?" Sarah was sure she was instantly beaming.

"The kind of surprise that means I'm not going to tell you because it's a surprise."

"But...what...what?" she asked.

"Don't worry, I'll take care of everything we need. As soon as I'm done here, we'll head out, okay?"

He waited until she slowly agreed, "Okay, I'll be ready."

"Good." He ran his fingers up through his hair, moving it from his forehead.

Sarah furrowed her brow at the sight of his movement. Seeing him rake his fingers through his hair and push it back, only to have it fall back, seemed familiar to her for some reason. She tried to recollect if she had seen him do that since she had been there. But she seemed to think that if she had, then this wouldn't have struck in her such a way. She wondered if the explanation was as simple as how incredible he looked as he did so.

She watched him go back with Henry, and wondered what he had planned for her. Just as the anticipation began to build, it just as quickly came crashing back down all around her. The excitement of going somewhere with Will was instantly replaced with guilt as she thought of Adley. Her thoughts had, of course, bounced between everything she was experiencing in Colorado, and everything she remembered about California. She missed him, she missed his touch, and how he could send her into a realm of pleasure that she never knew existed. Every night her prayers centered on keeping Matty and Adley out of harm's way. She couldn't bear to think of anything happening to either one of them, and she would force herself to think only good thoughts, and not let her imagination run away with itself. She knew she would go mad if she dwelled on everything that could possibly happen to them fighting in a war that had no qualms about taking them away from her, forever.

But, why the guilt? She hadn't done anything to betray Adley. Whether she remembered it or not, Will had been a part of her life since she was a girl, and he was family, more or less. She told herself that again as she continued to watch him. She couldn't deny his attractiveness. His body rippled with the strength of his defined muscles, yet with her, his hands had only been gentle with every touch. His looks were devastatingly handsome; there were no bones about that. But nothing was as alluring as how he looked at her. The heat that one look from him could produce in her was unsettling. She couldn't explain it, and yet couldn't wait for the next time he would focus his gaze on her. Therein lied the guilt. Another man, other than Adley, could stir a fire deep inside of her. It was a man that she didn't know, but somehow remembered. It was a man that she wanted to know, but was afraid of what that knowledge would do to her. Despite the nagging contradictory battle inside her mind, she knew she had no choice if she were to discover her past. That discovery was going to come one piece at a time. Just as a rainstorm begins with just a few lone drops of precious water, her memories had begun to splash onto her arid landscape in her mind. The drops quickly absorbed, leaving her craving more. There would be no way to turn away from the impending rain clouds that held more of what she needed. Guilt surged again as she realized that if Will was the rainstorm, it might be worth getting caught in it, even though she knew she was completely unprepared for it.

CHAPTER 23

The rest of the day had crawled to pace that tested Sarah's patience to the brink of sanity. She had tried to occupy her time, and most importantly, her mind, while Will and Henry worked throughout the day repairing the corral. They had taken a break for lunch and seemed grateful for the egg-salad sandwiches and lemonade that she had made for them. She and Will managed to eat despite their eyes never leaving each other for long, or a smile that would cross their lips when they caught each other looking. She couldn't deny that the anticipation was a delicious feeling, growing from deep inside. She tried to predict what the evening would entail, but every time she did, the flurry of a thousand wings would make her stomach rise and fall, leaving her breathless.

But now, the time had come. She was about to find out what she had imagined all day. She and Will were finally walking down the driveway, together. He had changed clothes and cleaned up, but Sarah would've taken him just the way he was. Hard work looked good on him. The warmth of the day was carrying over a bit longer into the early evening, but Sarah had learned by now that the minute the sun began its descent, it would get cold, and she remembered to bring her sweater. She still had not fully acclimated to the coolness of Colorado, unlike Will who seemed completely comfortable in his short-sleeve blue-plaid shirt.

"So, where are we going?" she asked, unable to keep from noticing how his blue eyes stood out, especially against the bright blue of his shirt.

He smiled slyly, "I guess you'll just have to wait and see, won't you?"

"Oh, come on, Will. Just a hint? You can at least tell me something," she pleaded, her smile growing.

He turned his attention to the gravel driveway, and then, back to her. "Hmm...I don't know. I kind of like that I'm in charge."

"Oh, really? In charge of what, then?" she asked, trying not to over exaggerate the innocent tone in her voice.

"You're not going to get it out of me that easily, Sarah. Good try, though."

They had reached the end of the driveway where they stopped before stepping out to the county road. Sarah looked in both directions, "Which way, right or left?"

"Neither."

"So, where then?" she asked, confused by what he could have planned.

"Straight." He pointed directly across the road.

Sarah followed his gaze to the field that was just beyond the bar ditch. The large rectangular field was filled with bright green grass, that hadn't reached its full length yet this early in the spring. "The field?" she questioned.

"Well, not really the field. Just stop with the questions, and follow me, okay?"

She nodded her head. There was something in her that knew he could suggest just about anything, and she would follow him without a moment of debate. How she knew that he would never lead her into harm, she didn't know. If her instincts were right, like they usually were, she knew she could trust him. If he wanted to take her to a field, then she would go. What she slowly came to realize throughout the course of the day, was that she would be happy to go wherever he wanted to; she just wanted to be with him.

A genuine smile of relief coupled with excitement played across his face, and his eyes glinted mischievously, as if he'd just won a victory, "Good, let's go."

They crossed the road and stopped before descending into the steep bar ditch. At the base of the ditch a barbed wire fence framed the field. Will stepped down the embankment first, stood sideways, and held out his hand out for Sarah. "I know you could do this on your own, but I'd feel better if you let me help you."

She knew she could do it easily on her own, too. But, that didn't matter to her. The fact that Will was so blatant about caring for her was even more endearing than the small gesture of helping her down the hill. She placed her hand in his and together they sidestepped down the hill. She couldn't help but feel the unusual sensation of his hand around hers. It seemed to encompass more than just her hand; she could feel the warmth race up her arm and into her chest. There was simply no point in denying that Will had a hold on her alright, and not just by holding her hand.

He held onto her, noticeably longer than he needed to at the base of the hill. She left her hand in his, curious as to when he would let it go, but even more so, to keep his hand, so gentle and secure, guarding hers. But, now that they faced the barbed-wire fence, the necessity to release her hand forced Will to slowly let her go.

"Are you up for this?" he asked, looking at the fence. "You're going to need to go through it."

"Of course, I am. The day a fence keeps me from doing just what I want, is going to be a sad day, Will."

His eyes shone with approval and he stepped to the fence, stepping on the lower wire and pulling up the wire just above it with his free arm, providing a wide gap to squeeze through. Sarah smiled and bent under the wire with ease. Once through, Will released the tension and let the wired spring back to their position. Walking to the nearest post and balancing himself with one hand on the top of it, he walked up the wires as surely as if it were a ladder, and jumped down to the ground with one leap.

The confident, gorgeous smile radiated from him, and Sarah could feel the rush of nerves at what he had planned for her. The emotion she was feeling was a welcome diversion to all that she had been feeling since the accident. Whether she ended up remembering any of her past or not, the fact that she was once again experiencing the tingle of happiness creep across her heart, was making the decision to come back to Colorado worth it.

Reaching for her hand, Will interrupted her admission of contentment.

"Ready?"

She looked at his hand, and without a second of hesitation, placed her hand in his. She glanced down at their hands, now enveloped in each other, and was almost so overwhelmed, that she felt frozen in place. The way they seamlessly fit together, with his strong hand securing hers, was too much for her to ignore. It was such a simple gesture that carried with it a message to Sarah, telling her everything she needed to know. She could feel the surge of what she meant to him course through her body. He squeezed gently, and she looked up into his blue eyes that were patiently waiting for hers.

She smiled shyly and nodded, "I'm ready."

They crossed the field of clover and grass in a few short minutes, and Sarah was sure that if she could've concentrated on anything but her hand in Will's, she would've noticed the simple, quiet beauty of the blades of grasses swaying in the slight evening breeze. As they approached the edge of the field, she couldn't help but be taken by towering pine trees that beckoned to her. She slowed her pace, and finally stood, staring into the shaded boughs. The grove of pine trees was impressive, and the white bark of the aspen trees that surrounded the grove gave a bold comparison of color, of light and dark. She felt Will's hand slightly tense around hers, and noticed that his expression had also changed.

"What's wrong?" She hadn't meant to, but her words came out in a whisper, perhaps because every other noise seemed to disappear and anything louder than a whisper would've awakened an entire forest.

Will forced a smile, "Nothing's wrong, Sarah. I guess I just didn't expect to feel nervous."

"You're nervous?" She smiled, and tried to lighten the expression that still creased his face. "Don't you think I should be the nervous one?"

"I don't want you to be nervous about anything, Sarah. That's not why I brought you here. It's just that, I haven't been here for a long time."

"Why did you bring me here, then?"

He turned his body toward hers and looked straight into her eyes. "I brought you here, to help you remember. I brought you here, because this was one of your most favorite places to be."

Now, true nerves had begun to swirl in Sarah's gut. Up until now, she had only been at Will's house, not somewhere like here. Yet, she was somewhere that had held a significant meaning to her, and she was about to find out if any of it was still there, somewhere in the depths of her mind.

"Show me, Will."

He smiled again, "These are the pines, Sarah." He turned smiling at the grove, his expression relaxing. "Come on."

They turned and stepped from the grassy field onto soft black dirt that slightly sank with each of their steps, as they ducked under the low-hanging boughs that guarded the entrance. Sarah couldn't help but allow her gaze to follow the thick trunks of the trees all the way to their tops, where only small patches of the blue sky could be seen. She slowly scanned her surroundings, in awe of the complete change from the grassy field just a few feet away. Everything was quiet, and the air was noticeably cooler. She took a few steps onto an obvious path that snaked around the trees. The crunch under her feet was barely audible, yet against the silence, it pierced through the air. She looked to the forest floor, and under her feet lay a blanket of rust-colored pine needles. Realizing the connection between the pine needles at her feet, and the same ones that had been kept the little pine box with the carving, she paused. She knelt down to pinch a few in her fingers and brought them to her nose. The fragrant little leaves still housed a powerful scent, a scent that when she closed her eyes, seemed to stir more than her sense of smell. A slight churning in the pit of her stomach made her both excited and anxious. There was a definite reaction her body was having to being here. Smelling the sweetly-scented needles, and most noticeably, Will by her side for the whole thing, it just felt right.

It wasn't a definite memory, but she was certain that she could sense having this experience at some other time in her life. She could feel the memory. Every reaction of her body was sending the same message. This was a place of happiness for her. This was a place that was still very much a part of her. Now, if she could just pinpoint the exact moments in her past to this glorious place, she could begin to connect the dots.

"Why do you not come here anymore? This place is," she paused, search-ing for words that could do the pines justice. "This is like a gift, a secret gift."

Will walked to her, and she slowly stood to meet him. He was so close to her that once again, she wondered if he might touch her. When he was in front of her, it seemed as if his broad shoulders and arms could circle her, and she could melt into the safety of his strength. He did not touch her, but she felt the intensity of him, even through his stare.

"It just got too hard to come here, without you, Sarah. Too many mem-ories, and everywhere I looked, I could see you. Every tree I looked at, I could see you next to it. Every time I breathed in, I could smell you. The pines were you, Sarah. The pines were us…when we were together. Being here without you was…torture."

Sarah's eyes searched his, letting his words sink to the depths of her being. He held her gaze, letting her fully absorb his confession. She reached up to touch him, and still, his eyes remained locked on hers. She laid her palm against his cheek, and let her fingers slowly trickle down his jawline. "I'm sorry, Will. I had no idea." The pain was still fresh in his mind, as she could clearly discern by his expression. The need to comfort him was overwhelming, and whether she could remember the pines or not, she felt compelled to erase the ache that he couldn't hide.

She let her hand drop to his shoulder, and he closed the gap between so that there was merely a thin, narrow space separating them. He raised his hand to her face, and let his fingers trace her cheek as she had done to him. He slowly brought his hand up again, and gently traced her cheekbone with his thumb, but he did not take his hand from her. The soft caresses down her cheek trailed down, and back up again, causing Sarah's mind to swirl and her body to tingle with awareness. With each caress, his hand seemed to pull her into him further and deeper. He leaned more and more into her, and she could feel herself being drawn in, not only with the physical connection, but something even more powerful. She and Will were connecting on a level so profound, that she could feel it in her mind and body.

She lifted her chin to him, allowing him to continue his touch. There were no words, only each other's eyes that said everything. This moment, this place, something was happening. There was no denying that all of it was igniting an ember that had been fading to the point being extinguished. But, everything about this moment was breathing life back into it, and the ember had awoken, a flame was eminent, and the danger of getting burned seemed uncontrollable.

CHAPTER 24

Touching Sarah was intoxicating. Touching her skin was like touching silk. Touching her was like a moth drawn to a flame. But, unlike the moth, he knew better. He just didn't care. The feel of her skin against his would be worth whatever consequence might come. For now, there was no consequence. There were only the two of them, in the pines, and Sarah was not pushing him away. A lot had changed in the last several days. He wouldn't have guessed by the way they were reunited, and Sarah having no qualms in using the frying pan to defend herself, that she would be resting her cheek in his hand at the moment, without one hint of fear. For as long as this moment would last, he was going to savor every second. Nothing else mattered right now; nothing else existed. The most rare and precious gift had found its way to him. Sarah had found her way back to him.

If not for the nagging noise of reality in the back of his mind, he would have kissed her. Everything about her was beckoning to him. Her eyes on him were soft and permissive. His hand against her face was delicious, but only made him ache for more. The feel of her lips against his, would be like pressing them into an angel's whisper. The thought of feeling her kiss him back was maddening, and if he could've escaped the realization that breathing her in would never happen again, and most certainly would only add to the anguish of knowing that he could not have her, he would've done it.

But, damned reality would not relent, nor disappear. The momentary pause of this reminder was enough to bring the building churn of desire back down to a simmer as Sarah bit her lip and looked down, causing his hand to drop from her cheek.

She looked back to him just as her eyes began to fill with tears. "Will," she whispered.

He sighed heavily, letting the moment release its hold on his breath. "Sarah," he said slowly, "do you remember any of this?" He wanted to hear her say yes, with all his being, he wanted her to remember. Wanting her with all of his heart, knowing that if she did remember, his heart would surely die a thousand deaths knowing that he could not have her. His heart had calloused with time since she had left, so much so, that he thought it could never be hurt again. But, with the one touch of her skin against his, the rough shield around his heart had begun to melt away.

Sarah kept her eyes on him and slowly shook her head. "I...I don't know."

He looked at her, waiting for further explanation. How could she not know? Either she remembered, or she did not, and bringing her here accomplished nothing more than bringing a glaring light to the fact that he was still in love with her. There. He admitted it, knowing that denying it any longer was futile. He was still in love with her. He had never stopped loving her.

Sarah pleaded with her eyes for some sort of understanding from him, "I've never felt this before. I mean, what just happened, with us. It was like nothing I've ever felt, except it seemed like I had felt it before, I just can't remember when. Will, I," she paused again, blinking away the tears, "I must remember, because there is no other explanation for how I feel now. If I didn't remember, this would just be a forest of trees, like every other tree in the world. But, it's not. I can feel it; there is something about being here, in the pines, with you. My heart remembers this, I'm certain of it."

She remembered. The words he had hoped, and in the same instant, feared, made him want to pull her into him and kiss her until she knew he would never again let her go. However, he found himself asking what he'd done to deserve this cruel hoax. But, the true love he felt for her won out, knowing that she deserved to remember her past. He survived losing her once to California; he would have to survive losing her again, to fate's will.

She held open the palm of her hand, revealing the pine needles that were all part of the concoction that brought the memory, or at least the remembrance of feeling something, and that would have to suffice for now. "Will, I know I've been here, I can almost see it in my mind." She shook her head and looked to the ground, "Unless it's just me wishing that I could see it, I don't know. This is all so, so much for me to try to understand."

He wrapped his hand around hers, gently folding her fingers around the delicate needles once again. "Stop trying so hard, Sarah. Just let it happen, just let yourself feel."

"I want to, more than anything now. I wish I could explain what that felt like, to remember."

Will released his hand from hers and ran his hand up the length of her arm. "I remember it, too. I remember everything, a little too well. You don't have to explain anything. We never needed words before, we don't need them now, either."

Sarah looked at him in such a way that made him feel as if no time had passed, there had never been the move to California, there had never been the fire, and there had never been the arrangement with Margaret. She didn't need to tell him with words, her eyes told him everything. Whether she knew it or not, didn't matter at this point. He knew it. She was remembering, he'd be willing to bet his life on it.

He slid his hand back down her arm and clasped her hand in his. "It's getting late, and I can tell you are cold. Are you ready to go back?"

Sarah's slender fingers nestled into his palm, "I don't know. I like remembering. I like being here, with you."

Will's pulse quickened, and he instinctively pulled her hand closer to his body. Her words, her presence, everything about her could still drive him to the brink of throwing all good sense to the wind. It was all he could do to resist showing her how much he liked being here with her. To hear that she wanted to be there with him was just the kind of fuel the ember in his heart needed.

"I'll be with you anywhere you want to be, Sarah. I'll take you everywhere; everywhere there is a memory. I'll be with you when you remember."

"Do you promise?" she whispered.

A promise. Another promise to make to her. She had no idea what she stirred with those three words. He had promised her everything he had to give. He promised to love her, to make her happy. He promised to spend his life with her. Me Ware Wo. I shall marry you. The flash back in time, when everything was simple, instantly replayed in his mind. Nonetheless, the time for keeping that promise had long since passed. It was no longer a promise, it was a broken dream, and no matter what he promised her now, nothing would change the fact that the promise he made at the tree stump could never be kept.

"I promise, Sarah. I promise I will always...." He stopped himself from continuing. He couldn't say what he wanted to. It would only hurt them both to hear the words out loud.

"You'll always, what?" Sarah's soft voice prompted, and her eyes pleaded with his very core.

"I'll always...help you remember. I promise to help you remember."

She smiled and he couldn't help but trace the outline of her lips with his eyes. Son of a bitch, Will! How the hell are you going to get yourself through this? He couldn't help but to ream himself inwardly. This was going to be some version of hell on Earth to never taste Sarah's lips and breathe her in like he ached to do.

"Okay, good, I don't think I could without you. I don't think I would want to, without you. There's just something that tells me that as long as you're with me, remembering my past will be okay."

Will swallowed hard, unable to respond. Once Sarah remembered, and if she remembered everything, he was pretty sure it would be anything but okay. He promised he would be with her when she remembered, but he knew that would be one time when he wouldn't want to be by her side to see the look in her eyes when she did.

"Let's get you home." He had to change the subject before he could let himself completely fill with dread. That moment wasn't now, and there was the chance it wouldn't come at all, so there was no sense borrowing trouble.

"Okay." She smiled, and shivered slightly. He felt her hand squeeze his, and it sent a wave straight to his heart. She had some kind of power, just like she always had, to drive him crazy with desire by just the slightest gesture. "I'll make some coffee, that'll help warm us up."

She looked around the pines one last time, already gazing at it like a long-lost friend, before nodding to Will. Still hand in hand, they turned down the slight incline back toward the field. In a moment, they would be out of the sanctuary, into the world that held more than just the two of them, and he hoped that once they stepped out into the fading daylight, that what they had felt in the pines would not disappear.

Just as they bent to duck under the last bough guarding the entrance, Will froze in place and pulled Sarah's hand back. He stepped back and pulled her back under the cover of the shadows.

"What? What's the matter?" He hated the instant look of fear on Sarah's face.

He pointed across the field to the truck that was turning up his driveway. "It's Margaret," he said flatly.

They watched the truck lurch up the driveway, and then he turned to Sarah. "I'm sorry, I didn't mean to scare you. It's just that I wasn't expecting to see her. I don't know why she's here."

"I'm sure she came to see you, Will. Why wouldn't she?" Sarah's voice trailed off, and only because he knew her so well, he could detect the slightest hint of annoyance.

"I told her that I would be busy today. I told her that I had plans." He had a lot of plans, more than just fixing the corral; he knew he would have this day to spend with Sarah. The last thing he was ready to do was cut the day short by involving Margaret in it. But, in true Margaret fashion, she had decided what his day would, and would not, include. He hadn't realized how much he truly did not want to see her until he stopped short and pulled Sarah back into the pines, shielded by the towering trees. He could only hope that they hadn't been spotted by Margaret before she'd turned into the driveway.

"How long will she stay?" Sarah's tone had changed dramatically, and he cringed. Their moments in the pines were just what he hoped they would be. Instead of continuing their evening next to the fire with each other, they would have to wait for Margaret to leave. There was no way he was willing to bring the two women together again. Once Margaret found out he wasn't home, and moreover, that he was somewhere with Sarah, there would be hell to pay. He would have to be the one to diffuse Margaret's wrath at a later time, he refused to subject Sarah to it.

For now, he was still with Sarah. Despite the nagging in the back of his mind of what it would take to inevitably convince Margaret that he had done nothing wrong, he would not waste the moments of being with Sarah.

"I don't know. It's hard to tell. Hopefully my dad won't tell her anything, and she'll be on her way."

"You...don't want to go home and see her?" The hopefulness in Sarah's voice was so much more revealing than any words ever could've been.

He turned to her once again, wanting her. The want was becoming more and more evident every time he looked into her eyes. He slowly shook his head and answered quietly, "No. I want to be here, with you. I've waited all day to be with you."

He watched her expression carefully. He knew her so well, and despite the time and distance apart, they were seamlessly falling back into place with each other as easily as their two hands clasping together.

"I have too, Will." Sarah voice trembled.

Once again there was no stopping the force that brought his hand to her face. He gently rubbed his thumb against her cheek, brushing the tear to the side. He needed to kiss her. He needed her to know that he still loved her, and he knew he could tell her everything she needed to know with one kiss. His eyes trailed down to her mouth, and he was suddenly ravenous to feel her mouth, and her soft lips against his. He leaned down to her face, feeling her soft breath against him. He was a mere second away from feeling her; from tasting the sweetness that he knew would be waiting for him. One short second and he could have what he dreamt about having since the day she left for California.

She parted her lips slightly, as if to welcome his imminent kiss. The innocence in her eyes was doused with trust, and his heart pounded with that knowledge. In that moment, he knew that she trusted him, with no reason to, other than her heart must still recognize him.

He continued slowly with the downward motion of his face toward hers, but squeezed his eyes shut, just as his lips landed on her soft cheek. He couldn't do this to her. He couldn't have her, so he wouldn't hurt her, nor give her any reason to not trust him. It would be wrong. He knew once he felt her again, everything would be different. That was a price he wasn't willing to pay. He had survived many heartbreaks; but kissing Sarah, knowing that he couldn't fully have her, would be too much. More than the certain agony that he would have to endure, he refused to kiss Sarah, and then go back to being Margaret's future husband. He wouldn't do that to her. He also promised that he would always protect her. That promise, he could at least keep. He'd be damned to ever be the one to hurt her.

CHAPTER 25

Sarah scoured the frying pan, with each scratch of the morning's breakfast, breaking apart, she seemed to scour her own self and how she had allowed herself to be over the past couple of weeks with Will. The evening in the pines had been just the beginning. Now, the harder she scrubbed the more she condemned herself for allowing her feelings to come as far as they have.

The near kiss still haunted her. At that moment in time, she couldn't have had a coherent thought one-way or the other, let alone rationalize the right or the wrong of letting it happen. Had it not been of Will's accord, she would've let it happen. Or, would she? Would she have turned at the last second before her lips met his, knowing that no good could come from a fated kiss in the pines? She knew he was not available, and she wasn't a woman to steal from another. She pressed even harder into the pan, cursing herself as Adley flashed through her mind. The rationale of not allowing a kiss to happen would've been enough with the pure fact that Will was taken. But knowing her last words to Adley were that she would wait for him, and marry him, and love him for the rest of her life, was torturous. Adley was everything she could hope for in a man, and the love she had for him was true. Why then, could she so easily fall into a raging river of emotion whenever she was with Will? A silent tear couldn't be stopped as it fell from her chin into the dishwater. What she wouldn't give to have her mother at this very moment.

Fortunately, Margaret would only pick Will up in the mornings to take him to the lumberyard, and she had only seen Margaret a couple of times since the night at the pines, all of which were glimpses of her sour demeanor.

Most evenings, Will caught a ride with Mr. Wilkes, or Henry would go into town for supplies and time the trip for when Will would be getting off. She couldn't be certain, but she got the distinct impression that Henry didn't want Margaret around the house in the evenings any more than she did. In fact, she wondered about the motivation of Henry not letting on that Will was with Sarah that evening that they first went to the pines, and Margaret only stayed for a few minutes before leaving. Sarah was relieved for Will. She could only imagine the explaining he would undoubtedly be forced to do if Margaret knew that the two of them had gone off somewhere together. She knew, too, that if she had any hopes of spending time with Will, it would be better if Margaret didn't feel the need to check up on him, and deliver another surprise visit.

She didn't want to admit how she felt about spending more time with Will, but if she allowed the truth to seep into her inner heart of hearts, she couldn't wait for the next time she could be with him. Whether or not she was remembering anything, she didn't know. But just being with him felt so right. She felt as if she were home, even though the only thing of home she actually remembered was a thousand miles away in California. Since most of his days were spent in town, she busied herself with chores around the house until he returned home, but until she could scour the guilt from herself, she would take it out on the frying pan. The same pan she raised, and actually swung, at Will. Now, she found herself incessantly gazing out the window in the hopes of seeing the truck crest the hill, announcing his arrival. How much had changed.

Her day had played out like most. The laundry was washed, and swaying in the wind. She had scrubbed potatoes and had them bubbling in the starchy water to make into Will's favorite mashed-potato dish to go along with dinner. Now, she sat in the front porch swing, with one leg tucked under her and the other on its tip toe, pushing the swing back and forth until the squeak of the metal fittings had almost lulled her asleep. Lulu, who had quite easily let Sarah back into her life, sat asleep and purring, almost in time with the sway of the swing. Sarah let her finger float along

Lulu's nose as she gazed out into the scrub oak that lined the perimeter of the house. From this vantage point, she could see the tops of the pines. Just the thought of what had occurred under those pine trees made her stomach curl. She knew that the memory of the pines was not an apparition. What she had felt there had been real. But, the memory of Will moving down to kiss her was the startling revelation that day. If she had wondered about his feelings for her before, she no longer needed to. Henry's description of the relationship she and Will had before she left was somewhat skewed, and missing a few relevant details.

Imagining those details was interrupted when she heard a truck grab a lower gear and the engine whine to slowly climb the driveway up to the house. She straightened her posture, hoping it was someone bringing Will home. But, her shoulders sank back into the swing once she saw the blue Ford crest the hill. Will was coming home, but the fiery red hair that could be spotted through the windshield meant more was coming than what she wanted. Or rather, someone.

Her hopes of avoiding another uncomfortable encounter with Margaret were dashed as she noticed her coming up the walk, hand in hand with Will. Margaret's smile was as posed as if any minute her photograph was going to be taken. Will's eyes locked onto Sarah's, and he seemed to be holding his breath.

Lulu's yellow eyes opened and narrowed at the uninvited guests. She gracefully jumped from the swing and scampered off, just in time to avoid the encounter. It would've been nice if Lulu would've stayed, if for nothing else, but to give Sarah something to do with her hands. But cats did not put up with anything they weren't in the mood for, and Sarah couldn't blame her.

Margaret squealed and pressed against Will to avoid contact with Lulu as she skittered just past the base of her navy blue dress. "Oh! That cat! What's the matter with her? Is she rabid, or something?" She turned and looked over her shoulder, shooting Lulu one last disgusted glare, before giving the same look to Sarah.

Sarah smiled, exaggerating her sweet, relaxed tone. "Oh, no. She's just fine. You know what they say about cats."

"No, as a matter of fact, I don't." Margaret responded.

Sarah raised her eyebrows, and stated matter-of-factly, "They say, cats are a good judge of character." She cocked her head to the side, letting Margaret wonder exactly what she was referring to. Giving her no time to respond, she looked to Will, "Hi, Will, how was your day?"

She refused to look back at Margaret. She could feel the flicks of Margaret's annoyance being sent her way, but she would not give Margaret the satisfaction of seeing any of them land on her.

Will stammered but finally answered, "Oh, uh, fine. Just fine. But I do have a lot of chores to get to, and it'll be dark soon. I should get started." He looked to Margaret expectantly, but her eyes were still narrowed on Sarah.

Without looking at him, she spoke. "Oh yes, by all means, darling. Go ahead and get the chores done. I'll stay and visit with Sarah for a bit." The air on the porch instantly became heavy and silent.

Sarah swept her gaze to Margaret. This all may have been new to Sarah, but she hadn't forgotten how to hold her ground. That had nothing to do with her head injury. That came from her gut. She smiled again, which seemed to infuriate Margaret even more than the comment about the cat. She turned back to Will, wanting to reassure him that she would be okay. She could see the look of concern on his face, and her stomach twisted again knowing his concern for her couldn't be mistaken.

"Well, that sounds lovely, Margaret. Will, I'll be out to help you with the chores in just a bit." She nodded her head to him, hoping he could feel some relief that she would be alright.

Will sucked in a deep breath and looked to Margaret. "Okay, I'll be at the corral watering the horses."

He turned to make his departure but Margaret snagged his hand before he could. She leaned in and pressed her lips against his. "Miss me," she demanded, once they parted.

As Will stepped from the porch and out of sight, Margaret turned to

Sarah. "Mmm. I just can't get enough of that man." With no response from Sarah, she continued. "So Sarah, how are the memories coming along?"

"Just fine, thank you." Sarah kept her eye contact steady.

"Really? Does that mean you are remembering your past? Do you remember your life here?" Just like Lulu, Sarah was a good judge, and picked up on the slightest tone of fear in Margaret's voice. What she couldn't decide was, why the fear?

"No, not yet. But I feel like it's coming. In fact, I'm sure of it."

Margaret walked the few steps separating the two and stood directly in front of her. "Nothing?"

Sarah shook her head, "Nothing specific. Why do you ask, Margaret?"

Margaret smiled wryly and sat down on the swing next to Sarah. "I'm just curious if you've been able to remember our friendship yet?"

"Our, what?"

"Friendship, Sarah. We were very close all throughout our childhood, and until you left for California. I've been waiting for you to remember. We haven't had a chance to spend much time together and we have so much catching up to do."

Sarah's eyes felt as if they were vibrating and her vision blurred as her mind grappled with such unexpected information. She quickly turned her face to the yard, searching in the darkness of her mind for any recollection of a friendship with Margaret. There was nothing, absolutely nothing for her to place her finger on. She spotted the tips of the pine trees, knowing she could remember them, at least the feeling of them. But with Margaret, there had been no indication of the feeling of friendship. In fact, just the opposite. Every encounter she had with Margaret over the last several weeks was tainted with an aversion to her personality. But suddenly, she was wondering if all of that stemmed from their first encounter when Sarah had returned to Colorado. Sarah had been so repulsed by Margaret's lack of compassion over her parents' accident, that from that moment on, she had nothing good to think about the woman. Had she been so hurt by that, that she truly hadn't given Margaret another fair opportunity? Just as she considered the possibility, another likely explanation entered Sarah's mind. Perhaps she loathed Margaret for the pure fact that she had what she couldn't deny what she was beginning to covet. Margaret had Will.

"I don't remember anything about our friendship." Sarah said slowly.

Margaret smiled again, "Well, we could start again, couldn't we? I'll need a friend like you, especially once I start planning the wedding. In fact, I think it would be quite fitting for you to be my maid of honor. With us growing up together, and all. It just seems so perfect. There's just so much to do, and even though you don't remember, I do. When we were young, we always talked about the day we would be getting married. Who would've guessed that it would be me first? Well," she laughed out loud, "as soon as William could have me for his own, he made sure he got to me before anybody else could. And who could resist him? I certainly couldn't. I've wanted him for as long as I can remember. And then, one day, the stars aligned and brought us together, almost as if my wish had been granted." The sickening syrup of her words dripped from her mouth and Sarah felt her stomach tighten in disgust.

Sarah listened, unable to respond. She could only look out to the trees, begging herself to remember: to remember any of this. But, she couldn't. It was as frustrating as if she had been in another country and didn't know the language. She heard Margaret's words, yet none of them resonated with meaning. None of this made sense. If it did make sense, she didn't want it to.

Either way, she didn't want to listen anymore, and she sure as heck didn't want to talk anymore. It was unsettling to doubt her instinct. One thing she had felt sure of, and clung to, was that she trusted her gut. She was an intelligent woman, with a God-given common sense. Now, with this announcement from Margaret, she was beginning to wonder. That was just one more reason to dislike Margaret. Sarah now had to contend with self-doubt along with everything else she was feeling.

"I think I'll go help Will with the horses now." Sarah stood from the swing, promptly followed by Margaret.

"Sure. We'll chat again soon, Sarah. It's so good to have you back home."

Sarah nodded and continued down the walk. The sooner she was away from Margaret, the better. The sooner she got to Will, maybe she could once again feel safe and in control. Nothing was adding up, and everything that Sarah was starting to feel prior to her conversation with Margaret, was suddenly as up in the air as the treetops of the pines.

She spotted Will at the horse trough, the watering hose sputtering and splashing cool water into the steel container. Gambler, the midnight black stallion, and Little Big Man, the coffee-colored young gelding, were already dunking their noses in and taking in long, slow slurps. He must've been deep in thought, as when she stood next to him, he was jolted out of his thoughts.

"Hey," he said, bringing his foot down from the bottom rung of the corral to turn toward her. "Are you okay?"

She wanted to either laugh, or cry, or maybe both at the question. But Will didn't need to worry about her any more than he already did. "I'm fine. Just wanted to come out here, with you."

"Where's Margaret?" he asked, glancing back toward the house.

"I don't know, maybe still at the swing. That's where I left her."

"Did she say something to upset you?"

"No, Will. Really, everything is fine."

"Alright," he said reluctantly. "I'll be right back. Are you okay here?"

She nodded and he turned, walking stealthily back to the house. She hoped he would convince Margaret that it was time to go. As soon as she left, she could start to sort out what just happened to her fragile world.

The spigot nozzle squeaked as she twisted the handle to turn the water off. She looked back to the house, hoping to see Will, and only Will, coming back. She needed him, a feeling that was finally beginning to feel real. The short conversation with Margaret had managed to loosen her already tentative grasp on her life now, and the only thing she felt certain of was that Will could make her feel better. He may not be able to make her understand, but he had a way of holding onto her, and not letting her slip down the slope she was so desperately clinging to.

She waited a little longer, and still, no Will. She ducked under the posts of the corral and walked to granary. She filled up a black-rubber bucket with a little grain for the horses, and stepped back into the pen, with Gambler and Little Big Man following close behind her. Little Big Man was the first to jam his nose into the bucket, and it took nearly all her strength to keep the bucket in her hands. He wasn't a big horse, but he didn't know that.

When she heard the truck start up, and head down the driveway, she let out an audible sigh. She was sure that Will could put some of the missing pieces together for her. But, as soon as he approached her, the look on his face told her he was in a decidedly worse mood than when he left. She wondered what caused the change in demeanor, but more than that, she just wanted to change the scowl on his face, even though she couldn't help take note that the scowl didn't diminish the handsome features that she was precipitously coming to adore.

"Will? Is...everything alright?" she quietly asked, as he walked to her side.

He pursed his lips and rubbed his hands over Little Big Man's ears, which did little to dissuade him from getting to the bottom of the grain bucket. "Everything's fine. As fine as it can be, I guess."

Sarah pinned her eyebrows together. She could sense that he was anything, but okay. "Is it something that I said?"

He turned and looked at her, the scowl dissolving as he met her eyes. "Sarah, it's not you. I need you to know that no matter what memories come, or what happens from here on out, the way things are..."

He paused, swallowing hard. "The way things are, aren't because of anything that you did, or didn't do. I need you to understand that, to know that. Sometimes our lives become headed down a path, and that's just the way it goes."

Sarah shook her head, "What are you talking about, Will?"

Will took the empty bucket from her hands and set it on the ground. He wrapped his hands around hers, pulling her a step closer to him. "Sometimes in life, we can choose our path. Other times, fate chooses for us."

Sarah moved her gaze to each of his eyes, searching for an understanding of what he was trying to tell her. His eyes were piercing, but when she looked into them, they made her feel as if she was sailing into a safe harbor after years of being lost at sea. "I know, Will. Believe me, I know."

CHAPTER 26

It had been three days since Will last saw Margaret. She hadn't been in to work at the lumberyard, and Will knew by now, that she never stayed away from him for too long. Only to himself would he admit that the lull in keeping her happy was a welcome break, but now he knew it was getting to the point that he would need to step in before any real damage control would be necessary.

Margaret had left furious at him after their heated discussion at the swing on the porch. After Sarah had left her there, he went to find that Margaret was no longer in her upbeat mood that she portrayed when they arrived home. He had no idea what the conversation entailed between Margaret and Sarah, but he knew it wasn't reconciliation. Margaret proceeded to pressure him to settle on a wedding date, spouting her patience was growing thin. Once he made the mistake of asking why the big hurry, Margaret could not be calmed down.

But now, he had a new vision that would not leave his mind, and made him sick to his stomach recalling the memory. The Vice President of the Mountain Spring Savings & Loan had paid Henry a visit the night before. Apparently, Henry had ignored a few too many notices from the bank stating a past due amount on the farm loan. The house call was a notification that couldn't be stuffed into a drawer, and Will again watched the spirit of his father twist hopelessly in the wind.

He knew what needed to be done, and he dreaded it almost as much as setting a wedding date. There was only one person who could help him, and it was the one person he never wanted to ask for a thing. It was the one person he knew who would be more than happy to hold a favor hostage; just waiting to cash in repayment of the service in God only knows what fashion. Will had made his prior deal with him feeling there was nothing to lose, only to gain, in saving his family's farm, and hopefully, what remained of his father's life. But, now that Sarah was home, everything was different, except that nothing had changed.

His legs were heavy climbing the stairs to Vernon's office, and his arm even heavier as he raised it to knock on the door.

"Who is it?" Vernon's typical growl came from behind the door.

"It's William," he yelled back with confidence. If there was anything he had learned by now, it was that Vernon could sniff out weakness like bees swarming to fear. William wouldn't give him that advantage. He wasn't afraid of Vernon. He knew for as much as Vernon was helping him, he was equally doing for him by keeping his daughter happy, and taking that burden off his hands. This wasn't fear he was feeling, this was a revulsion for the man that had festered ever since the day of the community picnic. He wouldn't ever forget, or forgive, the disrespect Vernon showed his mother.

"Come in."

William pushed the door open to see Vernon sitting behind his desk, leaning back in his chair with his arms crossed over his chest.

"Do you have a minute?" William asked, striding across the room to Vernon's desk.

"Oh sure, I've got all the time in the world. I'm not trying to run a business or anything. I'm supposed to have a partner in this whole shittin' thing, but so far, that ain't working out too well for me, is it?" His eyes narrowed and his head jerked toward William's arm, still wrapped in the sling.

William looked down, and slightly lifted his arm, which actually had been becoming more and more pain free with such movements. "Yes, well, I'll be sure to think about that the next time I save a kid's life."

"And what a life that was." Vernon curled his lip in disgust. "Shit-for-brains Wilson," he said, shaking his head.

"I have an appointment with Dr. Paul in a couple of days, I'll know more after that, but I think I'll be out of this sling soon," William said, changing the subject.

"That sure as hell would be helpful, now wouldn't it?'

"Yes, it would. I'm as anxious as anyone to get back to normal."

"Ha! Not as anxious as your future wife, or haven't you noticed?

William nodded his head slowly, "Yes, I've noticed."

"Well, then surely you must've noticed that you gone and done something to piss her off. She's sore at you about something, boy. And you better be figuring it out soon."

William sucked in a long, deep breath. His suspicions were correct; she was off pouting about their discussion. Or rather his underwhelming need to set a date for the wedding. Either way, she was sending a message to him, and to her father.

"That's what I'm here to see you about. I know Margaret wants me to focus on the wedding, but with my father's farm needing so much of my attention, I'm just not able to do it all."

Vernon's eyed narrowed, and his words slipped from his mouth without it hardly moving. "What, exactly, are you trying to say?"

"I need an advancement, on my share of the business. My father needs some equipment and supplies to get the farm functioning again. Otherwise, I'm not sure it'll make it." His words sounded like he was implying the farm, but in his heart, he was referring to his father.

"An advancement. On your share of the business, huh?" Vernon was obviously amused by the suggestion, but William steadied his gaze, giving no indication of recanting.

"Yes. If I'm going to be able to give the attention to Margaret that you want," he paused briefly, "and that she deserves, I've got to get the farm producing some sort of income. That can only happen if I can buy another tractor, and get the seeds in the ground."

Vernon pushed his chair back from the desk and stood up. He walked around to the front of the desk and leaned against it. "That's quite a demand from a one-armed partner who's not even in the family yet."

"It's not a demand. It's a means to an end. That being, a wedding that can be planned."

Vernon rubbed his fingers over his mustache, while his eyes pressed into slits. "Yes," he hissed slowly. "I'm sure you're right. I'll tell you what. I'll let Wheeler know that you have a line of credit at the feed store, under my name. You get what you think you need to once and for all, get your father on his own two feet.

"Thank you, I appreciate it." William felt the relief soar through him, yet held his expression steady.

"Just so we're clear, Harston. Once this is done, you'll have nothing else to distract you from taking care of Margaret's needs, am I right?"

Sarah's face glimmered through his mind. All he wanted was to be distracted by that face, by that body, by that love, that still pounded through him, and had been every minute of every day since her return. But, that was a distraction that he would have to keep to himself, and most definitely keep from Vernon and Margaret. He knew the trade-off was unavoidable. He got what he needed for his father's farm, but he gave up the only viable excuse to keep the wedding at bay. Once the farm was showing signs of recovery, there would be nothing for William to arm himself with. In that moment, his chest ached, knowing that the new deal struck with Vernon, was just one more step away from Sarah. The plan had been set in motion, there would be no stopping it, and he only hoped he could still find a way to slow it. It would be a slow torture knowing he couldn't have Sarah the way he always thought he would. But, being with her, being next to her, breathing her, would be worth every bit of it. He never dreamt he would welcome cruelty like this. But he did. The agony of being so close to her, and not having her, was nothing compared to the suffering he endured when she was taken from him. It was simple. The pain of knowing he couldn't have her, although excruciating, was tolerable as long as he could escape reality and sink into her eyes, and into her soul. That would have to be enough.

William's eyes snapped into focus at the abrupt clap of Vernon's hands in front of his face. "You hear me, boy? We better have an understanding here. I personally don't give a rat's ass about your father's farm. But, I do care about my daughter and her happiness, and Margaret has decided that you are the one she wants. So, I'll keep playing along, as long as you keep playing along." Vernon stood and stopped a few inches in front of William. "Understand?"

"I understand," he answered, mustering everything he could to avoid telling Vernon where he could shove his understanding.

"Good. I suggest you start by stopping by the house and making up with my darling daughter. Mrs. Thornton has Bridge Club tonight, and I'm sure I'll be here working late since I've got a new line of credit to pay for at Wheeler's."

CHAPTER 27

Sarah's eyes squeezed shut before she allowed them to open to the sunlight that had barely crept in through the small window of her room. Her eyes burned in protest as she forced them open. She couldn't even be sure how long she had been asleep. It couldn't have been long, considering she could not beg, or borrow a moment of peace long enough to allow herself to drift off to sleep. Her mind could not be quieted, and she had spent the longest night yet, since coming to Colorado.

She had spent her day in her normal routine, gauging the time by the completion of her chores. She hoped Will would take her back to the pines, or another place of their childhood that might beckon to her memory. To her dismay, she still had not been to King's Creek. If she allowed herself to admit the truth, it didn't matter if they went somewhere or not. It was becoming clear that as long as she was simply with Will, she was content. Even more than content, she felt awakened. With, or without her memories, she was at home with him, and when he looked into her eyes the way he did, there was only the two of them in the whole world.

It did not take her long to realize that her evening would not materialize as she had become accustomed to. Dinner with Henry and Tommy was excruciating as she tried to join in the conversation and seem normal. But, failing miserably, she could only nudge her dinner around her plate with her fork, trying to reassure Henry that everything was alright, and that she was feeling fine. Instead of spending the evening in front of the fireplace, she retired early to bed, but couldn't concentrate long enough to even read a book. Will hadn't come home, and instead of being worried, she was sickened by the reality of knowing exactly where he was. Henry told her, that Will had already gotten a ride from town to Margaret's house.

She dropped her arm across her eyes and shook her head. What exactly was she so upset about? She had no right to be. Will wasn't hers, and she was Adley's. Whatever this emotion was, she better reel it in. Will had made his choice to marry Margaret, who he clearly, still wanted. He chose to be with Margaret last night, and not her. And why wouldn't he? He was engaged to a beautiful woman who probably gave him everything he could want, and then some. She didn't know if Will had even come home at all. The more she thought about it, the tighter her throat became, making it physically difficult to swallow.

She flung the covers from her body and stalked to the mirror. Her mission in coming back to Colorado had become muddled with her bewildering feelings for Will. She yanked her hair to one side and quickly twisted it into a braid that draped over her shoulder. She was here to remember her past, to know where she came from, and then go back home, to California. Go back to be Adley's wife. How could she do this to him? He was off in a God-forsaken war, and she was here, struggling to deny the feelings for another man that seemed to consume her. She scolded herself, how could she be so horrible? Her feelings for Will would have to be limited to that of achieving her goal in coming here, and nothing else. He would go on to live his life with Margaret, and she would go on living her life, with Adley. But, just as she solidified her resolution, she stared into the mirror as the next thought sliced through her core. He would go on to live his life with Margaret, and she would go on living her life, without Will.

She quickly dressed, still fuming how she could've let her life spiral out of control, even more so than what it already had. As she exited her room, the house was silent. Good. She didn't need any early morning conversations; she needed to get out of the house and into the world that was large enough to drown out the noise in her head: a walk, the birds, the trees, anything to distract her from her own mind. Anything that could distract her from imagining Will with Margaret.

She tiptoed from her room, avoiding the boards she had learned would give her away. The kitchen was quiet, no coffee brewing, the dish towel still draped over the sink from last night; everything untouched. She turned the corner to the living room, realizing that she would need to borrow one of the coats hanging on the hook by the door. The house was chilly, and she knew that the morning air would be twice as such.

Before she could think anymore of her exit, she froze the moment she entered the living room. She sucked in a breath and felt her heart instantly pound against her chest. She hadn't planned on seeing him so soon. But, there he was, staring out the window into the quiet morning sky. The fire had dwindled to a few glowing embers underneath the blackened wood giving very little light, and his silhouette was strong and striking, framed by the gray morning. Her mind tried to convince her not to be stirred by the vision of him, but her heart and her body completely disagreed. Her mind completely lost the battle once he turned from the window and his eyes sought her – penetrating her core.

He paused only for a moment and walked toward her. "Sarah, you're awake?" His voice deep and smooth. Quiet, but strong.

She nodded, and whispered, "So are you." She hesitated as she noticed she was spinning her fingers around each other. She moved her hands to her side to still them. "But, maybe you were never asleep to begin with."

The surprise on his face from her tone paled in comparison to the pain her sharp tongue brought her. She didn't want to talk to him in such a way, but she knew herself too well. She would not be able to hide the angst inside of her knowing that she needed to distance herself from the feelings that he effortlessly could conjure in her. The sooner she could do that, the more likely it would be that she wouldn't have to suffer any more heartache in her life than she already had. Unless, it was already too late.

"Sarah, I'm sorry," he said, moving closer to her.

"Sorry for what, Will?" She tried to steady her voice, but her high-pitched question could not hide how difficult this was. She knew she was fighting the tears. How could she be feeling this way for him, someone she hardly knew? None of it made sense, and all she felt now was an ache so profound that she couldn't catch her breath.

He was only inches away from her now. "I'm sorry I wasn't home last night. I wanted to come home, and take you to the pines, or wherever you wanted to go. I wanted to come home, but..." His words trailed off, and he could no longer look her in the eye. "But something came up; there was something that I had to do."

Sarah's eyes moved from his and watched his lips as his words about coming home to her spilled over her. As much as hearing that made her heart beat that much faster, it didn't change the fact that he didn't come home to her. He was with Margaret, and had every right to be. He had not kept his engagement a secret from her; there had been no misunderstanding about that. She, on the other hand, had failed to mention her own engagement, which made her even more remorseful about her unkind tone that she used. Her eyes were drawn down to his neck, not knowing why, until her gaze landed on dark purple bruise. Margaret had been sure to leave her mark, on her man, for all to see.

Sarah's stomach twisted again, this time sending a physical pain that she thought might actually cause her to grimace. "Yes, Will. I'm sure you were thinking about coming home the whole time." Now the tears could not be stopped as they pooled in her eyes. She refused to blink; she could not let him see the tears fall.

Will creased his brow, confused with her accusation. He touched his hand to his neck, where Sarah's eyes still blazed, when the memory flashed across his face. She could only envision what his memory recollected. She could imagine Margaret's red hair spilled across Will's chest as she pressed into him, delivering the kind of kiss powerful enough to leave evidence of a passionate encounter.

Against every bit of will, she closed her eyes, hoping the vision of the two of them could be erased. She felt the warm drops slide down her cheeks, and she quickly turned toward the door. She didn't want to have to explain to Will what she was feeling. The only explanation that existed was one that couldn't be possible.

"Sarah, wait." Will rushed to her side, stopping her before she opened the door. "Don't go. Please, don't go. Stay, and talk to me."

She bent her chin to her chest, and slowly shook her head. "I can't, Will. I don't know what to say to you."

He gently lifted her chin, forcing their eyes together again. "I can't stand to see you cry. Please, talk to me."

She sniffed and wiped her cheeks, "It's nothing, Will, really. I don't even know why I'm crying. I just really want some time alone, that's all."

"I don't want to leave you alone, Sarah. All I've ever wanted…was to be with you." He ran his hand over her shoulder and down her arm. She felt his hands gently pulling her toward him.

She looked up, the sincerity beaming from his eyes. She knew he didn't like seeing her upset, and she didn't want to feel this way, which was exactly why she needed to get out of the house and clear her mind of all it. But, her feet couldn't move. Instead she felt herself being drawn into the power that he seemed to possess, like a daisy turning toward the sun just to fully bask in its warmth. His eyes followed the movements of his hand, which continued to caress her bare arm. It was amazing to her how every time he looked at her, it was as if he were relishing the moment. He moved his gaze back to her eyes, and again the same force she felt in the pines wrapped completely around her. It would've felt as natural as breathing to let him kiss her. But, a single kiss would not change their reality, and the moment the kiss ended, they would be right back where they were now. Except that she would most certainly have a new memory to contend with. It would be a memory that would only complicate her future. If there was one thing she was certain of, it was that she already had enough obstacles in her life.

She turned her shoulder away from him, breaking their connection, and reached for the coat hanging next to her. "I'm going to go," she whispered. "Please, Will, just let me go."

"I don't know if I can, Sarah." Will's voice was quiet and strained.

She looked back at him, for a moment wishing she could ignore everything that she knew, and let him take her to a place that only his kiss could conquer. She pushed her arms through the sleeves, and again reached for the door.

His hand found hers. "Wait. Just, can you at least tell me where you're going?"

Crazy. She was going crazy. She shook her head, knowing that he was genuinely concerned for her. "I don't know. I thought that I would take Little Big Man, and go for a ride. Is that alright?"

"By yourself?" he asked, incredulously.

"I'll be fine, Will."

Will sighed and nodded. "I know, but I just don't like you going by yourself. Let me at least help you saddle him."

Sarah pulled the door opened and took a few steps, his hand still wrapped around hers. "No, really, it's not necessary. I can do it, Will. I think I just need some time alone, okay?"

He nodded and reluctantly released her hand. "Well, can you at least tell me which direction you're heading?"

He had never made it a secret that he worried about her. She never wanted to worry him, and it tore at her heart even more to know that he was so protective of her, and yet she needed to get some space away from him. Or at least, get away from how she was feeling. She hadn't even thought about where she would go, but she knew Will would never let her go if she didn't tell him. "I think I'll go ride down along Cow Creek. Okay?"

Will thought for a moment and breathed deeply. "Fine, but that trail leads deep in the forest, and then branches off into different trails that will take you everywhere but back home. It's easy to get lost up there if you don't know what you're doing. Just promise me that when the trail branches, you'll turn around and come back."

"Okay, Will."

"No, Sarah, promise me. Promise me you'll remember."

As quickly as lightening can slice a jagged scar through the sky, an unforeseen rush of emotion blazed through Sarah's body, so much so that she actually took a step back, trying to regain her balance.

Will grabbed her arm to steady her. "Sarah. Are you okay?"

"I...I don't know. I swear, Will. I swear you've said that to me before. As soon as you said it, I saw you in my mind saying the same exact thing; only you weren't saying it in your house. I saw you, in a forest." She closed her eyes, shutting out all other influences to her senses. "I just can't seem to remember what else." She waited, hoping her mind would reveal more, but she could only see Will against a backdrop of trees, and his words, "Promise me you'll remember." "Oh, this is so frustrating!" She clenched her jaw and rubbed her forehead.

"It's okay. Relax, Sarah, relax. Take a deep breath." Will's voice was calm and she tried to hold onto it as she breathed slowly in and out.

"What was it, Will? What was it that you asked me to remember?" The tears were now fully streaming down her cheeks, and she didn't even try to hide them or wipe them away.

"Shhh," he soothed. "Don't force it, Sarah. It'll all come back to you in due time."

"Will it?" She demanded. "When?"

"I don't know the answer."

"I don't know, either. I don't know about anything, anymore. Actually, I know that I need to go. I need to go and be by myself. I hope you can understand that."

"I do. But, please, just be careful, and remember what I told you about the trails."

She agreed one more time before stepping into the brisk morning air. As soon as she ran down the steps of the porch, she stopped to wipe the tears and calm her breath. She was in a hail storm, with nowhere in sight to shelter. Memories were coming, feelings were overwhelming, and realities were settling in.

She saddled Little Big Man quickly as he was in an amiable mood, and was riding down the driveway before too long. She prided herself on being a woman that could saddle a horse by herself, and never more so than this moment. Normally, she would welcome the help from Will, but today she just needed to have some space to breathe. She hadn't been out by herself much, and never too far off Henry's property. But, she had driven past the turn off from the county road that led to a crude trail that wound through a heavily wooded forest of aspens and ferns, and a seasonal stream. It had a certain allure to her, like it was somehow taken straight out of a fairy tale book. It would be the perfect place for her to go to now. It could be her escape, if just for a while.

CHAPTER 28

"Son…of-a-bitch," William said out loud. He tilted his head, posturing to get a better view of his neck in the mirror. No wonder Sarah reacted like she did. Margaret had left an unmistakable mark of their night's activities, and Sarah had to be the one to discover it. He shook his head, wishing he could do anything to go back in time, just long enough to have discovered the mark before Sarah, and think up something to hide it. He already felt guilty enough for not coming home after work. But, after his conversation with Vernon, it was clear that he had very little choice in the matter. Making a deal with the devil did not come without a price.

The expectation of smoothing everything over with Margaret was clearly set, and Margaret made sure he delivered. He initially thought that just coming to see her would be enough, but he should've known better. She was going to make her point that she was not happy with their last interaction, and that he would make it up to her, to say the least. All he could think about was Sarah, while he had to painstakingly convince Margaret that she was undeniably the only thing that occupied his thoughts. Fortunately for him, Mrs. Thornton arrived back home from her card game and interrupted their reconciliation before it had a chance to fully become what Margaret wanted. Will could only shudder now. He never looked forward to seeing Mrs. Thornton, but her arrival had spared him. He had no idea how he was going to force himself to be with Margaret in the future, when all he could see was Sarah's face and all he could feel was the consuming love he had for her. But now, as he cast one more look into the mirror, Margaret was the one to leave indisputable proof that they had done enough. Enough for Sarah to piece the evidence together, and enough for her to know what he had been doing. Something told him that the bruise would fade long before the horrid feeling that was left in him would.

He spent the next three hours pacing between the house, the corral, and even down the driveway waiting to see if he could spot Sarah and Little Big Man returning home. Three hours was plenty of time to get to Cow Creek, walk the trail, and get back. He could not keep the vision from his mind of the day she went to the creek and was trapped in Coon's Cove by a mother bear. She didn't listen to him then, and nearly paid for it. If she failed to heed his instructions again today by not turning around, he'd have a wall-eyed fit. He couldn't think about being mad at her now, he was too worried. If she decided to take one of those other trails, he was certain she was lost. As soon as she was home, he'd be sure to lecture her about doing as he asked. But, he'd have to get her home, first. Fear was rippling through him with each passing minute that seemed to double in length from the last. All that mattered to him now, was that she made it home.

After another hour passed, he kicked the door open to the tack shed and pulled a bridle from the row of hooks along the wall. He stomped out into the corral where Gambler stood, lazily swishing his black tail over his rump. Gambler's ear instantly pricked at Will's hasty entrance and his tail stilled. Will realized he better slow down, and calm down, if he was hoping for Gambler's cooperation. Most of the time the horse was agreeable, but it would be just like the animal to decide to balk at Will, just as he was in a rush like this. The urgency became unbearable, and he cursed under his breath for not leaving sooner. Four hours had felt like forty. Why in the hell had he waited so long to go? He couldn't stop from imagining how deep into the mountain Sarah might be by now. And worse yet, which trail did she take? They all led in completely opposite directions, and the thought of not being able to find her left him barely able to breathe.

Gambler, despite Will's uneasiness, stayed still as he ran his hand up and over his back. Will ducked under his thick neck, trying to quiet his pounding heart, which he was certain Gambler would pick up on.

"Easy boy, easy," Will coaxed, as he the rubbed Gambler's nose. "Come on, boy." Will placed the bit at Gambler's mouth, which he fought for only a second before Will was able to get him to bite down on it and he could slide the leather straps up and over his ears. He led Gambler to the gate and quickly unfastened the chain. The gate's hinges shrieked as he and Gambler passed through. It wasn't his habit to leave a gate open, but at this point, he didn't care. He pulled the reins to the back of Gambler's neck and grabbed a fist full of the thick black mane, hoisted himself up, and swung his leg over Gambler's back. He could've saddled him fairly quickly, but even that felt like a waste of precious time.

Gambler was not a horse to hesitate and he gladly broke into a gallop once Will guided the reins against his neck to turn left, and gave him a quick jab with his heel. Will held tightly to the reins and Gambler's mane, and squeezed his legs around the bare back. He dipped into the slight valley, passing Cow Creek Schoolhouse on the right. Normally, he would avoid the schoolhouse if he could, just to avoid the memory of the last time he was there with Sarah, and her father announcing that they were leaving: the night that stole his hopes for making Sarah his, forever.

But even that didn't matter to him right now. He could only focus on one thing, and that was laying his eyes on his Sarah. He clenched his jaw with even more determination. Yes, his Sarah. He realized in that moment that she still belonged to him. It had always been that way, and he had been a fool to think that it had somehow ended just because she left. He had tried to survive without her, and tried to convince himself that it was over. For a little while, he could live in that denial. He lived in that denial, long enough to allow himself to completely disregard what was meant to be for him. Sarah had been the one for as long as he could remember, and he thought that he could somehow rationalize his way out of that reality? That rationale landed him shackled to a woman that would never possess the power that Sarah had over him.

Even the deal with Vernon, that sealed his fate, didn't matter now. He would gladly suffer a lifetime with Margaret, as long as he knew that Sarah was safe. Gambler's pace had slowed to traverse the ruts and logs that impeded the trail, and Will furiously scanned the trees. The ferns next to the trail were formidable. The coolness of the shady forest and the recent rainfall were ideal conditions, and they had made their plea for the sky's attention by stretching taller than Will could remember ever seeing.

He leaned over Gambler's neck, pulling back on the reins to slow his pace. The softened soil was impressionable, and his pulse quickened as he recognized the curved imprint of a horseshoe. Surely to God, that must be her. The prints were too fresh to allow the coincidence of another rider on the trail today. His eyes strained to see through the aspens, hoping to see any shape other than the tall white pillars that felt like a prison he was trying to escape.

He urged Gambler on, though the horse fought to pick his footing much more carefully than Will's impatience would allow. He kept his eyes between the trail and brush, feeling only a slight glimmer of relief that the horseshoe prints could be seen every few feet. As long as he could see them, he would know which direction she headed. But, if she had decided to get off the trail, there would be no way to track her through the fern. Something inside of him told him she wouldn't do that. He told her to stay on the trail, and even though she was hurt to the point of a blurred vision by him not coming home, he still thought that she wouldn't do that. But then again, he told her to turn around when she got to other trails, and she obviously hadn't. She would've been home long ago if she had kept her promise. Damn it, Sarah! When will you learn? He realized he had no place to judge. He hadn't been very good at keeping his promises, either.

He crested a slight knoll, realizing that it would soon be time to choose a trail to follow. He prayed he would be able to still recognize the horse tracks and wouldn't have to guess. The knots tightened in his stomach, and he could only think that if he could find her, he'd be damned to ever let her out of his sight again.

He pulled Gambler to a stop. As he hadn't spotted any tracks for last several minutes, he began to fear that he'd lost her path. He quickly ran the options through his mind. He'd need to go back, get his dad, Mr. Wilkes, and anyone else to come out and join the search. That would take precious time. Time that Sarah would be out here, alone. Damn it, all!

He was about start Gambler further down the trail when a crackling sound shattered the silent forest. He realized then that he hadn't even noticed birds singing, or the rustling of wind through the leaves. Nothing could drown out the sound of his mind under the cloak of fear. But this was hard to ignore. A definite snapping of twigs, coming from the brush just slightly ahead him and to the right, couldn't be mistaken. Something was coming through the brush.

He nudged Gambler on, allowing him to descend to the bottom of the small hill. Finally, a shape stood out amongst the white and black. A sight that at the same time, gave him the relief he was begging to find, and filled him with a fear unlike he had fathomed feeling. Picking through the fern with a few steps at a time, was Little Big Man grazing quietly. The horse seemed completely unaware that he was being watched, or that anything at all was out of place. Little Big Man was found, but that meant nothing. Sarah was not on him.

Panic welled up inside of him. In pure desperation, he cupped his hands around his mouth. "Sarah! Sarah!" His voice was loud, and unrestrained. A horrible echo called back to him, as the sound of fear bounced all around him. His posture was rigid, and he closed his eyes to block out all influences but sound. He called out again, "Sarah! Sar—ah!" Why wouldn't she be on Little Big Man? He looked back to the horse, his reins hanging free down the sides of his face, swaying with each step. She would not just let him roam freely. This was his fault, not hers. He never should've let her go. Ever.

Just as he cupped his hands to his mouth again, he thought he heard a faint voice. He swung Gambler around to face the direction he thought he heard it from. "Sarah?" Again, he could hear the faintest of cries. It was her. He knew the sound of her by heart. He dug his heals into Gambler's flank, forcing him into a trot. "Sarah. Where are you?" He rode down the trail, but realized the sound of Gambler's hooves were too loud to discern any other noise. He stopped again, scanning the hillside for Sarah.

"Will. Will!" Sarah's voice was small and weak.

"Sarah!" Will jumped from Gambler's back, not even feeling his feet hit the ground, and ran at full speed toward her voice. "Where are you?"

"Will! Here, Will. Over here."

He spun, with each turn honing in on her location.

"Sarah! I can't see you." Again his eyes scanned furiously, but saw nothing through the thick fern. "Where are you?"

"Here, Will. I'm down here."

His ears and eyes zeroed in on her voice and he saw the tops of the ferns at the bottom of a gully begin to sway. His eyes widened and his heart pounded harder than he thought was physically possible. He found her. The relief was so massive and intense, but he had no time to relish in the feeling. He sprinted down the embankment, keeping his eyes locked on the swaying ferns.

"I'm coming, Sarah. Keep moving the ferns."

He pushed aside the ferns and stepped over the fallen logs and rocks that blocked his path to her. He was nearly there; a few more steps and he could start breathing again.

"Sarah!" He called out one more time.

"Here, Will. I'm here." Her voice was trembling. She must be terrified.

He pushed aside one more large spray of vegetation, and suddenly the entire world blurred, and all he could see was Sarah lying against a backdrop of broken ferns.

"Oh my God, Sarah! You're hurt!" He fell to his knees at her side. He could see that she wasn't okay. He face was scraped and dirty, and her shirt torn. Her neat, tight braid from the morning had loosened leaving locks of hair to fall around her face. He ran his fingers along her forehead and down her cheeks, grimacing at sight of the bright red blood tainting her velvety skin.

She reached up and wrapped her fingers around his hand. Tears fell from her eyes as she closed them. "You found me. Will, you found me." She pressed her cheek into his hand and began to sob. "I was so scared, I didn't think anyone would ever find me."

Will rubbed his thumb against her cheek, brushing the stream of tears to the side. "I would find you, Sarah. Come hell or high water, I would find you no matter where you were." His heart heaved with relief and pure love for this woman. He knew now what he'd known his whole life. There wasn't anything he wouldn't do to keep Sarah safe.

She looked up into his eyes and smiled faintly, "You saved me, Will. How? How did you know?"

"I just did," he said, fighting to keep his voice steady. He shook his head, "I can't explain it."

She smiled again and nodded slowly in understanding. She lifted her head and shoulders slightly to sit up, but grimaced in pain and fell back to the bed of ferns.

"Easy, Sarah. What...what the hell happened? Where are you hurt?" He breathed heavily. His eyes quickly taking inventory of her body, and any clues to the extent of her injuries.

Sarah breathed deeply and uncomfortably, and she squeezed her eyes shut in pain. "We were just riding along the trail," she said, opening her eyes and looking at Will. "We were walking, and everything was fine. But then, a deer jumped out from the brush and spooked Little Big Man. He bucked so suddenly; I didn't even have time to hold onto the saddle, or anything. I fell off, and down this ravine. And," she smiled weakly, "I've been here ever since. I tried, but I can't get up, Will."

Her once brave façade quickly faded as the fear seeped through her voice.

Will swallowed hard. How badly was she hurt? This was his fault. He never should've let her go. He knew better, and now she was hurt; he just hoped not too badly. The sting of guilt quickly surged through his body, and he let his mind retrace his steps the night of the barn fire. The last time he saw his mother, was his fault too. He hadn't learned a thing.

"Okay," he said, trying to steady his breathing, "tell me everywhere that hurts."

Sarah's eyes once again melded with his, and he instantly wished he could take away her fear and her pain for himself.

"It hurts everywhere," she tried to laugh, but again twisted her face in discomfort. "I think the worst is my ankle, and my back. I think my back hit a rock when I rolled down the hill; it took me a while to catch my breath once I stopped rolling. How's my face? I know it's scraped up, too."

Despite the smeared mud and blood, she still had the most beautiful face he'd ever seen. But he was more concerned with her injuries, and how he could possibly get her home.

"Your face is," he paused, assessing the damage, "your face is perfect."

"Well," she said, gingerly bringing her fingertips to one of her cuts, "I don't think that's exactly true, but thanks for trying to make me feel better."

The truth was, he meant it. Especially now that he was laying his eyes on that face, after his deepest fears had gripped his throat until he found her, he never felt more in awe of her beauty. He slid down to her feet and carefully slid her pant leg up on the leg she said was hurt. Her ankle was already swollen and bruised. After she was able to move it around, he felt fairly sure that it wasn't broken. He could only hope that her back wasn't as bad as he feared.

"Do you think you can sit up? If I help you?" he asked, as he moved back up to her side.

"I don't know. It hurts, Will."

"I know. Let's just take it real slow, alright?"

She nodded and looked scared. "Okay, I'll try."

He sat up to his knees, and pushed his arm behind her shoulders. She gritted her teeth, and he could tell it hurt her to move. He wanted the strength to carry her, to make sure she felt no pain. Every thought that entered his mind was that of her well-being. Period.

"Sarah, wait. Lay back down." He gently guided her back to the ferns. "I've about had it with this son-of-a-bitchin' sling." He looked back at Sarah, embarrassed. "I'm sorry, Sar. About the language."

She smiled and laughed. "It's me, you can say what you want around me."

He looked back at her. "I would never want to be disrespectful to you, Sarah."

"Will," she swallowed hard, "I don't know much, but I know that you would never do anything wrong by me. There's just something about you —about us—that I trust. I've tried to explain it to myself, but I can't. It's just a feeling, and I've decided to go with what feels right, whether it makes sense yet, or not."

How could she do that? How could she read the playbook of his soul so effortlessly? He knew the answer. His soul, her soul; they were both woven with the thread that time and distance could not fray. It was the thread that bound them together from the beginning. Now, it was the thread that would have to keep her with him, in whatever way it still could.

He pulled the sling from around his neck, and slid his arm from the fabric.

"Will," Sarah said, her eyes widening at his movements. "What are you doing?"

"I can't help you with this on," he said, matter-of-factly.

"No. Will, your shoulder. Don't."

"I'm fine, Sarah. It's had long enough to heal. Now, I'm going to help you sit up."

"But..." she began in protest.

"Look, we can argue about this for a while if it'll make you feel better, but either way, I'm going to help you up, and I'll need both arms to do that." He sat and stared expectantly at her until she finally relented and nodded her head.

"Okay, fine. But please, don't reinjure yourself, please?"

"Deal. Now let's get you up."

He wrapped his arms around her, and felt her arms come around his neck. To be honest, he was a little nervous testing his collarbone like this. But, if it took breaking it again to get Sarah home and safe, it'd be worth it. She buried her face in his neck, and he swore the slight twinge of pain instantly disappeared with her sweet breath on his skin. He allowed the relief to swell inside of him once he was able to get her to a standing position, even though he could tell how her body ached with each movement.

"There," he said, wrapping his arm around her waist to support her, "are you okay?" She nodded, and he was in awe of her strength. "We've got to get up the hill to the trail, are you ready?"

"I think so, but my ankle—"

"I know. I know it hurts, Sar. I'm going to help you."

With Sarah barely being able to put any weight on her foot, the climb was long and slow. Once they got to the trail, he gently sat her down on a large boulder to rest. "Stay here, I'm going to go get Little Big Man. He's just down in that draw," he said pointing.

Sarah nodded and put her head in her hands, "I thought he was gone, Will. I felt so bad."

"It wouldn't have mattered if he was, Sarah." He gently tilted her chin to meet his gaze. The moment her eyes focused on his, the rest of the world fell away. He felt relieved when he found her, but what he felt now, was very different. Now, he was overcome with realization that he hadn't lost her. He had another moment in time to spend with her, to look upon her, to touch her. There was no way to stop what that profound attainment did to his mind, body and soul. He bent down to her lips, wanting to show her more than anything else, how he really felt. He stopped before his lips could brush against hers and whispered, "All that matters to me is that I found you."

A few beats of their hearts passed before he could break his trance, and he rubbed his thumb against her tear-streaked cheek. He straightened his posture and took a deep breath. Looking toward the grazing horse, he said, "I'll be right back, you stay put."

Within a few minutes, he was back with Little Big Man following obediently. Sarah tried to stand but the minute she put pressure on her foot, she slumped back to the boulder. "You're riding with me, Sarah," Will informed her. "There's no way I'm letting you ride by yourself."

He untied Gambler from the nearby tree and brought him over to Sarah. He easily hoisted Sarah's petite body up to the horse and she swung her leg over. Using Gambler's mane, he swung up to sit behind her. She sunk into his body and he closed his eyes, realizing he had never been so close to heaven as he was right now. Sarah was safe, and his arms were around her. He couldn't help but to thank God. Especially after the same paralyzing fear squeezed around him at the thought of losing Sarah, just as he had lost his mother. He had been spared a heartbreak that he surely wouldn't have survived.

"Are you ready?" he said quietly, as she leaned against him.

She nodded, "Take me home, Will. Please."

He would take her anywhere, but he knew that right now, with Sarah pressed against him, and his arms around her, she was already home. She was right where she belonged. If only it were possible keep her there.

CHAPTER 29

Sarah leaned her head back to rest against Will's broad chest. She was nearly home from what had started out as a harmless ride. Even though every inch of her body was sore and stiff, she realized she was in no hurry to get back home. She didn't know if she was lightheaded from feeling Will's arms wrapped around her, or if her mind and body were succumbing to the trauma of her fall. Really, she didn't care. Gambler could take his time getting them home.

They hadn't spoken more than a few words since they left Cow Creek. Will kept one arm firmly around her waist, and one arm holding Gambler's reins, and Little Big Man's reins, keeping him in tow behind them. She interlaced her fingers with his, and hugged his arm to her body. For as weak as she was, she knew she was safe with Will holding her. He had rescued her, and the elation she felt the second she saw him coming through the ferns hadn't left her. She tried to understand why the feeling felt familiar to her. She closed her eyes, scanning her mind for a memory that would make it all clear. What had happened in the past that made her feel this way? It was a powerful sensation, one that was still coursing through her veins. A fleeting vision flashed behind her eyes. Water. She was in water, and afraid. But, of what? She squeezed her eyes tighter, but nothing more would come to her. Only knowing, that what she had felt then, was how she felt today, when Will found her. The feelings then and now were undeniably the same. Relief. Gratitude. Love.

Despite wanting to feel everything that Will's arm around her could easily conjure, and wanting to stay melded into his body, they were soon cresting the final hill of the driveway, and they were home. She had no idea what time it was, especially since everything had become a blur beginning with the doe that sprang from the brush. The fall was bad, but she knew she was lucky. Falling from Little Big Man, and then tumbling down the ravine could've resulted in far worse. Her entire body was aching in protest from sitting in one position for so long, and her ankle was clearly sprained badly. All of that paled in comparison to the ache in her heart. The fall from the horse, she would survive. But falling for Will? She wasn't so sure.

Will guided the horses to the front porch and pulled them to a halt. She was dreading the pain that would surely come from getting down from Gambler, but more than that, leaving Will's protective embrace. She didn't want to let go of him, so she didn't. She squeezed his hand tightly, and draped her other arm over his forearm that held her the entire ride home. She leaned her head back against his chest and closed her eyes. Will dropped the reins to both horses and brought his other arm around her. She had never felt anything so safe. He bent his head down to be next to hers, and she realized that they were as close as they had been since her return to Colorado, physically and emotionally. She turned her head slightly, baring her neck to him. His arms wrapped around her even tighter, and she felt his lips, tender and timid on her neck. She recognized the pounding of his heart was keeping exact time with hers, and her chest began to heave against his muscular arms as her breaths came in short gasps.

He lifted slightly from her neck and whispered, "Are you doing okay?"

She could only nod.

"I'm going to help you down, alright?"

She nodded again, but neither one of them loosened their grip on each other. She turned to him, his eyes soft on her, yet so obviously filled with desire. "Will," she whispered.

"I know, Sar," he said, before she could continue. "I'm not ready to let go, either." Her breath caught in her throat, and she was starting to feel lightheaded. She wasn't sure what was happening, all she could do was feel. "I'm going to take care of you, I promise."

She reluctantly let her arms relax, and he slowly let go of her. He slid off the back of the horse and placed his hand on her thigh to steady her. She looked down at him, his blue eyes never leaving hers.

"I want you to carefully swing your leg over, and I'll lift you down."

Gripping Gambler's main, she urged her body to move. Everything seemed to be sore, and every muscle ached, yet, all she could really concentrate on was Will. Her body might've been injured, but it could still recognize the desire that was becoming more powerful than any of the pain from her bruises. As her leg came around, she felt Will's hand grasp around her waist as he effortlessly brought her gently to the ground. She wondered if she could walk, but Will already had her arm draped over his shoulders, and his hand around her waist as she limped to the porch.

"Sit here on the swing, I'm going to go put the horses away, and I'll be right back, okay?"

Watching him lead the two horses away, she shook her head. On the one hand, she felt lucky, but on the other, she felt confused. Having left this morning to get away from Will, and the reality that her growing feelings for him had no ground to stand on, she knew that she also couldn't stand the thought of being apart from him. Nothing had changed, but everything was different.

Before she could think any more about it, he was back. She smiled as he walked to her, still with the same look in his eyes. In a short time, she had come to learn the various looks of his eyes. Now, she could see hunger in his eyes. She could see in him, what was still welling up inside her. Feeling his body next to hers all the way home, his arms, and mouth on her neck; it was too powerful to dismiss.

He said nothing as he bent down and lifted her from the swing. She wrapped her arms around his shoulders, feeling his muscles harden under his shirt. He pushed the door open and carried her to room. He laid her gently on the bed, and slowly pulled his arms from under her, but did not pull away from her. She knew she should release her arms from his shoulders, but she didn't want to. More than ever she wanted him to kiss her.

There had been the moments before that it could've happened, and each time it didn't, it only left the wanting greater. He lingered for a moment, his eyes on hers, still hungry, but now with a pained look of restraint. She let her fingers fall down the length of his arms, and he closed his eyes.

He took a deep breath and straightened. "How are you feeling? I'm worried about you. I think I should take you to the doctor."

She smiled and shook her head. She couldn't believe his sweetness, and everything he said or did revealed his feelings for her. "I don't think that's necessary, Will. I'm okay, just a little sore."

"Are you sure?"

She nodded and looked at his shoulder. She hadn't seen him without the sling and she couldn't help but let her gaze fall over his chest and shoulders.

"Then, I think I know what would help you feel better." He walked to her closet and pulled her robe from the hook. Laying the robe on the bed, he reached for her hands and pulled her to a sitting position. "How does a bath sound?"

She nodded again, "Sounds perfect."

"I'll go get the water started. Do you think...do you think you can get undressed?" His cheeks instantly flushed.

"I think so," she said.

"Okay, but if you need me, I'll be right outside of your door."

He turned and closed the door behind him. Her heart pounded again. She couldn't deny that not only did she need him, she was finally starting to admit that she wanted him, a realization that was going to leave her more scathed than her fall. This time, she was falling for a man she couldn't have. Every rational thought in her head screamed at her. She already had a man, a good man. Why then, was the draw of Will so powerful? It was clearly a feeling that couldn't have been helped, even if she tried. She was starting to doubt her ability to ignore what was becoming more and more apparent with each moment spent with him.

She painfully removed her clothing, and wrapped the robe around her. Carefully hobbling over to her mirror, she got her first look at herself. She was an absolute mess, still covered in dirt, and hard to tell where exactly the scratches were under the blood and mud. She pulled her hair completely loose from the braid and brushed it out.

"Sarah?" Will knocked gently. "Are you ready?"

"Yes, come in."

He circled her waist again and helped her to bathroom where the white iron bathtub was filled with warm water and the scent of lavender soap. The curtains were pulled so that only a soft light was sifting in through the fabric.

"My dad and Tommy are at the Wilkes's Ranch for the day, so you can relax in here for as long as you want."

She nodded and stared into the water. "Will?" He moved to her side and she reached out for him. He instantly held onto her, a look of concern creasing his face. She suddenly felt as if she could faint, and she might've if he hadn't have been there to steady her. He pulled her into his arms, and she wrapped around his shoulders again, letting him hold her.

"I guess I'm a little more shaken up than I thought," she said.

Will sighed deeply. "I don't want to leave you alone, Sarah."

She pulled away to look at him. "I don't want you to, either."

"Is it okay if…if I help you?"

She nodded, and swallowed hard. She trusted him implicitly, even in this moment of uncertainty. She knew that even in her most vulnerable state, that Will would never to anything to betray her trust. "Yes, Will," she whispered.

She felt his hands slide down her back and around her waist. He slowly pulled the end of the fabric ribbon that held her robe closed, releasing the bow. Pulling the ribbon completely loose, her robe parted slightly. He moved his hands to her face, and gently caressed her cheek before pushing her hair behind her shoulders.

His eyes filled with a yearning desire mixed with want and need. He led her to side of the bathtub. "Hold on to me, as you step in."

He braced his arm for her to hold as she slid the robe from her shoulders and let it fall at their feet. He took a deep breath and turned his head to let her step into the tub. She let her body slowly sink into the warm water and let go of Will's arm. Sarah's mind couldn't be quieted. It was hard to believe that she was in a bath, with Will just a few feet away her. He proved, again, what she already knew. He was a gentleman.

Still looking away, he asked, "Are you okay?"

"Yes, Will. I'm in."

He slowly turned, but only to look into her eyes. As he knelt at the side of the bath and pulled a wash cloth from the rack, he dipped it into water, wrung it out and gently dabbed at the mud on her face, carefully cleaning her cuts. She closed her eyes, allowing him to continue. She concentrated on his touch. Soft. Loving. She reached up and put her hand over his. Their eyes never left each other as she guided his hand and the cloth to her neck. She lifted her chin slightly, revealing her neck to his touch. Her fingertips were light on his and she guided him along her collarbone and to her shoulders. He continued the motion, dipping the cloth under the water and running it along her arm. He slowly brought it back up and across her shoulders to the other side. She no longer needed to guide him with her hand. Everything she needed him to know was in her eyes.

He continued down her other arm. Her body, every nerve, awakened at his touch. As he submerged his hand in the water, she felt the back of his hand graze against the side of her body. Her body instantly responded and she felt her muscles contract. Her breaths quickened, and she parted her lips to gasp at the sensation of his hands on her body. It nearly sent her into oblivion as his hand traveled back up her arm, and he brushed against the side of her breast.

She looked at him, noticing the same hunger he had for her. He dropped the cloth into the water, and reached for the soap. Cupping the bar in his palm, he continued to glide against her skin, moving slowly, deliberately. She couldn't help but to rise to his touch, consenting to his tentative exploration of her. He slid his hand down the length of her arm until his hand clasped around hers. His fingers entwined with hers, and their hands easily slipped into each other. His hand enclosed around hers, squeezing gently. Their hands swirled and slid against each other, moving together in unspoken recognition, as if they had just been reunited with the only hand that knew how to hold the other perfectly. The only hand created especially for the other.

He gently placed her hand back into the warm water and moved to the end of the bathtub. He placed his hand on her bent knee, and slid down her silky leg until his hands landed softly on her ankle. His eyes traveled back up the length of her leg until his eyes fixed on hers, and their silent, but heavy breaths hung in the air. He broke away from her eyes to watch his hands continue caressing her skin. She felt the soap glide smoothly from beneath his hand as he rubbed any muddy remnants of her fall from her skin. He repeated the gentle massage on her other foot, before sliding up the length of her leg until once again he was at her bent knee. His eyes met hers again as he moved back to be directly in front of her. She could no longer concentrate. No longer control her breathing. Will's touch had taken over her mind, and her body.

His hand brushed just under her collarbone and he closed his eyes. The momentum of his hands against her body had built to the point that she wanted his hands everywhere on her. She didn't want to be rational. She knew it was wrong to want him, but something so deep inside of her told her that if ever there was a right time to be wrong, it was now.

She lifted her hands from the water indicating that she needed his help. He stood, and once again his strong arms easily lifted her from the water. He steadied her and reached for the robe. He turned his head again while she wrapped the robe against her wet skin, and waited for her to reach out to his arm. She gingerly stepped out of the tub and stood facing Will. With neither one of them saying a word, Will swooped her up again into his arms and carried her from the bathroom. Her pulse was beating rapidly. His breaths were uneven.

He carried her into her room, but paused to use his foot to swing the door closed behind them. He gently laid her on the bed, pulled his arms from under her, and kneeled onto the bed. As he brought his body directly over Sarah's, she looked up at him, both of their eyes pleading with the other for permission.

No words would come. The emotion flooding her body now was something completely new, yet so unbelievably familiar. It was as if she were under a spell. A wonderful, scary spell. She reached up to his shoulders and ran her hands to the back of his head. She gently weaved her fingers into his hair. Her robe opened slightly with the movement of her arms. It was time. Time to surrender.

He moved slowly toward her and stopped just above her waiting mouth. "Sarah," he whispered, so quietly that she barely heard. "I've dreamt of this for so long. Please tell me I'm not dreaming, now."

She ran her hands through his hair again, and shook her head. "Maybe, it is all a dream, Will. If it is, I don't want to wake up. Please, Will," she said, as tears filled her eyes, "please, kiss me."

Just as the words left her lips, his mouth descended hard onto hers. It left her breathless to finally feel him. His mouth engulfed hers with such urgency and passion that she wasn't sure she would ever catch her breath again. She opened her mouth to him, and pulled him deeper into her. His tongue meshed with hers as she allowed him full access to explore her kiss. This felt like a moment she had been waiting for a long time. Ever since she and Will were in the pines, there had been a lingering desire between them. Until now, she wasn't sure if Will had felt it as intensely as she did. But now, there was no doubt.

Will's kiss slowed, but his urgency persisted. She felt him slowly taste her lips, savoring each sensation, taking in the inexplicable pleasure that their breaths were the same. She became soft and pliable to everything that his mouth wanted from her, and moved her tongue lavishly along his. His hand slowly crept from her cheek and along her collarbone. Her body began to respond to this long-awaited moment. Her mind crept back into the moment. As much as she knew this was going to end badly, her heart overruled her mind, and her body surged with craving. She admitted it.

She craved him, everything about him, and he was leaving no room for interpretation that the feeling was mutual.

CHAPTER 30

Finally kissing her was like surfacing from underwater and breathing in a lung full of air. Each minute that passed once she left Colorado, and each minute since her return, had been just as suffocating not being able to feel her lips on his. The air, the kiss, was intoxicating, and left him wanting more. He never wanted to be underwater again. He never wanted to not be able to kiss her again.

He closed his eyes and moaned softly into her mouth. He couldn't help it; it was the most luscious taste he'd ever experienced. Her kisses before she left were wonderful, no doubt, and what he thought was the pinnacle of happiness, but there was something about this kiss. This kiss was never supposed to exist. It was a kiss plucked from fate's fingers. It wasn't stolen; he was only taking what was rightfully his. He just never expected to have it back. But now, as his tongue encircled Sarah's, and his breaths were her breaths, he wasn't certain he would be able to let it go ever again.

He slowed his kiss momentarily as his ruthless reality crashed down onto his head. What the hell was he thinking? He couldn't have Sarah, not anymore. Lifting away from her sweet lips, he needed to look at her, just to make sure he hadn't conjured this whole thing in his mind. But, there she was. Beautiful and radiant, and he had just kissed her. They had spent years apart, and in those few delicious moments, the years had been erased. Nothing had changed. Except, that he wanted her even more. Now, on top of refreshing his memory on just how sweet it was to taste her again, he would have to push her away, for her own sake. He was a son of a bitch for doing this to her. He let his kiss move from her mouth and down to her neck. Pausing, he breathed deeply against her, not wanting to stop, but knowing he had to. He moved his body off hers and rolled onto the bed next to her.

They lay silently together, catching their breath, both clearly reeling from finally getting what they both hungered for. Sarah lifted herself to lie on his chest, and he wrapped his arms around her.

"I...I just don't want to hurt you, Sarah," he finally said.

Sarah looked deeply at him. "I'm okay, really I am." She gingerly touched the contusion on her temple, and tried to sound reassuring.

He brushed her hair from her face, and ran his hand down her cheek. "That's not what I meant."

She lay back down to his chest and whispered, "I know."

It took every ounce of sense not to pull her back up to his mouth again. If he couldn't tell her with his words how much he still loved her and wanted her, he knew his kiss would have communicated that for him. But, he knew he couldn't do it again. This was a one-time encounter. Even though, he half thought that it would be able to snuff out the desire that had been building between the two of them, he knew that was completely untrue. At least for him. How many times had he imagined the feel of her body against him? With her robe still slightly open, he could feel the warmth of her soft, beautiful skin. This was torture. That kiss did not extinguish his need for Sarah; it only strengthened it. He ran his fingers through her hair until she was asleep and breathing softly.

Even after a week had passed, and he was still tasting Sarah's kiss with every breath, he could only operate in a dazed confusion. Once Henry had seen Sarah and her injuries, he was so upset that he made her promise not to leave again by herself. It was unnecessary, as Will had already vowed to never let anything like that happen again. But, it didn't hurt to have her promise to Henry. Whatever it took to help keep her safe—to keep her close to him—was going to happen.

He hoped their interactions wouldn't be awkward after their kiss. Hell, it had been more than a kiss. It had been a revelation. But, they were still fine together. Something had changed, though, that much was obvious. For him, he couldn't look at her without looking at her mouth and reminiscing about what her lips felt and tasted like. He decided to keep it a secret a little longer about his collarbone, which had seemingly healed in good shape, just as Dr. Paul had projected. Until he was cleared from the doctor, he didn't want his father to worry about it. The only glitch he was forced to deal with, was that of an impatient bride. He had held her off for as long as he could, but he was starting to fear that time was running out. Now that Vernon had given him a line of credit to use at Wheeler's, he was sure that Margaret would be cashing in on the interest. But for now, he was going to keep a promise that he made to Sarah. It was time to help her remember. It was time to go to King's Creek.

"Are you nervous?" he asked, as they walked the trail that led to the creek.

Sarah looked at him and squinted in the sun. "A little."

"Why are you nervous?"

She looked down at the trail before she answered. "I guess, because I know how it was a favorite place of mine. Where there are a lot of memories, a lot of things that should be familiar to me. I'm just afraid that they won't be."

Will reached over to hold her hand. "Let's just wait and see how it goes once we get there."

She nodded and they walked quietly together. Holding her hand felt so good to him. He hadn't touched her since their kiss, and it was starting to drive him crazy. Living together, and seeing each other each morning and night, but not being able to touch her, was challenging his willpower. So, now with her hand in his, he would be sure to savor every second of it. Holding her hand would have to be enough, since another succulent kiss was out of the question. He resigned himself that he would take whatever he could get, and be happy as hell about it.

The small trail that wound through the aspens gave way to another grove of pine trees. The evergreens were spaced further apart, and twice the size of the pines of their childhood. He watched Sarah's reaction closely, hoping a glimmer of recognition would cross her beautiful face. He was pleased that her cuts and bruises from her fall were healing nicely; he hated the reminder of the fear he felt when he thought she might've been seriously injured. As difficult as that memory was, it was also the day he never wanted to forget. A wish had been granted to him. He felt Sarah's kiss one last time. As he watched her, here in this place that they had made their first fragile promise to love each other forever, and then had to say goodbye alongside the same creek, his mind went to his hopes of that day. He begged her to never forget the promise they made. And now, as much as he knew that her memory returning would cause undeniable confusion and pain for her, he couldn't help but wonder if that somehow, it could change the path of their future. If Sarah remembered, and still felt the same about him as she did the day she left, would it be enough to change the downward spiral his life would certainly take with Margaret as his wife? Would it be enough, would the power of their promise and the depth of their love be enough to challenge fate's design, and come out the victor? It was a huge gamble, but he knew he had to take it. It was a risk that could result in splitting both of their hearts, but he would take it knowing that Sarah deserved to be loved utterly and completely. He could only hope that if she remembered their promise, it would prove strong enough to somehow let him be the one to do so.

Sarah squeezed his hand as she looked up to the towering pines, pulling him back into the moment. The sky was a brilliant hue, almost too blue to be real. A slight breeze brought the smell of the forest to their senses, and provided the coolness on a day that was proving to be unseasonably warm. She smiled, still admiring the trees, "This is beautiful, Will."

"If you like this, just wait," he said, pulling her toward him. He wasn't planning on letting go of her hand, and he wanted to be holding her when she remembered the creek. If she remembered the creek.

She looked at him in anticipation, "What do you mean?"

"C'mon, it's just around this bend."

They walked for another minute under the canopy of trees, when Coon's Cove finally came into view. Will hadn't been here for a long time, and even for him, it looked more striking than he remembered. The cove was filled with water that rippled slightly with the current, and the willow tree seemed to have grown since he was here last. If the sky looked unreal, Coon's Cove might as well have been painted with the same brush.

Sarah stopped, her expression showing she was clearly entranced by the vision of the cove. "Oh my goodness, Will," she said quietly, putting her hand to her chest.

Will waited. Had she finally remembered something? Did she remember that this is where they had said goodbye to each other? "This is Coon's Cove, Sarah." His instinct was to tell her everything; everything from this being her favorite place on the creek, to everything that had ever happened here between them. His eyes were drawn to the stump where he carved their symbol all those years ago. He wanted her to know everything, but more than that, he wanted it to be because she remembered. There would be a difference between being told about the past, and being touched by the past. Only a memory could fully explain what he wanted her to know about Coon's Cove.

She took a timid step forward, and looked to Will as if she were unsure about letting go of his hand and continuing. He nodded in understanding, "I'll be right here, go ahead." She took another step, their arms stretching apart, clearly indicating that neither one wanted to let go. He gently released his grasp, and their arms fell. She looked at him again, and he thought he could see the emotion welling in her eyes. Her eyes were wide, with tears threatening to fall. She seemed in awe. Mystified. But, was it recognition of their past and the significance of this place, or just the acknowledgement of the beauty around her?

He watched her as she slowly approached the bank of the cove. Her ankle was still clearly causing her pain as she limped slightly. It was a testimony to her inner fortitude that she hadn't complained of any pain. She stopped at the bank and stared into the water. Despite nature's beauty surrounding him, he couldn't take his eyes from her. Her silhouette was stunning against the backdrop of willows. The way her body curved and dipped against the straight rigid lines of the branches beckoned his eyes to float over every inch of her shape.

He stepped to her side and waited for her reaction. A look of peace washed over her expression and her lips curled into a slight smile. He was convinced his heart suddenly skipped a beat. He was certain that the Sarah's expression was one of recognition.

"What is it, Sar?" he asked, although his breathing was jagged.

She looked to him, almost in disbelief. "I remember, Will." She smiled and nodded, "I remember this," she whispered.

Will sucked in a breath. The words he hoped to hear, out of love for her. Whether it changed anything or not, he wanted her to have her past back. "What...what do you remember?"

She looked back to the water that was as serene as her voice. "I remember being in this water. I do, I can almost feel it." She closed her eyes and continued, "I can feel the muddy bottom, the cold water. Right? I've been in the cove, right?" She opened her eyes, looking for confirmation from him.

He nodded his head slowly. "Yes, Sar. About a thousand times, you've been in this cove."

Sarah let out the breath she had been holding and jumped into his arms. She squeezed her arms around him and buried her face in his neck. He could only hold onto her as their hearts pounded against each other. Her muffled cry came from his neck, "I'm so happy, Will. I remember. This means that I can remember. This place feels like a part of me."

He held her for a long time until they both released their embrace. He would've held her for an eternity. Gladly. He could only think about the last time they were here, holding each other as they were now, and the irony of the promise they made to never forget. Now, she remembered the cove, but that didn't mean she remembered their promise.

Sarah loosened her grip, but did not remove her arms from his shoulders. She moved directly in front of him and allowed their eyes to lock. "Will?" she whispered.

"Yes, Sar?"

"Will you do something for me?" she asked, her voice tinged with hesitation.

"Anything," he replied, without a hint of reluctance. He allowed himself only a moment to fantasize about everything that he would like to do for her, but stopped himself before he got too carried away. He knew that every image that just seared through his brain wouldn't happen.

CHAPTER 31

Sarah felt her heart jump at Will's words. He didn't have to say it, she already knew. He would do anything for her, and that knowledge was a feeling that was unmatched by anything she had ever felt. She was shaking, and wondered if Will could feel it. She remembered this cove. Finally, a piece of her life in Colorado was coming into focus.

She gently slid her arms from Will's shoulders, but stayed directly in front of him. "I want to feel the water. Will you come in with me?"

"You want to go in? Are you sure?" Will raised an eyebrow.

Sarah smiled, she still couldn't calm the rush of remembering, and she wanted to be as submerged in the memory as possible. She nodded, and this time, couldn't contain her laugh. "Yes."

Will slowly shook his head and cocked a sideways grin. "Okay, Sar, but you first."

She slightly pushed against his chest, "What? No. You said you would…."

Will put his hands on her shoulders and interrupted, "Calm down," he said, his eyes glinting with humor. "I will do anything you ask. And if it's a swim deep in ice-cold water, then by all means, let's do it." He reached down and pulled the hem of his shirt up and over his head and threw it to the ground. He began unbuttoning his pants and looked at her expectantly. "Well? Are we doing this, or not?"

Sarah pursed her lips and smiled back. Following his lead, she peeled off her shirt and threw it on the ground next to his. She wore an eyelet lace bra and her pulse quickened as Will's eyes skimmed over her skin. His playful demeanor had quickly melted with the heat from his eyes. He bent down and unlaced his boots, as she quickly stepped out of her pants, kicking them into the growing heap of clothing on the ground. Will quickly followed, and now it was her turn to admire Will. His chest was wide and muscular, and his stomach rippled with muscles as his waist narrowed. He stood wearing his boxers that hung against his hips, leaving very little for Sarah to have to imagine. She bit her lip, and forced her eyes back to his. She was almost bare to him, her skin barely covered by modest underclothes. She expected to feel shy, or embarrassed. But all she felt was warmth: warmth from Will's gaze, and warmth emanating from his body that was merely a few inches from hers.

She might've stayed staring permanently, if hadn't been for Will reaching for her hand. "Okay," he said, with the smile that could, by itself, cause her to breathe quickly. "Let's do this."

She let her breath rush out and smiled, "Lead the way."

She wrapped her fingers around his as they stepped down the small embankment and to the water's edge. The water lapped at their feet, and Sarah was surprised at the unexpected coolness. She looked at Will, widening her eyes, "This is going to be cold, isn't it?"

"Cold? No."

"Oh, good," she said, relieved.

"It's going to be freezing."

Before she could respond, Will scooped her up in his arms and was holding her against his body. "It's best if we just get right in," he said, in response to her squeal.

She wrapped her arms tightly around his shoulders as he proceeded into the water slowly. "Will! Oh my gosh, don't drop me." Suddenly, she was second-guessing her idea of getting in the water.

"Don't worry, I won't."

Sarah's body and mind were both in a complete state of shock. She didn't know which sensation was more arresting; the coldness of the water, or the delicious heat of Will's body next to hers. The water was something she could experience any time, but Will was a different story. Without even pretending to debate any longer, she resigned herself to only concentrating on the sensation of her skin against his.

Will stepped further and further into the cove until she could feel her toes begin to dip into water, and slowly, despite still being cradled in Will's arms, her body was skimming the surface. She tensed against the sting of it and closed her eyes.

"It'll be okay, Sar. Remember, you've done this a hundred times. It's always cold at first, but you'll get used to it." He stepped even deeper, and now, the water splashed against his chest and most of her body was immersed. Will slowly twisted from side to side, still holding her against him.

Slowly, Sarah felt her body ease as the temperature settled in against her. She laughed, "Whose bright idea was this, anyway?"

Will dropped his arm from under her knees, but steadied her as feet settled into the soft mud. Sinking into the dark softness with her feet only brought the memory more into focus. She closed her eyes and breathed deep. For the first time since being back, she finally felt like her heart and her feet were in the same place. She was home.

Will's hands were gentle against her hips, and she imagined him pulling her into him. Now that she was not touching him, the absence of his body left her instantly craving its return. "Are you good?" he asked, trying to stifle his grin.

"I'm good, I think," she said. Although, to say she was good, was a lie. She felt exhilarated. The water's bite had lessened, and it was becoming comfortable and refreshing.

His hands dropped from her waist, and she slowly turned to inspect the cove. The water flowed from the cove into a narrow opening that had been littered with branches that beavers had meticulously stacked for years, keeping the water calm and deep. Upstream from the cove, she watched the water flow over the rocks into the small creek, glistening and gurgling. Just above the creek, an old, weathered log bridged the two banks, and laid quiet and strong above the lively water. The log was certainly impressive, but she recognized something inside of her stir as she stared at it. There was a history to that log, not that she knew what it was at that moment. But, something deep inside told her there was history there.

Between the dam and log, centered in the cove, a large willow tree left its black shadow in the water. She waded closer to the tree, almost expecting to see something once she reached it. She closed her eyes, beckoning the memory to come in to her mind. She let the quietness enter, she let her mind be open, and she breathed deeply. She could see the willow tree in her mind, it seemed smaller though. She could feel the hot sun, and the heaviness of pants in the water, and she could feel her toes sinking in the mud. In her mind, she focused on the tree. Something about the tree. No, something in the tree. Breathing deeply, an image, like headlights coming through the fog, slowly came into focus. She could see it now, and more importantly, she could feel it now. It was terror that she felt, and it was a bear that she could remember.

Her eyes shot open and stared at the branches of the willow tree. A bear had been there, and she had been in the cove. She implored her memory to give her more, but the curtain had dropped. There was no more for her to see. She turned to Will who had come even closer to her.

"Will!" she said breathlessly. "A bear. I remember a bear."

He ran his hand along her cheek, a seriousness embedded in his expression. "Yes, Sarah, you're right."

"But, how? What, what happened?" she stuttered.

He took a deep breath, "Well, you came to the creek to gather rocks, and decided to wade into the cove. It was warm, just like today. A mother bear and her cub came to the cove, too. They were right there," he said, nodding to the willow.

Sarah looked down, but nothing more of the incident would come to her. "Then what? How did I get away?"

"Someone came looking for you, and they saved you from getting eaten by a bear." Will's eyes glinted again.

A soft smile crossed her lips and she cocked her head slightly. "Someone, huh?"

Will smiled and nodded.

"You. You saved me. So, you've saved me from a bear, and from falling off a horse."

He nodded again, and she took a step closer to him. "How, Will? How do you always know when I need you?"

Sarah felt his arms come around her waist and he pulled her close until their bodies were connected under the water. She sucked in one last breath before she knew she would no longer be able to catch it. She looked up into his eyes and wrapped her hands around the muscles in his arms. She thought she would surely faint if he wasn't there to support her. "I don't know, except that all I've ever wanted to do is take care of you. It's all I wanted then, and it's all I want now."

Her chest heaved against his, his arms wrapped tightly around her, pressing her into his hard body. She darted from one blue eye to the other until her gaze fell onto his lips. No sooner than she parted her lips to speak, Will's lips met hers. She opened her mouth and let him caress her tongue with his. Heaven. She tilted her head, giving him even easier access. She pulled his lips into her mouth, and gently sucked until his mouth ravaged hers. His hands slid down her thighs until he pulled her up to a straddling position against his hips. She hooked her ankles together behind him, her body now completed embedded in his. He wrapped his arms around her back, embracing her so completely that they were now one. She brought her arms around his neck, and let her fingers weave through his hair. His kiss was proving to her that he meant every word. Whether she needed him because of a bear, or a fall, he was there. Now, she wasn't sure why she needed him, but it didn't matter. He knew. Just like all the other times, he knew. She needed him, and he was going to take care of her. She needed this kiss more than air. Because of him, she could breathe.

But that breath was coming in short gasps. She felt Will's body between her legs, and felt his desire for her harden against her softness. There was only a fine layer of fabric that was separating everything that she felt.

Her body instantly clenched and tightened with every bounce of her body against him. The current in the cove pressed them into each other, and with each wave, it pressed her into his hips. With each wave, she felt his hardness at her entrance, and if it weren't for the fabric, the waves would've brought him into her. Her body reacted as if there were no fabric. Her body reacted as if the next wave didn't come soon, she would unravel from sheer rapture of feeling him against her. She felt his body surge up, as her body pressed down. She wrapped her fingers tightly in his hair, just to keep herself even more securely against him. She felt the tightening of her womb build each time Will's body caressed her. He was hard and significant, and completely unable to be ignored. Feeling him inside of her was all she could think of. This moment, this water, this man. All of it felt right. Her body knew it would feel unbelievable. She wanted him, her body wanted him, and she was slowly building to the point of no return. Nothing would be the same after he made her feel this way. She broke away from his kiss, but only long enough to whisper his name before he descended once again to claim her with his mouth.

CHAPTER 32

Hearing her say his name, as he tasted her kiss was almost enough to encourage the ecstasy that was surging through him to explode. If it weren't for what was nagging in the back of his mind, it would've been pure pleasure in its complete form: mind, body and soul. He wanted her in every way possible. The emotion of the moment had brought them to this point. Sarah wrapped in his arms, and his body in complete disregard of what his mind was telling him. What would it take to stop something that his mind knew was wrong, but that his body and soul could not deny was right? He was powerless against this force. Two out of three forces won out, and he kissed her in the cove like there would only be this moment to live in for the rest of his life.

The current in the cove kept their bodies in constant motion against each other. Her breasts were pressed against him and he fought to keep his hands from them. With each movement, he felt himself rub against her body; her own amazing cove that his body was ready to explore. The softness and warmth. Sarah's body. Divine. Had it not been for the indescribable gratification of feeling Sarah's hand dig into his hair as she succumbed to her own body's will, he might've been able to take the moment needed to slow this experience. Her arms tightened around him and her body stilled as she let out a soft, long moan of pleasure into his mouth. He had never heard a sound so breathtaking in his entire life. The sensation of her body just brushing against his, her legs clenching tightly around him, and knowing that he had brought her to the point of such sweet ecstasy, was more than he ever could've imagined. He closed his eyes and felt his own release shatter against her body.

They both held onto each other, and for the first time since they arrived at the cove, Will felt like he finally took a deep breath and was able to take notice of their surroundings. He began to hear the bird calls through the forest, felt the breeze against his face and the cool water swirling around his waist. Nothing compared to the sensory overload of what he and Sarah just shared. She still clung to him, her body trembling and her breathing rapid against his neck. He closed his eyes and shook his head. He could think of only one thing to say. "Sarah," he whispered.

She didn't respond, and held tightly around his shoulders. "Sarah, look at me," he urged gently.

She lifted herself from his neck and looked into his eyes. He tried to read her expression, but there was too much going on in her eyes to be able to decipher just one reaction. He leaned into her and kissed her mouth gently. He was relieved to feel her welcome his kiss, and return with her own lavish strokes against his tongue. Her kiss was completely delectable; there was nothing more exquisite. He wanted to kiss her slowly, as if by slowing down, this moment wouldn't come to an end. Their lips slowly parted and he looked at her with desire and love, both emotions soaring through his body. "What are we doing?" he whispered.

She slowly shook her head, a sadness invading her eyes. She nestled back into his neck, not answering. But, her eyes had already answered the question, acknowledging all that he had just thought, she had thought, too.

He didn't have the answer either. The worst part was that whatever it was, he sure as hell didn't want it to end; he only wanted it again. He never wanted something so much that he knew he couldn't have. He held her tightly, begging the feeling of her body against his to sear into his memory. There was a time in his life when he thought he would have this feeling forever. At this cove, in fact. They had given each other their promise to be together forever at this exact place. A promise that brimmed with love and desire. At the time, he could've never known that their promise would not be kept. Except for this one moment in time, fate allowed them a fleeting glimpse of what true contentment could've felt like. Of true bliss. Love. Of what forever could've felt like.

But the brief hint of happiness that fate teased them with was over too soon, and leaving the cove was a necessary evil. They eventually climbed the muddy bank and pulled their clothes over their wet bodies. Will couldn't help casting his glance to the stump, but Sarah never caught his gaze long enough to notice. He swore to himself that he would let her remember in her own time—on her own terms—about the stump and their promise. After what they both experienced today, the cove held new memories that rivaled the old.

Walking back home was like a strange dream, mixed with elation and heartache. He and Sarah walked most of the way in silence, but held tightly to each other's hands. Every minute that he spent with Sarah, and every precious second that his lips could touch hers, led him further and further down the path of a love beyond anything he had ever dared to dream. His body could not forget the sensation of Sarah so close to him. They brought each other to such planes of pleasure by mere touch. It was too much to even think about what it would actually be like to make love to her. The first visit to Coon's Cove proved to be so much more than he thought it would. He thought that it would be for Sarah's sake, for her memory's sake. How could he have known that it would've altered everything in his own mind?

He pulled her to a stop at the base of the driveway. They would be home in a few minutes, and everything would have to go back to the way it was before. It was an impossible task, but he would be forced to pretend that nothing had changed, except the fact that Sarah had regained a memory. "Sarah, wait." He didn't know exactly what to say, all he knew was that he wasn't ready for this feeling to end.

She turned and looked at him, her beautiful face unable to hide the same duality of emotions that he was feeling. "Yes, Will?" She smiled and looked as if she would cry at the same time.

"I'm not sorry...about the cove." He held both of her hands, but wanted so desperately to pull her into another kiss that would make everything else just fall away.

"I'm not either," she whispered back. "But..." she paused, her eyes now clouded with pain.

"I know," he interrupted. "We can't..." He stopped again. He didn't want to say the words out loud. They both knew they couldn't be together like that again.

She nodded and looked down. When she looked back up, she smiled to hide the tears. "Will?"

"Yes, Sar?"

"I loved the creek. Everything about the creek."

Will's chest tightened, and he was suddenly so angry at the course that led to this moment. Life wasn't fair, and there wasn't a damn thing he could do about it.

He breathed in deep, forcing the memory of the creek to become permanent in the forefront of his mind, ahead of anything that ever had been, or ever would be, a memory. "I will always love the creek, Sarah. The creek is more important to me than you know. Today was just one more reason why the creek will always be a part of me."

"A part of me, too, Will. I promise you, I will never forget today."

Will pulled her hands to wrap around his waist. He ran his hands along her arms slowly and leaned down to her expectant gaze. He pressed his lips against hers, closing his eyes tightly, as if by doing so, the memory could never escape. The anger slowly left him as he realized that he never expected to be able to do this again, and for that, he could be grateful. Some of Sarah was better than none of Sarah.

CHAPTER 33

Sarah finished hanging the laundry but couldn't make herself move from the shelter of the sheets waving in the breeze. It had been several days since her and Will's trip to King's Creek, and she felt an inexplicable amount of relief knowing that it would be possible to regain some of her memory, and maybe even all of it. For, as much as she felt some of the pieces fall into place, just as many shattered all over again. There was no way to explain what was happening between her and Will. It was dangerous to be around him, as she felt completely out of control. He was betrothed to someone else, and so was she. But, when they were together, the force that drew them together couldn't be ignored. The fact of the matter was that she was playing with something far more dangerous than fire. She was risking a heartbreak that surely couldn't be recovered from. The guilt that wound around her throat was overwhelming and paralyzing. How could she continue to betray Adley? Somewhere, in a scary and threatening place, Adley was holding on to the promise she made him. She cringed at the thought that she might be the only thing keeping him going. He promised her that he would come home and marry her. She told him that she would be waiting. She told him that she loved him. All of that was true. How then, could the connection to Will supersede everything she had sworn to give to Adley? She buried her face in her hands trying to subside the twisting in her stomach and the tears she had fought so often. She had cried enough, and it never changed anything. It wouldn't change anything now. If only she were here in the laundry with her mother. The pain caused from the absence of her mother never dulled, not that she had expected it to. She wasn't sure how she was going to get through the rest of her life without those magic hands to brush her tears away.

"Sarah? You out here?" Tommy's voice broke through and temporarily froze the grip of grief that was squeezing her heart.

She brushed aside the tears from her cheeks and breathed deeply. Hoping to sound like herself she called back, "In the sheets, Tommy." Tommy was just what she needed right now. Just when she was feeling the claws of despair begin to drag her into the depths of utter pain, a reprieve arrived in the form of someone she had come to trust.

Tommy was the kind who was completely happy to be left to his own accord. He was satisfied to be on his own, but he never turned down the opportunity to be others, either. Since he and Sarah were usually the only ones around the house during the day, the two had formed a friendship easily and quickly.

"Hey, are you all done out here?" he asked, moving a sheet to the side to reveal Sarah amongst the swaying sheets.

"I think so," she said. "Unless you plan on wiping your dirty hands on all of the sheets."

Tommy jerked his hands from the pale yellow sheet and turned them over frantically inspecting them. "What? They're not dirty."

Sarah had to laugh, "I'm just kidding, Tommy." She already felt better.

"I'm going to go brush the horses. Wanna come help me?"

"Yes, I do," she said. This was exactly the kind of distraction she needed. "Let me go put the baskets away and I'll meet you out there."

Tommy nodded, "Sounds good."

By the time Sarah had put the baskets away and straightened a few things in the house, Tommy had the horses tethered to corral posts outside of the tack shed. This would be good for her. She needed something else to think about instead of Will and Adley. That, and the ever present gaping hole in her heart from missing her parents and Matty so much, that it was hard to breathe. Will had left for the lumberyard, which meant he was most likely going to be seeing Margaret. She was especially anxious for

Will's doctor appointment today with Dr. Paul. She couldn't shake the fear that she had somehow reinjured Will's collarbone with everything that had been happening lately. Not only had he carried her after her fall, but, almost immediately she was taken back to the memory of him lifting her and carrying her into the cove. Her face flushed and she physically shook her head. It was no use trying to get that day out of her mind. Every time she did, she was only pulled deeper into the memory and her stomach would actually twist and turn. She was beginning to feel like Will's touch on her skin was an addictive drug. She could feel herself going through the waves of craving something that was not good for her, and the inevitable withdrawal that follows when you can't have it.

She pulled her hair back and tied it into a ponytail as she slowly approached the horses. Little Big Man snorted and whinnied as she approached him to rub his nose. She didn't have any ill feelings toward him after her fall. She knew it wasn't his fault, and he was a good horse, for not running away into the mountains after it all happened.

Tommy was already brushing the glossy black mane of Gambler when he nodded to the bucket on the ground. "There's another brush in there if you want it."

Sarah nodded as she found the large wooden brush with black bristles that looked as if it had brushed a few hundred horses over the years. She slowly ran it through Little Big Man's mane, carefully pulling through the knots.

"So," Tommy began. "You doin' okay?"

"Oh yea, these knots aren't too bad. I'll just go slow. I don't need him bucking me off again in some sort of revenge. Huh, boy?" she said, smiling and patting Little Big Man's neck.

"I don't mean that, Sarah. I'm talking about everything since you've been back here. I know that you've been going through...a lot."

Sarah silently kept her brush going through the coarse hair. Tommy was wise beyond his years; very observant, too. She wondered if he somehow knew about her and Will. Had she and Will done a good enough job keeping their secret, or had he picked up on the connection that she couldn't keep squelched no matter how hard she tried? But then again, Tommy was sweet and caring, and he may just be asking a general question. Her guilty conscience was starting to get the better of her.

"Yes," she managed to stammer. "I'm doing okay. I don't know what I would do without you three, though. Taking me in like you have." She shook her head, "It's meant a lot to me. I really want to remember my life here. And," she paused, "I think my memories are starting to come back."

Tommy stopped his brush and looked at her. "Really? Good. That's good, Sarah."

"I remembered the creek. Not everything, but I could definitely remember it."

Tommy raised his eyebrows and nodded, "Yep, that's a big one. You loved the creek. We all spent a lot of time there. But, you and Will probably spent the most time there. Together."

The creek. Her and Will. Together. The memory of her body shattering into pieces of pleasure from being against him washed over her again. She ducked under Little Big Man's neck to avoid Tommy seeing the crimson hue that was surely flooding her face.

"Mmm," she simply responded.

"You know, a piece of him died the day you left."

Now Sarah had to look straight into Tommy's face. She knew that she and Will were close growing up, but she never had figured out all of the details of their friendship. "Really? What do you mean?"

"I mean that he was never the same. Didn't laugh. Didn't joke around. He moped around here for months. He never came right out and said it, but I think he thought that he would never see you again. He held out hope for a long time, like he was waiting for you, but then…." He paused and shook his head. "Anyway, I haven't seen him like he is now, for a long time."

"Like what?"

"Happy. He's happy again, Sarah. That can only be because of you, don't you think?"

Sarah continued to brush out Little Big Man deep in thought. She changed the subject to the weather, to the steers coming, to anything but what she couldn't stand to think about anymore. If what Tommy said was true, Will was finally happy again now that she was back. For some reason, it gave her a glimmer of hope that he had never been truly happy being with Margaret. But, a hope for what? Hope was a dangerous thing to allow into her heart. But then again, not letting hope into her heart was not an option. She would rather die than to never have the one thing that could never be taken from her, the one thing that was truly within her control. No matter the circumstance, she had always found a way to let hope guide her. The only question now was, what exactly did she dare to hope with Will?

CHAPTER 34

It was nearly noon when Will finally walked through the back entrance of the lumberyard. The store was busy; always a good sign that the better times folks had been looking for might actually be coming to fruition. A good sign, too, that the lumberyard was making money. Yet another thing to keep Vernon happy, and preferably, keep him from taking out his frustrations on the employees. The store had lost a good employee the day Jake was fired. As far as Will knew, Jake was working where he could, but still hadn't landed a steady job. If he had anything to do with it, he'd hire him back in a minute. Jake made a mistake the day of the logging accident, but Will wasn't one to hold a grudge, and he sure as hell wasn't one who couldn't forgive. Everyone in town knew the same couldn't be said about Vernon. Truth be told, he wasn't sure Jake would come back even if he had the chance. He had escaped Vernon once, and Will was pretty sure Jake would keep it that way.

Will hung his coat in the back room and went out to the sales floor. He glanced around, nodding and smiling at the customers, asking if he could help them find something. He turned the corner of an aisle and noticed Dan restocking the fencing staples.

"Hey there, William," Dan said, standing from his kneeling position. He gave Will a friendly pat on the back. "Look at you." Dan had been at the lumberyard for years, and everyone in town knew him. He was the kind who could fix anything, would help anyone, and always had a story to tell. He had learned long ago how to put up with Vernon's bullshit, and kept the lumberyard running as smoothly as it did. He was good at managing the employees, and taking care of the customers. Vernon would be completely lost without Dan running the store, and everyone, including Dan, knew it.

Will looked down at his arm and slightly raised it. "Yep, the doc said I don't need the sling anymore."

Dan smiled, "That's good, Will. I'm real happy for you. Glad you're gettin' better."

Will nodded slowly, "Me too." He was happy to be healing, but with the good report from the doctor, came the end of excuses as far as Margaret was concerned. There was nothing now to keep her from planning the wedding.

"Is Vernon here?"

Dan shook his head slowly, "No, I don't think he's back. He had to run some errands over at Wheeler's."

Will nodded again, a familiar wave of nausea seeping in. That really was his last excuse. Once his dad's farm was able to produce again, thanks to the line of credit at Wheeler's, he would be fully able to concentrate on Margaret. At least that's what Vernon thought.

"But, I do believe Margaret is in his office if you're lookin' for her."

"Alright, thanks, Dan. I'll see you later."

Dan turned back to his work and Will headed to the stairs leading to Vernon's office. What was it about climbing these stairs that had conditioned him to feel dread? He knew the answer. Walking these stairs felt like the path to an ominous life sentence. Each step just one more link in the chain that was tightening around him. Soon he'd be completely bound, his arms tethered to his sides, and completely unable to reach out and hold Sarah ever again.

"Come in." Margaret's voice answered the knock.

She stood from behind her father's desk and came running as soon as he walked in. "William. You're back. What did the doctor say?"

He gently pulled her arms from around his neck, and kissed her cheek when she gave him a look of confusion. "Well, he said that he thought I was doing pretty good. I'm still not completely healed. I'm going to have to take it easy, build up the muscles, and not strain myself with any heavy lifting."

He wondered if he sounded convincing. The truth was, that Dr. Paul thought he could resume normal activities, within reason. He wasn't sure why he didn't fully divulge the truth to Margaret, especially since he knew for a fact that his collarbone had healed quite nicely, and had allowed him to hold Sarah just fine.

"Well, thank God! I was getting so tired of seeing that sling. And now, you'll be able to fully use your arm for...other activities." Her eyes glistened with suggestion as she stepped toward him, placing her hands on his chest. "You've been at a disadvantage lately, wouldn't you agree?" She ran her hands slowly down to his waist.

Will's mind searched for something, anything to halt where this was headed. But Margaret's hands worked quickly and she was already pulling his belt loose from the buckle. He quickly clasped his hands around hers, stopping her before she could continue. "What are you doing?" he asked, in a hoarse whisper.

"Don't you worry, William. Daddy's going to be gone for at least another hour. No one will bother us up here. Besides, I can lock the door."

He held onto her hands and flexed his jaw. There was no way he would be able to do anything with Margaret. There was not one ounce of desire for her. Margaret could be convincing, he knew that much. But, it didn't matter. She had no power over his needs or cravings. He could still taste Sarah's kiss, and feel her body wrapped around his from being together in the cove. The last thing he was going to do was taint that memory by touching Margaret. He was in a fine mess, now.

"No, it's not that," he said, stopping her from walking to the door.

She stopped and turned sharply to look at him straight on. "What is it then, William?" She slowly started walking back to him, the flirtation gone from her voice. She looked at him, with frost invading her green eyes. She clearly wasn't pleased to be denied by him.

He needed to come up with something. Anything. And fast. Margaret was closing the distance between them and he was beginning to feel like he was running out of air. But in that moment, as if a hand reached into the pool he was sinking into and pulled him to the surface, the image of his mother's face came into his mind. Her soft, knowing eyes, looked into him, and he felt a rush of warmth pour over him. His mother. His mother was the answer he was looking for.

"Margaret," he began slowly, "I haven't treated you like I should have."

She narrowed her eyes and tilted her head slightly, "What are you talking about?"

"Something happened, something that has made me realize that I've made a mistake."

"William?" Her voice raised as if she was asking something, but really, it was laced with a sharp tone of warning.

"Last night, something happened. I had a dream about my mother. It's the only dream I've had since, since she's been gone." He fell silent, wishing that he actually had dreamt about his mother. The truth was, that each night before he slept, he asked for her to visit him in his dreams. He longed to see her one more time, to talk to her, to feel her presence. To apologize to her for letting her go to the barn instead of him. To apologize for the tone he spoke to her in. But, she had not come. Now, he was again spinning a web of lies.

"And?" Margaret's impatience was growing.

"And, in my dream, my mother told me that she was disappointed in me."

"Disappointed in what?"

"She told me that I had disrespected you. She was disappointed that I would, you know, have relations with you, before we were married. She told me that she raised me to be a gentleman, and that she thought I should try to make it right, if I could."

"That's ridiculous." Margaret huffed. "So what are you saying?"

"I'm saying that, out of respect for you, and for my mom, I don't think we should, you know, be together anymore until we are officially man and wife. It's the right thing to do. You're a lady, and I should've known better."

Margaret put her hands on her hips and stalked to him. "Are you trying to tell me that until we are married, we won't be together anymore?"

William nodded. "I'm sorry, Margaret. My dream was so real, it felt as if my mom were really here. When I woke up, I knew it was a dream, but my mom was right. We should've waited."

Margaret ran her hand down his chest again, dragging it down until her hand was between his thighs. "Are you telling me that you're going to be able to resist my touch until we are married?" She slowly moved her hand to his manhood and began massaging him through his pants.

He quickly grabbed her hands, and held them. "Yes, Margaret. Please, I know it's the right thing to do." At her look of astonishment, he brought her hands to his lips and kissed them lightly. "Please try to understand that I'm still trying to deal with my mother's death, and that I'm to blame for it. If I can do this, and somehow feel that I'm making her proud, I feel like I should."

Margaret pursed her lips and shook her head. "I've never heard of anything so crazy, William. But, I can see that I'm not going to be able to change your mind."

William let out a silent sigh. He hadn't had a dream about his mother, but his mother saved him anyway. "Thank you for understanding."

"Oh, I don't understand, William. But, if that's how you want it, then it's time for me to get what I want."

He looked at her, waiting for her to continue. He knew that his latest revelation would not come without a price.

"I want a date, William. Once and for all, I want us to set a date for our wedding. You've made me wait long enough, don't you think? I've waited for you to get out of that awful sling, and you have. And now, if you're going to make me wait to feel you touch me again, then I'm not willing to wait very long."

The price. The price was steep, but it was inevitable. It was worth not having to force himself to be physically involved with Margaret. He couldn't bring himself to be. Not until he could somehow get Sarah out of his every waking thought. It was a task he was certain would be impossible, but necessary.

"Of course," he replied, swallowing the dry lump that had formed in his throat. "When were you thinking?"

A smile finally cleared the scowl that seemed etched in her brow. "Well, a summer wedding is out of the question, now that it's already June. I suppose a Fall wedding will do."

She quickly passed by William to her father's desk. Pulling the calendar from the wall, her eyes scanned the weeks. William held his breath, knowing that with each flick of her eyes, another day of his freedom was numbered and just as quickly, being erased.

Her eyes finally stopped, and she looked up. "August twenty-third should work, I think. It's a Saturday, and that should give me enough time to plan everything. What do you think?"

He nodded, knowing he needed to share her enthusiasm. "That sounds fine. Whatever you would like, you know that."

CHAPTER 35

"This nation owes you a debt of gratitude, son. What you've gone through," Dr. Gregory shook his head, "well, it's been through hell and back, hasn't it?" The doctor gathered his stethoscope and light, and placed them back into his black bag.

"Yes, sir. It has." Adley's voice remained steady, but his eyes flashed with painful memories.

Ellie came to Adley's bedside, and ran her hands over his forehead. She took a deep breath and looked from Adley, back to the doctor. "How do you think he's doing?" Her voice was nervous.

"Well," Dr. Gregory said, slowly as he continued gathering his belongings, "he's been home now, what? A couple of weeks?"

Ellie nodded, "A little over two."

"I would say in that time, I've been very pleased with his progress. His concussion is better. Pupil dilation is normal, and his abrasions are showing no signs of infection. Overall, I would give him an excellent report. He should be able to slowly regain normal activities as soon as he feels up to it." He directed his attention to Adley, "But, I still want you to let yourself heal, don't push it, alright?"

Adley's eyes never left the spot on the wall across the room that he had been focusing on. "Yes, sir."

Dr. Gregory took one last look at him before clearing his throat, "Yes, well. Call me if you need me. I'll be checking in on him in another week or so."

"Thanks for comin' out, Doc. We appreciate it." Oscar extended his hand to the doctor, "We'll walk you out."

Oscar, Ellie and Dr. Gregory left the room and Adley lay quietly in his bed, hearing their muffled voices as they descended the stairs. He reached up and rubbed his temple. For as much as he had healed, he still had a constant searing headache to remind him of what had sent him home. He closed his eyes, unable to erase the last image of his memory before the Screaming Mimi hit his foxhole. Sergeant Sway, looking at him and screaming. Something. Everything was so loud that he couldn't hear him, even though he was only a couple of feet away. The barrage of artillery was everywhere, and the look on Sgt. Sway's face told Adley that this might be the day he died. Sgt. Sway was the last thing he remembered before everything went black. Silent.

They told him once he came to, that he had been knocked fifty feet from where the bomb hit. He had been unconscious for ten days and spent a month in the hospital before the Army gave him his papers to go home. His concussion rendered him too impaired to continue any further, he'd be more of a liability than anything else. His hearing still hadn't completely returned, although the ringing in his ears was loud and clear. But, he was still alive, and by the grace of God, was sent home. They never did find Sgt. Sway.

"Thanks again for coming out. It sure has been nice of you to keep your eye on Adley." Oscar said, as they all three stepped out to the porch.

"It's the least I can do, and you know I'm happy to do it. He's lucky, and I'm real glad he's home."

"Do you really think he'll be okay?" Ellie folded her arms across her chest nervously. "He just doesn't seem like himself, and it worries me."

Dr. Gregory raised his eyebrows, "Well, like I told you before, a concussion is an injury that still has a lot of mysteries. You can expect him to have drastic mood swings, and even personality changes. It's hard to know exactly how this has impacted him. But, try not to worry too much, Ellie. I think he'll come around."

"I hope so," she said quietly, rubbing her arms.

Oscar sighed deeply, "Well, it's hard to know if it's from his injury or just plain ol' being pissed off."

Dr. Gregory nodded in agreement. "Well, it could be that too."

Ellie said goodbye once more and Oscar walked the doctor to his truck. When Oscar returned to the porch, Ellie still looked uneasy. "Do you think he'll ever forgive us?"

"Well, I think it would sure help our cause if Sarah got back here." Oscar put his arm around her, and they walked back into the house and up to Adley's room.

"Are you hungry, dear?" Ellie asked, sitting on the side of his bed. "I have some soup if you are."

Adley blinked, and looked to his parents. He could see the worry carved into their faces. "No, I'm not hungry. But what you can do is explain to me how in the hell you could've let Sarah go. How could you have done that? I still can't believe you would do that to me."

Oscar and Ellie looked to each other, but it was Oscar who spoke. "Son, we've tried to explain it to you. It was not our choice. Sarah made the choice to go back and try to regain some sort of memory of her life. We just felt that it was the right thing to do to let Edward and Anne's best friends know about the accident. We had no idea that Henry would come, and we sure as heck didn't know Sarah would choose to go back to Colorado."

"Why didn't you stop her?" Adley sat up and swung his legs over the bed. He took a deep breath, and stared at his parents. "Don't you understand that she is the reason I survived everything that I did? Knowing that I had her, knowing that I had a life to come home to, knowing that I had her to come home to and marry?"

"Yes, son. But—" Ellie began.

"No, I don't want to hear it. You've told me already." His voice rippled with annoyance. He sat quietly for a moment before he spoke again. "She did this, too. The last thing that she said to me was that she would be here, waiting for me until I came home. She promised me." Adley clenched his water glass in his fist and cocked his arm to throw it across the room. Ellie gasped in shock, and he halted his movements. He slammed the glass on the bedside table and put his head in his hands and stared at the floor. Without looking up, he said quietly, "I'd like to be left alone, now."

"Oh, Adley, please..." Ellie began, as tears filled her eyes.

Adley looked up to her, his voice filled with tension, "Mom, just please, please just leave me alone."

Oscar put his arm around her shoulder and gave her a nod to go to the door. "Alright, son. We're here if you need us." They turned and left the room, quietly closing the door behind them.

Adley stood from his bed and walked to his window. He had a perfect view of the little house that now sat vacant. His mind battled between all of his emotions as his eyes then moved to stare at the garden. Holding on to the memory of Sarah was the only thing that kept him from going completely insane over the last several months. The only thing. Every day he dreamt about coming home to her, marrying her, and finally having her as his own. And, what really stuck in his craw was that she had agreed. She said she wanted all of that, too. He was extremely sorry about her parents not surviving the accident, and he knew what that must've done to her. With Matty being gone too, he knew she had to have been going through hell. But why couldn't she have waited for him? He would've made everything okay again. He would've taken care of her, and been good to her. All he knew, was that he did not just go through everything that he did, to come home to an empty house, where his future wife should've been waiting. Sarah should've been here, like she promised. Apparently, she didn't understand the fundamentals of a promise, but he did. He promised her that he would come home, and make her his own. He had never broken a promise before, and he sure as hell wasn't going to start now.

CHAPTER 36

"Where is he, boys?" Sarah asked, as Little Big Man and Gambler came over to the fence of the corral. She brushed their soft velvety noses with her palm, but was too distracted in her thoughts to enjoy her time with the horses. Will had come home from work, but they still hadn't connected like they usually did at the end of the day. She thought he must've been out doing the chores without her, but when she realized the horses had already been fed and watered, she was left with even more questions. It wasn't like Will to avoid her, but she was suddenly very self-conscious, that maybe he was. A pit was growing in her stomach with each passing minute. Not only had she become dependent on being around him as much as possible, she now worried that he was distancing himself from her. That was a thought that she couldn't tolerate to entertain for another minute.

After searching the yard and corrals, she finally found him sitting on the porch swing. His elbows rested on his knees, with his hand clasped in front of him. His head hung, and the normally squeaky swing was silent. She walked to him, unsure if she was interrupting. She almost stopped to turn around when Will spotted her.

"Hey, you," he said, his troubled look softening as soon as their eyes met.

"Hey," she replied. "I didn't mean to bother you."

"You could never bother me," he said, sitting up straight.

"Are you sure? I could go in the—" She motioned toward the house but he stopped her before she could finish.

"I'm sure. In fact, there's no one I would rather be with than you. Come, sit with me, please?"

Will had a strange power over her with just his words. He had a power over her with just about everything, as she thought about it. Seeing him, talking to him, touching him, kissing him. All of it rendered her defenseless. Dangerously defenseless.

She walked to him, completely aware that his eyes were consuming her. He moved over, allowing her room to sit next to him.

"Are you okay? I looked for you at the corral, and when I couldn't find you, I was worried." She looked at him again, noticing heaviness to his demeanor.

"Yea, I'm okay. I just came out here to think."

Sarah nodded and looked out into the yard, happy to just sit with him; and the relief that he wanted to be with her washed over her.

"It's my fault, you know." He looked to her with such sadness in his eyes that Sarah wanted to wrap her arms around him.

"What's your fault?"

"My mom. I should've been the one to go to the barn that night, not my mom." Will shook his head and swallowed hard. "She never should've been there."

Sarah had only heard bits and pieces about Catherine's accident, but she never once heard what Will was so painfully pouring out now.

He looked at her again, "If I would've just gotten up. But I didn't. I let her go out into snow and the cold, and I slept. I slept, Sarah. I was too lazy to get up, and she went. She went, and, and I don't even know what happened. How could I have done that, Sarah?" His eyes filled with tears.

Sarah could no longer stop the longing to comfort him. She wrapped her arms around his shoulders and held him tightly. He wrapped his arms around her waist and pulled her into him. She squeezed with all the love in her heart, hoping to wrap his sorrow in her embrace and absorb it from him.

"Will," she whispered, "it's not your fault. I don't know exactly what happened, but I promise you, it's not your fault."

Will held her tightly. "I miss her, Sarah. I miss her so much."

"I know, Will. I know."

"The guilt has haunted me, every day and night. Not only did that decision take my mother, it stole my future. That one decision changed everything, forever."

Sarah could only let him hold her, wishing she could do anything to ease the pain that she, herself, knew only too well.

"If I could only have one more chance, one more chance to make that decision. But I can't, and every night I go to sleep wishing I could feel her kiss my forehead one more time, like she did that night. I had her right there," he said, reaching his hand out. "She was right there next to me, and I let her go. And now, I'll never be with her again, Sarah."

Sarah reached out and took his hand in hers. She knew she would never erase his pain like she wanted to, but she was suddenly filled with a glimmer of hope and felt her pulse quicken. "Stay here, I'll be right back, okay?"

His look begged her to stay, but he slowly nodded. Sarah stood from the swing and hurried into the house, letting the screen door slam behind her. The sadness that plagued her was wiped away with hope. Hope that she could help Will find some sort of comfort from the sorrow that never truly left. She entered her room and knelt by the trunk that had traveled with her to California, and now back to Colorado, holding all that was precious to her. Her hand landed soft on the lid and she closed her eyes. This was still hard for her, too. Even the smell that would waft from the trunk was enough to trigger memories of Matty and her parents, memories that for now, brought more pain than comfort.

She opened her eyes and took a deep breath. For Will, she could face the contents. The brass latches clanked open and she slowly raised the lid. Just as she knew it would, the open trunk awakened her own burden of learning to cope without the people she loved the most. She delicately moved the items to the side until her fingertips landed on her goal. The moment she saw it, the anguish of seeing the contents of the trunk faded into a gentle hope. Her only thought now was easing Will's pain. She would gladly give anything to do that.

With a kiss to her fingertips and to the lid of the closed trunk, she returned to Will. She smiled, as he opened his arm, indicating her place to sit next to him. She nestled against him, and relished in a feeling of optimism that she hadn't felt in a long time. Remembering how much she enjoyed giving gifts, there was no one she would rather give to, than Will.

"I'm glad you're back," Will said, leaning in against her hair.

"I have something for you, something that I want you to have," she said, turning toward him.

"All I want is you, right here, next to me." He looked at her tenderly and brushed the strands of hair that had fallen against her face, revealing her cheek as he slowly caressed her with his fingers. "Only you, Sarah, can make this ache in my chest bearable."

She leaned into the palm of his hand. It was such a small gesture, but the emotion that radiated from him filled her with a longing to always feel the way she did when she was with him. He was going to be a hard habit to break, and a heart breaking one on top of it. This connection, or reunion, that the two of them had been indulging in, would have to stop. Sooner or later, there would be a reckoning.

But for now, all she wanted to do was be with him. She pulled her hands from behind her, and held them out for Will. "This is for you."

He looked down to her hands, and pinched his eyebrows together at the sight of a folded, white fabric. "What is this?" he asked, gently taking it from her hand.

"Open it up," she said, suddenly feeling nervous about how he might react.

He unfolded the fabric gently until the inside was revealed. He stared at it for a long time before he responded.

"Always together," he murmured. He ran his fingertips over the embroidered sentiment. He looked to Sarah with the emotion flooding his eyes. "I remember her making this." He looked back to the tea towel, letting his eyes float over ever stitch of the mountain scene.

Sarah nodded, "It was my mom's most prized possession. She would take it from the trunk all of the time, especially when she was sad. I'm guessing that she was missing your mom so much, which explains why she couldn't even speak when she held this towel. Your mom made it to remind her that distance meant nothing, when you are joined by heartstrings that can span any distance. Now, I want you to have it. You and your mom will always be together, no matter the distance between here, and heaven. Nothing can break the connection of hearts that were brought together and joined together."

Will reached up, and ran his hands down Sarah's long, silky hair, and wrapped his hand behind her neck. He leaned in closely to her and whispered, "Thank you, Sarah. Thank you for helping me see something that pain had blinded me to." He moved in, brushing his lips against hers as he spoke, "I love...this." His lips gently pressed against hers with a kiss so charged with passion, that Sarah actually lost her breath. How she wished this could last forever; that he was actually hers, forever.

He reluctantly pulled from her lips, and rested his forehead against hers. She closed her eyes, realizing that the kiss, as seemingly simple as it was, was the most powerful kiss she had ever experienced. His words almost said it, but his kiss screamed it. He loved her.

"What about our heartstrings, Sarah?" he quietly asked, still pressed against her. "Did our heartstrings stay connected, no matter the distance between here and California?"

Sarah could actually hear her heart pounding. Her mind flashed images of the past several years, and the past several days. Memories of Adley's face, and Adley's touch, shot through her like a bolt of lightning. But, the past weeks with Will seared through her memory and went straight to her core. Was there a connection between her and Will before California that should've kept them connected? Something that was as powerful as what had obviously connected them ever since she arrived back to Colorado? How she felt about him now indicated yes. But, how then, could she have moved on to Adley, and Will moved on to Margaret? Will's suggestion that they too had heartstrings, only presented her with more questions that sent her mind swirling, and she could only remain silent, even though she wanted to say something, for both of their sakes.

"Nevermind," he said, interrupting her thoughts, "don't answer that." He leaned back into the swing and closed his eyes. "I'm sorry, Sarah." He shook his head, more to himself than to her, adding quietly, "It doesn't matter, at this point."

Sarah's confusion had reached a new high, and she looked at him, telling herself that crying now would not help anything.

He pulled her hand to his lips and kissed it lightly. "Thank you for this," he said, looking again to the tea towel. "You gave me a piece of my mother's love. I hope you know how much it means to me."

Sarah nodded, she understood. But, what she didn't understand, was what was happening between her and Will. Clearly, there was more to their story than she knew, or could remember. There was more that Will wasn't telling her. If she were to fully understand her past, she would have to know what Will was holding back from telling her, and why. She left California for one reason; to know her past, and her past included Will. She just needed to know what had happened in her past that so dramatically impacted her future. Of course, there was no changing the past. But, maybe knowing her history would somehow alter the course of her future.

There would be no more answered questions for now, as Will stood and pulled her to her feet. "Come on, Sar. You must be getting cold. Let's go in, and I'll build you a fire."

A fire sounded nice, but she knew that nothing would compare to the fire in his voice when he had asked if their connection spanned the thousand miles, that she was coming to realize, changed everything for them.

She took his hand gladly, silently vowing that she would not rest until she completely uncovered the truth about her and Will. For now, she would be satisfied knowing that she could at least ease his pain, and that the moment they shared would be safe in her memory for the rest of her life.

CHAPTER 37

Six tortuous days had passed since Sarah had given the tea towel to him. He had almost let his love for her be known that day, and he could still physically feel the ache to tell her. He wanted to tell her every minute of every day how much he loved her. He wanted to shout it from the mountain top, and let it echo for an eternity. But, that moment was quickly tainted by the guilt that hung over him. His decision the night of the barn fire set the course for his life, and he would have to somehow come to accept that. Sarah was not a part of that decision, and it would be unfair for her to have to bear the punishment. Telling her of his love would only hurt her. She would not be able to understand the burden that was now upon him to take care of his father and Tommy, and he didn't want her to understand it. It was a horrible sentence that he, and he alone, would have to serve. It didn't take his ache away, but he knew he was left with no choice.

Margaret had become completely obsessed with planning the wedding. Every time he saw her, it was the same incessant questions about the most minute details that couldn't have mattered less to him. He knew it was probably a normal conversation that two people would have regarding their wedding, but to him, it was just more of the reminder that he was marrying someone who he didn't love. Every time she wanted his input on what type of flower should be in her bouquet, all he could picture was Sarah walking toward him in a white dress, and what kind of flowers Sarah would've chosen. Every wedding question or idea proposed by Margaret brought only one image to his mind. Sarah.

His mind searched for an excuse to escape an exhausting conversation about various shades of peach that Margaret was debating over for her bridesmaids' dresses. He told her to choose whichever one she liked, as he explained that he needed to go to the back yard to organize the lumber.

"I can't believe you're not taking this seriously," she huffed, with hands on her hips, clenching the fabric samples.

"Margaret," Will began, already completely spent by their interaction, "all of the colors of peach are nice. Whichever one you like, is fine with me." He raised his eyebrows and held out his arms in complete desperation. "Okay?"

"No. It's not okay. Every time I ask you about the wedding, you don't have an opinion. Which, to me, says you don't care. Is that the case? You don't care?"

He wanted to sigh in relief that she finally understood. He didn't care. Period. This was not going to be the wedding of his dreams. The wedding of his dreams would only require one detail, and it had nothing to do with the perfect shade of peach. But, it had everything to do with the perfect woman, whom he couldn't have.

To end the misery that was this conversation, he held out his hand for the swatches of fabric that were still tightly held in Margaret's fist. A slight smile of victory crossed her lips as she handed them to him. He flipped through the samples finally stopping at one.

"Here. This one. I like this one."

Margaret took the samples back from him, her eyes widening at his choice. "This is the worst one of the lot. This would've been my last choice. Honestly, William. I don't know what you are thinking."

For once, he completely agreed with her. He didn't know what he was thinking either. The woman he loved, the woman he desired and needed more than air, was sitting in his home right now. She filled his every waking moment, and the slightest touch of her skin against his sent him into such a sublime world he couldn't have even begun to imagine to exist, until he touched her.

The most powerful sense of urgency that he had ever experienced coursed through him and he knew what he needed to do. There was no longer any doubt in his mind, and he cursed himself for waiting this long to do it. Time was precious, life was unpredictable, and he had learned all too well that the people he loved could be taken away in a heartbeat. He was guilty of a lot of choices that resulted in heartbreak, but he would not be guilty of this. He knew that everything could change from one minute to the next, and giving fate the opportunity to take that time away from him was not something he was willing to risk. Having no idea what would come the moment after he told her, he could no longer contain the secret that was bursting to be revealed. He would not let one more minute go by without telling her. It was time that Sarah knew everything. Their promise at the creek, and his promise to love her and take care of her, were all he could think of now. She needed to know that he still loved her, and had never stopped.

He turned away from Margaret without another word. The only words on his lips were those that he was dying to tell Sarah. Walking away from Margaret was certainly laced with consequences that at some point would need to be paid. But at this point, nothing could stop him.

He hurried to the farm truck and slammed the door closed. The thirteen-mile drive home would be the longest of his life. But, with each passing fence post out his side window, his heart pounded with the feeling of liberation. He was finally going to tell Sarah how he felt, and he could only imagine how amazing it would feel once she knew, and he no longer had to hide their history. He imagined her sweet lips curling into a smile once he told her, and how sweet that first kiss would be. Their first kiss after knowing the truth would be pleasure beyond all reason. Finally, after everything that had happened that was out of his control, he was going to decide his fate.

With billowing dust behind him, the old truck shot up the driveway to his house at a speed like never before. The truck had barely slid to a stop and he was already jumping out of the door and running up the walk to the house. He was almost there. Never before had he felt so strongly like he was coming home. This time, he was coming home to Sarah. And, wherever Sarah was, would be home. He knew that this would be one of the most unforgettable moments of his life. He was ready to change the course of his life, and it would all begin with telling Sarah that he was in love with her.

"Sarah!" he said breathlessly, as he flung the screen door open.

She had been rocking quietly, reading a book in his mother's chair next to the fireplace. She immediately rose to her feet, her face instantly pale with worry. "What's wrong?" she asked, walking toward him.

He quickly grabbed her hands and pulled her into his body. "Sarah, I couldn't wait to get to you." He closed his eyes, and tried to calm the nerves that were beginning to take over.

"Will, what is it? Is everyone okay?" Sarah's voice was beginning crack with worry, and he could feel her trembling in his arms.

He swallowed hard and shook his head. The last thing he wanted was for her to worry. "Everyone is fine. Everything is fine."

"Then...what's going on? Why are you home? It's the middle of the day." He could see the worry fade, but the confusion grow.

"Sarah, I had to come home. I couldn't wait another minute. I need to tell you something."

"Okay," she said slowly. "What is it?"

Still holding her hands, he looked down to gather his thoughts. For as much as he thought about exactly what to say once he got home, every thought in his head was screaming at the same time. He wanted to kiss her, but he knew he needed to say the words that he had been holding back all this time.

Looking straight into her eyes, he began slowly. "Sarah, you need to know something. Something about me, and you. I haven't told you everything that you need to know."

Her eyes darted back and forth between his, but she let him continue. "From my earliest memory, you have been a part of my life. We grew up together, but we also grew together in another way. In a way, that has never left me, even when you left Colorado, you never left me. You've been in here," he paused, as he moved her hand to his chest. "Do you feel my heart beating?"

She slowly nodded. "Every beat is because of you. Every beat is for you. It always has been. You are the most amazing person I've ever known. You are the most beautiful and exquisite woman ever created, and I've thought of nothing but you, since the moment I had to say goodbye."

"I have to say that I completely agree with you." A deep voice from outside the screen door shattered against Will's words.

They both took an abrupt step back, completely jarred by the uninvited guest at the door. Both Sarah and Will squinted to make out the face beyond the shadow of the door. The screen door opened without invitation, and the man walked in without any hesitation. His face came in from the shadows and was bathed in the sunlight from the windows across the room. The stranger locked eyes with Sarah and walked straight to her, never leaving her eyes. "In fact, I could say the exact same thing. Which is why I asked her to marry me, and last I knew, she had said yes."

Sarah gasped and pulled her hands from Will. She covered her mouth and looked in complete disbelief at the man standing in front of her.

"Who the hell are you?" Will demanded, moving to stand between Sarah and the man.

Slowly moving his gaze from Sarah to Will, he said, "I'll let Sarah tell you who I am, but I'm going to kindly ask you to keep your hands off of my future wife, if it's all the same to you."

Will turned to Sarah, hardly able to formulate a thought in his mind. Surely this must all be a dream. A nightmare. "Sarah?" The words were thick coming out. "Sarah, who is this?"

Sarah slowly moved her hand from covering her mouth, but no words escaped her.

"Sarah!" Will's voice was now splitting the air like an arrow.

Sarah blinked and sucked in her breath. "Adley," she whispered. She turned to look at Will.

Will looked at her in complete disbelief. "What is he talking about?"

Sarah could only shake her head, still unable to talk.

"Sarah!" Will continued frantically. "Is that true? Are you...are you engaged to him?" he asked incredulously.

Sarah's eyes filled with tears, and moved between Adley and Will. Her gaze landed on Will's blue eyes that were no longer looking at her with the hope and eagerness of just a few minutes earlier. She nodded slowly, "Yes, Will. It's true."

Will couldn't even respond. He stared at Sarah, realizing that his earlier prediction had come true. This was indeed one of the most unforgettable moments he would ever experience. The knowledge that the woman he was in love with was engaged to another man was a moment that would forever be seared into his memory.

CHAPTER 38

A blanket of nausea so thick washed over Sarah that she didn't know what to say, what to do, or who to run to. The look on Will's face as her words settled in on him was a vision that she knew she would never be able to erase from her memory. The devastation and disbelief that invaded his eyes was so intense, and she knew that she just single handedly accomplished what she hoped to avoid. She hurt him, and the damage looked to be irreparable.

Her own disbelief was just as formidable. She turned to Adley. How did he get here? Why was he here? The questions pounded inside her mind like a hailstorm against a tin roof. She wanted to rush to him, to feel him, to make sure her mind wasn't playing a cruel trick. She had spent so many nights praying for the safety of Adley and Matty. Now, she could see that her prayers had been heard, and at least, partially answered. Adley was home from the war, but the expression on his face toward Will proved he was still ready for battle.

Clearly picking up on her inability to move or react, Adley brushed passed Will's shoulder to stand directly in front of her. She looked into his intense green eyes as she had done so many times. The eyes that looked at her with longing before, seemed different, but still flooded with desire for her.

Adley lifted her chin to him with his finger. "Say something," he said softly. "I've just traveled from a world away to come home to you. But, you weren't home, like you promised. So, I came a little further."

Her breath was coming in short gasps. Her head was spinning. Still, none of this felt real. A few moments ago, her hand was over Will's heart, and her own heart, stirred to life, as if it had been awakened after a long slumber. Now, her heart was in her throat. Adley was safe, and he came all this way for her. "Adley," she managed, "I...can't believe you're here."

A smile crossed his lips. "Maybe this will help," he said, as he leaned down to meet her trembling lips. He pressed his mouth to hers, and for several seconds, she was paralyzed with what reality had presented her with. She felt his tongue tentatively circle around hers as he cradled her head in his hands. He slowly retreated from her lips and smiled again. "There. Now do you believe that I am here?"

Sarah could feel the blood drain from her face, and a buzzing sound was gradually getting louder in her ears. She closed her eyes, feeling her head start to circle. She blinked several times, looking between Adley and Will. Seeing the two of them together was more than her mind could grasp. Of all the possibilities in the world, this was one that she never fathomed could become a reality. She could sense that she had been troubled by choosing between the two men before. But, it had always been one, or the other, that had actually been in her life. Now, with the two of them staring expectantly at her, she found herself in a predicament that she was in no way prepared to handle.

Will's face appeared in her line of sight. A face that once looked at her with such love was now destroyed. "Sarah, please. Please tell me what is going on." His voice sounded so foreign to her. She didn't know who he sounded like. All she knew was that it held no resemblance to the voice she had come to know very well.

Still holding Sarah's hands, Adley turned to Will. "Since she is obviously too overwhelmed to explain anything to you, I will. Sarah and I have been together ever since she came to my family's ranch in California. We fell in love. Effortlessly." He paused to smile at her. "Before I left for the war, I asked her to be my wife, and she made me the happiest man alive when she agreed. We planned to be married as soon as I returned."

Will's eyes never left Sarah's, though he was speaking to Adley. "Together since she came to California, huh?"

"Yes," Adley quickly confirmed. "And you, must be William."

Now Will broke his eye contact with Sarah, and narrowed his eyes onto Adley.

In response to his silent questioning look, Adley continued, "Yes, in case you're wondering. Sarah told me about you."

"That's sure interesting," Will rebutted. "Because she hasn't mentioned a word about you."

Adley turned back to Sarah, brushing the tear from her cheek. "Well, I'm sure that's because she has a kind heart. Why would she tell you that her childhood crush was nothing but a distant memory to her, and that she moved on to experience what being in love really meant?"

Will's eyes hardened. "Well, being in love sure didn't keep her in California, did it?"

Sarah couldn't stand what was circling around her. "Stop. Both of you. Please stop."

"Is that true, Sarah?" Will looked at her, pain streaking through his voice. "A childhood crush?"

"No, Will. It's not like that," she pleaded.

Will just looked at her at shook his head. "You know what? It doesn't matter. Not anymore." He turned to Adley, jutting his right hand out to his. "Nice to meet you, Adley. I'm glad to hear that Sarah has realized what true love is."

Adley jammed his hand into Will's, although it was no secret than either was happy about the new acquaintance. Will shot Sarah a look that she never expected to be receiving from him, and it nearly caused her to buckle at the knees. "Will," she said again.

"No," he stopped her. "Really, I don't want an explanation. I think I've heard all I need to hear. I'll leave you two alone, I'm sure you have a lot of catching up do." He turned from her and walked through the door and out to the porch. The screen door had never slammed closed with such finality, and Sarah closed her eyes and cringed at the sound that slammed against her heart with equal force.

Adley pulled her in to his embrace again. She felt numb, like a puppet that was moving only because her strings were be pulled and yanked into position. She fell against Adley's body, still in too much shock to speak. She forced herself to concentrate on the sensations against her skin. Adley. His arms wrapped around her, and he stroked her back. She remembered this feeling, and everything about California came rushing back to her. She remembered his touch in the garden, and the barn loft, and in the farm truck. All of it stirred emotions that had settled, and had become overshadowed by everything that Will had stirred to life in her.

Adley pulled away and looked at her. "Sarah," he began, running his finger along her cheek. He shook his head and looked at her in amazement, "You are even more beautiful than I remember. And, the memory of your face is the only thing that kept me alive. That, and knowing that I had to survive, because I had you to come home to. Knowing I had the rest of my life to live with you, meant everything to me." He leaned down toward her to kiss her slowly, passionately. He closed his eyes after leaving her lips, "Mmm," he quietly moaned. "And that. Your sweet kiss, and knowing that there was so much more of you waiting for me."

Sarah looked into his eyes, her lips still tingling from his kiss. All of him felt familiar, in an instant, it all rushed over her like a river breaking through a crumbling dam. "Adley, I can't believe you are here," she finally stammered.

He smiled warmly at her, "Believe it. I told you once that you would find me wherever you are. Well, I'm here, and I'm never leaving you again. Ever."

SNEAK PEEK AT CHOSEN BY FATE

RELEASING EARLY 2014

Will stormed from the house and down the porch steps as fast as he could. He didn't know where to go, or what to do. He just needed to get out of that house. Even though he knew that walking away from the situation would change nothing. A lot had happened to him that was beyond his comprehension, but this, this was so far removed from anything he could've dreamt, that the minuscule grasp he thought he had on his future disintegrated into a fine dust of lies. After all this time with her, after everything that they had experienced together, this was the culminating event. The irony of the situation made him want to punch something, or someone. The day he decides to tell Sarah of how he feels, is the day he learns that the woman he loves has been deceiving him all along. They both knew that what they had been doing was because of a force more powerful than either one of them could define. The one thing he believed whole-heartedly was that he could trust Sarah. And now, that was all shot to shit. What bothered him the most was the unfathomable ache radiating from his chest. Was he more angry that Sarah had lied to him, or was it the pain from knowing that another man was going to have her? Either way, the fury and pain mixed into a debilitating concoction that he wasn't sure would ever fully recover from.

He stalked to the back of the corral, ignoring the horses for the first time in his life. His eyes landed on the rock where he and Sarah sat, where he felt that they were just beginning to come together like he remembered. Things were complicated then, but now, he would've gladly taken "complicated" over whatever it would be called now. This might be the final blow for fate to guarantee that he would not be with Sarah.

He picked up a fist sized rock and threw it as hard as he could into the scrub oak. Fine. He got it. How many more tricks, and how many more slices through his heart would it take for him to realize? Whatever he thought his life would be was nothing more than wisps of whispers to be taken from him with the slightest breeze. All of his plans, everything he wanted, ended up being a waste of time and energy. He ran his hands through his hair with the most devastating realization yet. He felt like giving up. What the hell was the point of hoping, planning, dreaming? What was the point of loving? It could be all taken, and for him, it had been.

Now that you have finished my book...

Won't you please consider writing a review? Reviews mean so much to authors, and they are a great way for readers to find new books. I would truly appreciate it!

http://amzn.to/19phdc3

I love to connect with my readers!

You can find me on Facebook at www.facebook.com/jacelynryeauthor and you can always drop me a line at jacelynrye@yahoo.com.

One Last Thing...

At the end of this book, you'll be greeted with a request from Amazon to rate this book and post your thoughts on Facebook and Twitter. Be the first one of your friends to use this innovative technology. Your friends get to know what you're reading, and I, for one, will be forever grateful to you.

Thank you so much!

Jacelyn